What is it about you, woman?

Michael's muscles twitched in response to his silent question because even in her rapidly declining state, the woman in his arms was irresistible. She was seductive in an ethereal, ultrafeminine way. Her gray eyes, her flowery scent and white face were lures he hadn't been able to resist. Hell, he couldn't resist them now.

In his defense, Michael concluded that a good excuse for his behavior was that she probably wouldn't harm a fly. Even if she discovered that werewolves still existed, it would be a shame for the world to lose such a small bundle. He just couldn't imagine the alternative. Because if she did live and decided to expose his kind, the job he faced was unthinkable. Saving her life would have been for nothing.

"Breathe," he said to her. "That's right. Now breathe again."

HALF WOLF

LINDA THOMAS-SUNDSTROM

MILLS
BOON

First Published in Great Britain 2016
By Mills & Boon, an imprint of HarperCollins*Publishers*

© 2016 Linda Thomas-Sundstrom

ISBN: 978-0-263-92178-6

89-0716

Our policy is to use papers that are natural, renewable and recyclable products and made from wood grown in sustainable forests. The logging and manufacturing processes conform to the legal environmental regulations of the country of origin.

Printed and bound in Spain
by CPI, Barcelona

Linda Thomas-Sundstrom writes contemporary and paranormal romance novels for Mills & Boon Desire and Mills & Boon Nocturne. A teacher by day and a writer by night, Linda lives in the West, juggling teaching, writing, family and caring for a big stretch of land. She swears she has a resident Muse who sings so loudly, she often wears earplugs in order to get anything else done. But she has big plans to eventually get to all those ideas. Visit Linda at www.lindathomas-sundstrom.com or on Facebook.

To my family, those here and those gone,
who always believed I had a story to tell.

Chapter 1

Pain, sharp-edged and nasty, hit Kaitlin Davies in an undulating wave, pulsing in time with the spike in her heart rate.

God, she thought. *Can this be happening?*

The guy who had just seconds ago seemed like any normal male—short hair, jeans, old white T-shirt—had her by the neck before she could shout. So fast she couldn't draw a breath. The asshole actually bit her, breaking the skin beneath her right ear. He kept his teeth clamped to her neck and seemed to get a kick out of it. He was making happy noises.

Shock made screaming impossible. The a-hole had her pinned to a tree with some kind of supernatural grip.

Her bags fell to the ground. A hideous sucking sound, like someone knocking back a smoothie through a narrow straw, caused her stomach to turn. Something wet trickled down her throat, forcing a gag reflex, but she was too stunned to do anything other than try to breathe.

The scent of blood saturated the air. Her scream was internal, silent.

No...

The last rush of her frantic energy ebbed with a sensation similar to a tumbling wave's retreat. And then another jarring spike in her pulse hit, fueled by adrenaline with nowhere to go.

Scream. Shove. Knee him. Fight.

That was what the rules of self-defense said to do if she were ever to find herself in trouble.

Yell. Make as much noise as possible. Draw attention.
Don't talk to strangers.

While it was a safe bet that every single female across the country had been given those same rules, no one had mentioned the fact that they might not work. She hadn't spoken to anybody, had just been minding her own business walking across university grounds from the library to her studio apartment.

Searing red flashes behind her eyes warned that she was going into shock, and still standing only because the creep held her upright. She no longer felt her hands or feet. Nerve twitches that should have instigated muscle movement produced no response at all.

Shit.
Help me!

She was so very scared, and cold, though she had started to sweat. Inside, she was fighting, struggling. Outwardly, she did zip. This attacker's maniacal strength and the speed with which he had executed it severed any prospects of a worthwhile reaction.

What sort of creature bit a person?

Pervert.
Animal.
Monster...

Her thoughts began to fuzz over. Blackness floated in from the periphery of her brain like spilled ink spreading on a flat white surface, threatening a last hold on sanity.

Would she ever see her family again?

Tingling sensations accompanied her blood pressure's plummeting descent. Dark thoughts dangled. The monster was going to kill her beneath the trees bordering the pathway. She was on her own here because this was Friday night, and everybody else would be either prepping for the weekend or hitting the books. She had walked here at least twenty times this past semester, thinking it safe.

And now she was going to die. Out here. Alone. Just weeks before presenting her doctorate thesis.

She did not want to die, not like this or any other way. Her life hadn't really started yet.

Don't deserve this.

She had no energy left to finish the argument. The night had grown darker.

Somebody help me.

Anybody. Please...

Kaitlin prayed, chanting inwardly and straining to keep her eyes open for the last few precious seconds of life. Nothing seemed real. Nothing felt real.

Stomach convulsing, head exploding in a last hurrah, she heard another sound break through the darkness, stirring an internal response. It sounded like the growl of a large animal. Low, guttural and unmistakably menacing, that growl rolled toward her.

But maybe, just maybe, this was merely the sound a soul made when prepping for flight.

Her soul.

No. Not that. God, not that, because the monster beside her also heard the noise. When he lifted his head, part of her T-shirt hung from his teeth, soaked in blood.

His sudden withdrawal was more painful than the initial attack had been. The world began to spin, mingling with the sound of another ferocious animal growl that came from right on top of them.

Can't hold on...

The monster released her. She fell, sliding down the bark of the tree, sinking onto numb buttocks with her legs folded. In the dullness of tunneling vision, she witnessed a blur of black on black, deeper than the night itself, approaching.

Like a whirlwind, the blur of fluid darkness swept her attacker aside, seeming to temporarily shift things in her favor. In life's favor. Too weak to make any kind of acknowledgment, Kaitlin fought the wave of light-headedness threatening to overtake her.

In her dimming periphery, squeals broke through the silence—sounds reminiscent of fierce fighting that seemed to come from every direction at once. A high-pitched whine was followed by a scream and the unmistakable sound of flesh tearing. But it wasn't her flesh being torn this time.

Not this time.

Kaitlin heaved up one final inward cry. Tears were running down her cheeks. When the night became quiet, the silence was scary. And then an artificial softness descended like a cloud, as if she'd been covered by a fur coat. That softness caressed her legs and thighs beneath the hem of her denim shorts.

After the terrible events of the past few minutes, sensation of any kind seemed odd. So, was this gentle caress a sign of Death knocking at her door?

With great difficulty, Kaitlin cracked open her eyes. Looking out through teary slits, she found the face of a man kneeling beside her—a half-naked man, his skin gleaming from the waist up in the dappled moonlight filtering through branches.

This wasn't the creep that had tried to steal her life force. This guy had broad shoulders and a sculpted chest etched with scrolling tattoos. His hair was dark, long, and a stark contrast to his face.

Could this be an angel?

Moonlight encircled his position as if he sat in the center of a searchlight beam, but his features were hidden by shadows. He didn't speak, just sat there looking at her as if appraising the situation. If this was a trick, if he wasn't to be trusted, well, there wasn't much left for him to take.

When gentle fingers touched her face she winced, because tenderness in the malignant moonlight felt wrong. Her visitor finally spoke in a deep, hushed voice. "It's all right now. That thing is gone."

He moved inches forward so that moonlight flooded his face with a wash of pure silver. Kaitlin couldn't see much past the splashes of blood on his lips and chiseled cheeks. That blood was as black as his hair.

She did a quick reassessment, wanting to understand what kind of an angel would appear like this. Fear made a comeback. Rattles of protest welled up in her chest. Was the blood on his face hers?

The man's fingers slipped to her chin, which he tilted slowly upward. "You're safe."

I'm dying, she wanted to say.

As if he had heard the words, he brought his face close to hers. From inches away, he observed her with the brightest eyes she had ever seen—eyes that glowed a light luminous green and shone with intelligence and understanding. Beautiful eyes. Kind. Sympathetic. Not quite human.

His attention made the last wisp of her consciousness flicker way down deep inside her, almost in a sexual way. Kaitlin wanted to reach out and touch those angular cheeks. She wanted to wipe the slashes of crimson away and thank him for helping her.

She couldn't do any of that.

He spoke again, slowly, so that she could hear and comprehend.

"You can be healed."

There just wasn't one bit of energy left to argue with him. Threads were separating. She'd been attacked, mauled, only to be saved by a what? Man? Angel? Madman? Beast? He hunched there like a predator, with radiant eyes indicative of some animal species. She sensed an edge to his sympathy. He hadn't picked up a cell phone to call for help.

His presence kept her from drifting off. Kaitlin willed her body to hang on for a few more seconds, afraid he would leave, afraid that if she closed her eyes she'd never open them again and die alone.

Please stay with me.

Help me.

Did he hear her plea? He nodded as if he had.

When he put his arms around her, a strangled moan erupted from her throat—the pain was so very great. Her head hit his solid, soothingly bare chest as he lifted her into his arms, high off the ground.

An odd thought wafted through her mind that it would have been tough for an angel to manage the saggy mess of a twenty-three-year-old woman. Yet if this was an angel, who was going to argue? If he were to take her to heaven, she was in good hands.

Or so she thought until he shifted her weight and the pain came crashing down—crushing, pulverizing, boiling—as though she had imploded.

But it wasn't over yet. He gripped her with care and

whispered assurances. As he turned, cradling her against his body, Kaitlin's soul-wrenching wail was finally freed. She screamed and screamed. Feral cries. Helpless noises.

The shouts didn't frighten this man, this angel, this questionable soul who held her. Taking a deep breath, he placed his mouth on hers and blew a warm stream of air into her lungs that tasted of grass and meadows, not the bloody brutality of a savage monster.

His lips lingered on hers, forcing her to swallow past the pain, quieting the riot. She took in each breath he gave her. His long hair brushed her cheeks with a silkiness that was as light as day.

Who could have anticipated a kiss on death's threshold? The intimacy of their mouths touching and their breaths mingling held a surreal beauty that continued until Kaitlin was able to breathe on her own. Soon after that, the mouth she had depended on left hers.

Wait, she wanted to cry. With his kiss, the pain had lessened. She'd felt as though she actually might survive.

The heat radiating off this stranger's bare chest brought another level of awareness to her broken body. Her rescuer was muscled and extremely hot. Being held by him was like confronting a bonfire.

She parted her lips for speech that didn't come. The hovering unconsciousness, temporarily held at bay by a pair of green eyes that continued to stare into hers as if urging her spirit to continue, floated on the sidelines.

"You have to be willing," he said. "That's the way this works."

What did that mean? What did any of this mean?

"There's no time to explain. But it's the only way you'll make it. Nod your head if you understand."

In the end, it didn't matter what he might be suggesting, since she'd do anything to stay alive. With great effort, Kaitlin lowered her chin.

"I'll take that as a yes," he said. "Be brave. Hang tight and remember that I gave you a choice."

His finger tracked a tear sliding down her cheek. Then he nestled his face into her neck, right above the attacker's deadly wound.

Oh, God, she thought. *Not this.*

Taking her skin between his teeth lightly, he paused as if waiting for her to change her mind. After that, he bit down.

The sky collapsed in on itself. The earth rose to envelop her. And somewhere between the two, Kaitlin Davies became one with the dark.

What he was doing was a sin, and unforgivable. So why had he considered it? Why, on the spur of the moment, had Michael Hunter broken every rule governing Lycan behavior to try to save a human female he'd never met—when no human had ever done anything to help him, and in fact had left him with his greatest heartache to date?

His pulse was racing. He knew better than to cross the line.

And just couldn't help himself.

The woman in his arms was slender, and small-boned to the point of being fragile. But she was no child. Behind the torn T-shirt, her shape was visible. Lean legs, lightly tanned, were shown off by a pair of shorts.

Blood spatter covered everything, and the scent of that blood had already been dispersed through the air. If he didn't hurry, other bloodsuckers in the area—if they dared to show their fangs to a prowling werewolf—would come calling.

She was seconds from death. He recognized the signs. But death wasn't the worst scenario here. The worst-case outcome would be hearing her last strangled breath, and then watching her morph into the same kind of monster that had savaged her.

Vampire saliva was highly toxic. The ultimate poison. All it took to kill and then resurrect a human being to the dark side were four or five drops dribbled in an open wound. Rogue vampires didn't even wait around to see the rise of the night creatures they created. New vampires with no idea what had happened and nowhere to turn except to the raging thirst would be a threat to everyone.

There had been a rash of missing people near Clement College lately, and law enforcers were taking stock of those disappearances. Cops were nosing around. This didn't bode well for the other secretive nonhuman species living alongside the so-called normal folks. Something had to be done about the recent influx of vamps. Fast.

Michael looked down at the woman in his arms.

Her face was oval-shaped and bloodless. She had long hair that was a unique combination of red and brown, and her skin was soft and lightly scented with the fragrance of flowers, despite all the damage the vampire's fangs had done. Her tears tasted like sunlight.

After all these years, he still would have given anything for someone to have comforted his mother like this as she lay dying, and helped in any way they could.

This little human had sorely needed help.

Replacing the vamp's saliva with Lycan blood had been of paramount importance in order to save her life. Wolf blood was volcanic, and immensely alive. If she was lucky, that blood might counteract and overpower the other chilling version of poison put into her by those fangs.

With the miraculous healing powers Lycans possessed, if this female survived the night, the gaping edges of her wound would draw together and mending would begin. On the outside, anyway.

Odds were less than fifty-fifty that she'd pull through no matter what he did or how timely his actions were. Yet purebred Lycan blood, strengthened over the centuries, was one of the strongest medicines on the planet, and he had just given her system a jolt.

Blasphemy?

Hell, yes.

As Alpha of his pack, his other pack-mates might argue with what he'd done. Then again, a couple of them had been on the wrong side of a bite or two, so maybe they'd feel sympathetic.

She was light as a feather. Her breath escaped as a sigh through quivering lips, though her eyes remained shut. Michael's heart thudded with unanticipated empathy as he carefully scrutinized her expressionless face, deciding that she wasn't beautiful, exactly. *Striking* was a better word. She was quite striking for a human so near to death.

"Breathe, little one," he directed, knowing that humans didn't take well to their DNA being rearranged. Human women were especially vulnerable to the sudden change in their body chemistry.

"There's a chance, if what I've given you takes and you somehow manage your system's rewiring, that you won't thank me."

Although she'd be alive, she might also be angry, and that was a concern. Telling someone about this rescue attempt, or letting the world in on the secretive presence of werewolves, would place his pack in the spotlight. Hunting season would begin again, as it had for so many past centuries after humans got a whiff of werewolf—in spite of how humanlike Lycans were most of the time. In spite of the fact that this city's friendly local doctors, mailmen and cops might become something else when the moon was full.

There was another potential problem.

By getting too close to the woman in his arms, he could be instigating a bond between them that for Lycans was a greater event than placing a ring on her finger. Imprinting was something he had carefully avoided for all of his adult life. Imprinting with a human…well, that would be bad. Lycans only mated with Lycans. As werewolf royalty, pure Lycan blood was not to be diluted by the weaknesses humans possessed.

Yeah. So…it was too late for regrets. And hindsight was always a bundle of joy.

He had just committed a sin without thinking twice, and now had to deal with the consequences. Something about this female had captured his attention after merely a look, and that just wasn't usual fare for an Alpha with a badass reputation.

What is it about you, woman?

Michael's muscles twitched in response to his silent question because even in her rapidly declining state, the woman in his arms was like wolfnip. She was seductive in an ethereal, ultrafeminine way. Her gray eyes, her flowery scent and white face, were lures he hadn't been able to resist.

In his defense, Michael concluded that a good excuse for his behavior was that she probably wouldn't have harmed a fly, even if she knew about the existence of werewolves, and that it would be a shame for the world to lose such a small bundle.

"Breathe," he said to her. "That's right. Now breathe again."

It's a damn shame that if you live and decide to threaten

*or expose my kind, it will be my job to kill you. Saving your
life tonight would have been for nothing.*

Her lashes fluttered, which was a good sign. He said to
her, "Some of the pain will ease temporarily, though probably not nearly enough."

He watched her face for another reaction without finding one.

"The pain will return and get worse. I won't lie about
that. You'll have to hold on, ride this out, if you want to
survive. You'll have to prove yourself stronger than you
look."

The woman's pale lips, beautifully shaped and so close
to his own, were stiff with shock. Her temporary respite
from the agony—either of losing her life altogether or
losing life as she'd known it—was as fragile as the rest
of her. Michael lowered the odds of her ever opening her
big gray eyes.

Still, he held her possessively, liking the feel of her
body against his despite her chance of surviving. Liking
the velvety softness of her hair against his chest, and how
her silky legs dangled over his arms.

Seemed even badasses weren't immune to an attractive woman.

Something inside him stirred when she moaned. His
thoughts grew softer. *Is someone waiting for you to come
home?*

No response came from the prize in his arms. She
wasn't yet alive enough to speak. Possibly she didn't even
hear him.

"I don't know you. Don't know your name," he said.
"But here we are, about to either become allies or enemies. Provided that you gain back the strength to open
your eyes."

Michael felt his pulse skip again as he carefully observed his unintentional captive. His victim. His new, awkward responsibility. He wondered if maybe it was only the moon causing the hum in his chest.

Glancing up at the sky, where that nearly full moon blazed a luminous silver white, he held off the muscle burn that urged him to shift shape.

"Hold on," he whispered to the woman nestled in his arms, willing her to hear, commanding the few drops of his blood, now inside her body, to obey their codes and offer assistance.

His voice lowered to a growl as his internal wolfishness finally rushed to meet the moonlight. "Hold tight, little wolf, and pray for a miracle. If we're very lucky, maybe you'll actually thank me someday."

Chapter 2

"Are you awake?"

The voice was close enough to be inside her mind. Kaitlin struggled to place the words, found meaning and instantly, in some distant part of herself, recognized the tone.

"Can you speak?" the man asked.

Don't move. Don't you dare move or answer him. He could be anyone. Another wacko. Seriously ill.

This guy had hurt her, too, Kaitlin remembered, after he had actually asked for permission first. That's what had gone down.

Willing herself to stillness, to silence, while her heartbeat shuddered uncomfortably against her rib cage, Kaitlin desperately wanted to know what was happening. But she was afraid to find out. She was afraid to move.

She was lying down, curled up in a fetal position with her knees almost to her chin, and she hurt everywhere—head, body, skin, and all the way to the roots of her hair.

Pain lashed out each time she attempted a shallow breath, that pain just barely tolerable.

The urge came to whimper, shout, cry. But not to die. No matter what, she did not want to die, or be dead already.

"Can you answer me?" he asked.

Above her pounding heart she perceived another beat— slower than her own, steady against her shoulder blades. Puffs of air skittered along her neck, telling her that the guy was very close to her. She nearly cried out against this kind of intrusion as a fresh wave of panic struck.

Struggling to keep her eyes open, she looked straight ahead at something that had to be a length of chocolate-brown fabric. She was almost positive it wasn't dirt.

Fire sang through her skull when she tried to place even that one small thing. Her lungs ached. Her eye sockets throbbed. She welcomed the discomfort because those things had to mean she was alive.

Focus.

The brown surface had white lines that looked like stitching. White thread. She was on a blanket. This was good. She hadn't been left in the park for early morning foot traffic to find.

More relief and another round of chills accompanied a further perception. She wasn't cold. She rested on a blanket, and the man who had rescued her was here. She remembered the hardness of his chest in what still seemed like a dream. Though she had stopped shaking, she felt like she might throw up.

"Can you speak?" he asked again.

Was he casually posing a question when she had no idea where she was, who he was or what had happened to her? When she couldn't have uttered one word if she'd wanted to? Her throat was tight, raw and constricted, because a fiend had chomped on it.

Yes. A fiend. I remember that, too.

Swallowing was a chore. Something tight had been wrapped around her throat, from which a distinctive smell arose.

Gauze?

It was a scent out of childhood memory—of scraped knees and knuckles. In this instance, it was the smell of a treated bandage and implied that not only had she survived, but the man beside her had to be a good guy. Still… hospitals didn't have brown blankets or intimate sleeping accommodations.

More panic threatened with a dangerous undertow. Why hadn't she been taken to a hospital?

Kaitlin waited to find out if she was wrong about her rescuer and if this guy might have saved her for nefarious purposes of his own. She'd have to rally somehow. She would have to run.

"You're in my room," her companion explained, his voice producing a familiar tingling vibration inside her chest. "I didn't know where else to take you. Didn't know where you belonged. In truth, taking you anywhere else might have been bad for both of us."

His voice had the mesmerizing quality of a dangerous animal temporarily appeased. While the words themselves were gentle, they were underscored by a hint of something scary that chilled Kaitlin to the bone.

She gasped and managed to suck in a lungful of daylight-filled air. Stripes of light filled with dancing dust particles lay across the blanket beside her, she now saw. Sunlight was seeping through curtains or shutters.

She withheld a shout of relief. Daylight would chase the nightmares away; keep the horrors out of reach.

Any time now.

"Hospitals are out of the question," her host continued.

"I'm afraid they don't deal well with people like us. Their physicians wouldn't know what to do or what we'd need."

People like us. Kaitlin hoped to God he meant doctorate students without health insurance. She hoped with all her might this guy would turn out to be from the campus police.

She was twenty-three years old and felt terribly small and inadequate. More than anything, she wanted to hear her parents' voices. Without the people she loved, sunlight and fresh blankets weren't completely normal things or as comforting as they could be.

She fought back tears.

Squeaking bedsprings made her heart flutter. Her center of gravity shifted as the man behind her moved on the bed.

"You will heal, though it will take some time. The worst is over, but there will be more trials to come. That can't be helped. That's just the way it is."

"No," Kaitlin sputtered with a ferocious effort. *No more of this.*

"Luckily, you rode some of this out while unconscious. Our bodies are quick to repair and you'll soon find this to be true. Your body is trying to adapt right now."

Kaitlin moved her lips. "Thank you."

This had to be the man who had come to her aid in the park, and had put her on a blanket. Whatever else came to pass, she was grateful for that.

"You're welcome," he said hesitantly, sounding both relieved and wary.

"Angel," she managed to get out, her throat throbbing like crazy with each uttered syllable. "You?"

His response came in the form of a deep cascade of laughter that sent more dust motes dancing. "No angel," he said. "Not by a long shot. I'm Michael. Can you tell me your name?"

"Kaitlin."

"Right now you're still very sick, Kaitlin. But it's a new day and you're mending."

Taking a chance, encouraged by his kind words, Kaitlin unfurled her fingers slowly, glad when they soaked in the blanket's softness.

"Don't worry about anything right now," Michael soothed. "Rest. Heal some more. Get used to what's going on in your body."

Squeezing her eyes shut, Kaitlin whispered, "Afraid."

"I know."

"Home."

"In a while," he said.

"Home," she repeated.

"As soon as you're feeling better, I'll take you there."

His words were immensely reassuring. Why, though, when he could have an agenda of his own?

"Sleep now," he suggested. "Heal."

"Heal," Kaitlin echoed, wondering how she could sleep when she had been mauled by a monster and nearly killed. She would be screaming right now if her throat worked properly, and be running if she had the use of her legs.

"Sleep a while longer," he directed with a lulling, rolling purr. "You're safe here. No one will harm you while I stand guard."

Hell. Did she need guarding? If so, did it mean the monster that had nearly killed her might come after her again? Having sampled a taste, would he seek her out?

The roaring noise in her ears was like distant engines getting progressively closer. She actually felt her brain go dark. And for the second time in Kaitlin Davies's personal history, she just…slid…away.

* * *

She ran.

Barefoot. With the night wind on her body and moonlight in her hair. Sucking in air. Devouring the night. Blood pumping wildly in her veins.

Stars were luminous overhead. The night tasted like licorice and smelled like old wood. Running through the dark, inhaling it, Kaitlin felt driven, free, uninhibited and exceptionally fast. She felt joyously different somehow. More alive.

Noises followed her as she moved: a creak of branches, the rustle of leaves. Close behind those things came other sounds, like the racing beats of her heart and the snap of overextended muscle and bone. Each movement she made was a symphony.

Trees were dark shapes she rushed past. She knew them all, could name them and count the animals sheltering beneath. She could see in the dark. Outlines, shapes, were clear and slightly alien.

She wasn't alone. Someone ran with her, his strides in sync with hers. They moved as a single unit, in silence, with some distance between them.

Her companion called out once with a word Kaitlin didn't recognize, though she chased the sound of his voice into an open field. And suddenly, Kaitlin no longer felt sure of foot. She stumbled, teetered, struggled with her legs. Faltering, she fell to her hands and knees, sliding several inches, carried forward by momentum.

Strong hands yanked her upright, spun her around and lifted her off the ground as though she were as light as a cloud. Whoever this was carried her into the shadow of nearby tree cover and dropped her onto her feet. Warm hands pressed her to the bark of the closest tree in a hazy repeat of another time and place she couldn't quite recall.

"Not so fast," her companion advised.

The body leaning into hers was male, extremely warm and completely naked, though she didn't glance down to make sure of that. He was tall and light-skinned, with features that gave him a regal air, and rippling abs of steel.

"Take your time," this naked man advised.

His dark chin-length hair brushed her face, sending meaningful vibrations downward and toward a spot between her thighs. Bursts of energy spiraled outward from a spark deep inside her—barely containable energy. Highly unstable stuff.

Kaitlin couldn't keep her legs still, or her arms. It felt as though her internal engine's idle had been set too high and she waited nervously at a starting line for the gun to go off.

Did she know this man beside her? Her body did. She had a new and raging hunger for him that added to her shakes. She wanted to crawl under his skin and stay warm. The desire came to nip at his marvelously sculpted chest, half of which was etched with spirals of inky-black tattoos that swirled each time he moved.

Being with this guy felt exquisitely erotic, even though somewhere inside her mind red warning flags were waving with questions about who he really was and what she was doing here.

"Have to move. Have to run," she said breathlessly.

His piercing green gaze held her captive. "Go ahead. Run," he said, beaming silent messages Kaitlin swore she understood in some strangely telepathic way. "Stay close to the tree cover tonight. Taking small steps is the way to go."

The gravelly quality of his voice sent a cascade of thrills through her that set off another adrenaline rush. Her body was responding to this guy's closeness as though she knew him better than she should and much more than she recalled. Or maybe her anxiousness was translating this dream into some kind of twisted sexual wishful thinking, because she had a nearly overwhelming desire to trace those inky tats with her tongue.

"I'm fast," she said, exhaling pent-up steam.

"And cocky for a newbie," he countered. "Hell, you're only two days old."

"I merely stumbled."

"You'll do so again if you don't listen. Your muscles have to get with the program."

Kaitlin glanced around, needing to look anywhere but into the green eyes observing her. "Why are we standing beneath the trees?"

"You've got to avoid staying for long in direct moonlight. It all takes time. You'll thank me later if you listen. It's a miracle you're here at all."

Each word he spoke in that mesmerizing tone served to spread the wildfires already kindling inside her. Only this guy, whoever he really was, could affect her like this. His powerful body, chiseled face and incredible eyes were a turn-on that made her want to jump his bones.

She felt like an animal.

If she could just wrap her arms around his broad shoulders, then lift her legs to encircle his strong thighs, the place inside her that was thrumming with a need for intimacy would perhaps be appeased. As inexplicable as it was, she was tethered to this sexy beast by an invisible chain. His breath had meant her survival. Part of him was already inside her.

Or had she made that up?

"Tell me your name," she said.

"Michael."

Michael. Like the archangel. She remembered hearing him tell her this before in a conversation that seemed to have taken place a long time ago.

"Two days old?" she said, remembering what he'd just said.

He shook his head. "Explanations later. For now, it's enough that you're alive and walking."

More than alive, Kaitlin thought. And how could she think about *later* when Michael's expression told her he shared her hunger and was fighting to keep from letting his hunger out? Weren't people supposed to live in the *now*? Experience each moment as if it were their last?

Had she confronted that last moment recently?

"I want to feel," she whispered hoarsely, afraid to think back. "I need to know everything life has to offer."

"Yes, but for you tonight is merely a dream."

"That's why you're here, Michael? I've dreamed you up?"

He took her hand in his and placed her open palm on his chest, making his remark about dreams seem ludicrous. This guy was solid sculpted male goodness through and through.

"Enjoy this while you can because if it's all good, you'll be back to reality tomorrow," he said.

Another word floated through Kaitlin's mind as if Michael had conjured it. *College.* Not a totally unfamiliar word, yet too distant to capture with a focus that already moved back to Michael's taut body and the hardness below his waist that she knew was in her honor.

"You want me," she whispered.

"Like I said, you know nothing." Michael reached up to move a tangle of her hair back from her face, showing off arms corded with power and tension. No tats covered his biceps. His skin was actually sun-bronzed.

Waves of lust struck Kaitlin so strongly that she would have swayed if he hadn't pinned her to the tree.

"I know this isn't normal," she said.

"Not for you," he agreed. "Not yet. Your feelings are tied to what happened."

Do not think back, her mind warned. *You'll be sorry if you do.*

Kaitlin glanced sideways. "No one is around?"

"No one you can see."

Michael's remark triggered a memory she had just warned herself not to find. Things hid in the dark. Bad things.

Catching a whiff of some new scent, Kaitlin struggled to place it. She reached for her throat, found the rough surface of the bandage and pressed there. The sharp-edged pain beneath that touch caused the night to close in.

"Oh, no, you don't." Michael's hands tugged her fingers from her neck.

"What…" Nearly breathless, Kaitlin started over. "What's wrong with me?"

"Nothing we can't deal with." Michael's voice deepened further as he glanced up at a patch of night sky visible through the branches.

Kaitlin followed his gaze. "Will I remember this dream?"

She ran her palm over his chest, outlining one scroll of the tattoos. Michael twitched, stopped her progress with a tight grip on her wrist and shook his head.

"It wouldn't be fair for me to take you up on that," he said.

Her eyes strayed. "What does it matter, if it's a dream?"

"It matters," he said. "And you will remember it all eventually."

She pulled away from his grip and moved her hand to his shoulder, where moonlight helped to outline his exquisite muscular shape. He stopped her again with a firm hand and a nebulous whispered comment. "You don't, as yet, know anything. It's hard for me to…"

He backed up, stood tall, drenched in moonlight. The first *pop* Kaitlin heard after his little speech was a muted sound. There was no mistaking the second for anything benign. Or the third.

Like a series of pinging buttons on an overstretched shirt, the bones of Michael's jaw began to unhinge. The beautiful, sharp-featured face in front of her began to stretch. Michael's dark hair lengthened as if someone invisible had tugged at the roots. His muscles danced as though something alive under the skin wanted to get out.

As he dropped to a crouch, the scrolling tattoos on his chest began to spread, covering muscle, turning his skin dark. Then his legs furred up in fluid series of swishes and cracks.

One minute the man had been there, and the next minute, something else appeared that uttered a reverberating growl. When his head lifted, familiar green eyes looked out, but it was no longer Michael, the angel's namesake, facing her. It was an animal, dark as the night, tall as her thighs. Sleek. Primal. Down on all fours.

Michael had turned into a wolf.

And he had been right about one thing.

She didn't yet know anything about what was going on.

Chapter 3

Kaitlin woke up screaming, her body prepared to fight. Fists curled, mouth open, she felt trapped and unable to flee the nightmare because something was holding her down.

She kicked out with her legs and opened her eyes. Expecting to see a big wolf leaning over her, she instead found another image. Trees.

Hell, yes. There were trees in her sightline, and not the living kind. She was looking at a picture, a poster of a forest, on the wall above a desk that held a retro lava lamp, a silver telephone and an open laptop computer.

Hesitating, consciously attempting to quiet her churning insides, Kaitlin's mind filled in the gaps. These were her things. Familiar things. She wasn't outside, running in a moonlit field. Nor was she pinned to a tree by a naked man.

This was her apartment.

But she wasn't alone.

Fine hairs at the nape of Kaitlin's neck prickled with leftover panic as she turned her head. No wolf waited there with its black fur gleaming. A woman, a stranger, sat on the edge of her bed.

"Kaitlin, is it?" her uninvited visitor asked.

Kaitlin sat up to find that she'd been trapped by nothing more than a tangle of sheets. Eyeing the stranger, she scooted backward against the headboard. Quivers of muscle soreness accompanied her movement. She looked down to find her arms covered in red scratches already starting to scab.

Instinctively, Kaitlin reached for her neck.

"That bandage won't be necessary for long," the woman said. "You'll have a pretty little scar that I suppose you can consider your first war wound."

The woman was close to Kaitlin in age—maybe twenty-three or four, with deeply tanned olive skin and glossy black hair that hung halfway down her back. Nothing out of the ordinary presented itself in the woman's face or body. The problem was her eyes, which were an unusual shade of green that Kaitlin had seen before.

Fingering the bandage taped to her neck, Kaitlin's fear escalated. She tore off the bandage and winced at the raw, extremely sensitive puckered line of raised skin beneath her right ear.

That can't be right. I'm awake now.

Dizziness threatened as flashes of memory returned. Night. Blood. An attacker with incredible strength. In that nightmare, she had been mauled by a monster.

Her eyes swept the room in a desperate attempt to set things straight. No man, wolfish or otherwise, sat on the bed, or appeared anywhere else in the small studio apartment. Morning light seeped through the filmy curtains.

There was no brown bedspread. She sat on familiar worn floral sheets.

"Kaitlin?" her visitor repeated.

"You can't be real." Kaitlin avoided the woman's green-eyed stare.

"Really? Then I wonder why I bothered to brush my hair. Still, I guess you'd have to think that way, wouldn't you, since your reality is being inconveniently rearranged."

"Who are you?"

Her visitor tossed her hair, scattering a whole bunch of scents into the air at once: soap, lipstick and something else Kaitlin had no time to pin down. *Damp fur?*

Also, now that she thought about it, other smells came to her above and beyond those: dust, pencil lead, chemicals from the lava lamp and a pair of dirty socks stashed under the bed. She also smelled the iron tang of anxiety. Her anxiety. Because, hell...the crisp denim of this stranger's dark blue jeans had a unique smell. Also discernible was the scent of the worn-out fabric of her own T-shirt. Edging those smells was a lingering odor of badly injured skin, blood and matted hair.

Her hands fell like rocks to the mattress as she studied the scratches crisscrossing her forearms.

"Looks like you might have picked those up last night," her visitor said. "Sometimes puppies forget how vulnerable their skin really is."

"Who are you?" Kaitlin repeated.

"I'm Rena. And you, it seems, are Michael's little secret. Until now."

Michael. That name belonged in a dream. Kaitlin refused to let this woman see her shake. She swallowed a rising protest.

"He hasn't told us about you," Rena continued. "Since

Michael has been MIA for a few days, I got worried and followed him here."

Michael was here? Yes. With her eyes closed, Kaitlin found hints of her dream man in the room. There were scents of shaving cream, faded jeans and musky maleness.

"Who are you, exactly?" she asked Rena, her voice faint.

"Kind of a new relative. A distant cousin."

That made no sense at all. Kaitlin tried another tactic. "What do you want?"

"Merely to see you and find out why Michael would do something like this. I suppose he wanted to ease you through the process on his own first, before letting us know what he'd done."

"What process would that be?"

In Kaitlin's mind the word *wolf* kept flashing. Fragments of what she'd begun to worry had not been a dream began to coalesce. In it, the man this woman spoke of had turned into an animal right before her eyes.

The fine line between reason and insanity made Kaitlin's nerve endings fire. As she wrapped her arms around her knees and considered Rena carefully, fear continued to make her heart race.

She looked again at the scratches on her arms. Had she gotten those from being pressed to the bark of a tree, or from a madman trying to kill her in the park?

Rena's smile suggested that none of these panic attacks Kaitlin was having might be warranted. Whoever this Michael guy was, and whatever kind of trauma she had been through, she couldn't believe there were alternate species in the world. If she'd had an accident and some guy named Michael, acting like a Good Samaritan, had helped her home, possibly jealousy was what had brought Rena here today. Rena could be Michael's girlfriend. His lover.

As calmly as she could, Kaitlin met Rena's scrutinizing gaze. "Where did your friend go?"

"To the corner store, probably to bring you something to eat," Rena said. "We need to keep our strength up and require lots of fuel. More than usual."

"We, as in what? Wolves?" Kaitlin asked cynically.

Rena smiled again, flashing very white teeth that almost made the idea of wolves seem plausible.

"He didn't have to bother. I'm not hungry," Kaitlin said. In fact, she was sure she'd never be hungry again.

"You'll be hungry as soon as you smell the food," Rena told her. "Our metabolisms run hot."

In her dream, Michael had been hot in more ways than one. But Kaitlin couldn't turn inward to look for answers to the problems at hand with this woman staring at her. In another minute, she'd sprint for the door.

"It wasn't a dream, you know," Rena said as if she had the ability to read Kaitlin's mind. "You'll find that out soon enough."

Rena seemed to be waiting for her to say something, as if they were going to have a conversation that made sense. All Kaitlin could get out was, "What day is it?"

"Monday."

"That can't be right. I couldn't have lost two days."

With another glance at the discarded bandage, Kaitlin added, "What is going on? Really going on, I mean?"

Rena stood up. "I'm sorry I can't explain it to you, Kaitlin. For the time being, I guess I'm not supposed to know you exist. Imagine my surprise in finding out that you do."

Kaitlin was feeling stranger by the minute because Rena was fairly convincing. She decided to go for broke, hoping that when this woman she had never seen before heard what she had to say, Rena would laugh her head off and hit the road.

"Are you a wolf, Rena?"

"You can't tell?" Rena countered noncommittally.

"Hell, I'm not even sure I'm awake."

"Then the answer is yes."

Yes…

The room suddenly felt cramped. Too many ridiculous ideas were taking up space, and the air seemed to beat with a foreign rhythm. Kaitlin blinked slowly to get her bearings and went for round two of the most inconceivable questions possible. "So, that would make you and Michael part of a group of…wolves?"

The question sounded silly in a truly horrifying way. Rena didn't laugh, though. She said, "You call us werewolves. And we call ourselves a pack."

Werewolves. Pack. Kaitlin's stomach tightened. Her next question bordered on hysterics. "You believe that? For real?"

Rena held up a hand in a gesture that indicated she was telling the truth. Scout's honor, or some such equivalent thing for females.

Kaitlin stared at the pretty, rather feline-featured visitor. "How many of you are there in this pack?"

"Four. There are four of us here, and then there's you."

The hairs at the nape of Kaitlin's neck stood up. Chills iced her spinal column as phrases came back with a startling clarity—bits of words the Michael in the nightmare had used.

It's the only way you'll make it. And *Remember that I gave you a choice.*

She did not want to ask the next question and knew Rena anticipated it, because the scent of Rena's excitement wafted in the air.

"Are you hinting that I've become one of you?"

Glancing sideways to view her image in the wall mirror, Kaitlin found a pasty-complexioned, tangle-haired version of herself. But it was Kaitlin Davies who looked back.

Rena smoothed the creases from her jeans with both hands. "Not quite one of us. I suppose you'll be accepted by the pack if he wants you to be, though, since…"

"Since what?" Even short pauses in Rena's partial explanations were intolerable.

"Well, it's not my place to assume anything or tell you more. You're Michael's pet project, so he will have to explain."

"What is he, the king?"

"Alpha," Rena corrected, walking to the door. She opened it before anyone had knocked, and then stepped back to make way for the man who suddenly filled the doorway.

Chapter 4

Michael stopped on the threshold of Kaitlin's apartment. He looked first to Rena, who nodded her head before slipping past him. Damn it. Rena knew about Kaitlin, which meant they probably all knew.

His gaze slipped to the waif on the bed who had compressed herself into a tight ball near the headboard. The auburn-haired beauty was staring at him with a wide-eyed, stunned expression, as though she'd seen a ghost.

Because the bandage he'd taped to her neck had been removed, he knew what was coming. Hard questions and demands for explanations would be the next things out of her mouth.

Really, this nursemaid routine didn't suit him. He was better at chasing bad guys. And Rena had no right to jump on his parade.

"I see you've met Rena."

He leaned against the doorjamb, not quite sure what

to say now that Kaitlin was fully awake. She was staring. Her eyes were clear and focused.

"I didn't tell the others about you because I wanted to make sure you were all right first. Otherwise…"

She finished the remark for him in a voice that was stronger than he would have expected. "Otherwise there might not be any me to tell them about, since I'd be dead."

He could sense the fear radiating off her in waves similar to the rippling heat of a desert mirage. Only colder. He felt that fear from six feet away. Yet Kaitlin was showing an inkling of the spirit that had attracted him to her in the first place. Even half-dead, he'd sensed she was a fighter.

He couldn't look away from the tight, pale face that wasn't quite like any other human's face he'd seen. Light, this time from streaks of morning sun, seemed to caress Kaitlin's delicate contours. He'd noticed those contours from the start, too. What he'd failed to remember correctly was the impact she had on him when those big eyes of hers were open. This fragile flower took his breath away.

And if he admitted that to anyone, or took it too seriously, he would no longer resemble the wolf he'd always thought he was, and he would dishonor his fallen mother's memory.

Humans were a fickle, dangerous species. Some were even his enemies. And here he was, protecting one from things that went bump in the night.

He observed Kaitlin steadily. "You're pale, but looking better. Does your neck hurt very badly?"

"Bad enough," she said.

Life pulsed beneath her skin. In this case, he could sense anger, an indication of her turnaround, and yet Kaitlin looked even more waifish than before. Already thin, she'd lost more weight in the past two days—a sign of her new, faster metabolism kicking in. If she didn't eat something soon, her nerves would fry.

Michael lifted the paper bag in his hand and watched her glance at it. "Breakfast."

She didn't acknowledge that.

"Do you feel sick, Kaitlin?"

She shook her head. "I'm not sick, I'm scared. I'm not sure who you are, why you're here or what's going on."

He nodded. "I do realize how difficult this must be. Let me just say that I found you in the park, injured pretty badly, and that I helped in the best way I could."

She pointed to the bandage. "You did that?"

"Yes."

"You brought me here?"

He nodded. "As soon as I found out who you were and where you belonged."

Her hand went to her neck. "I can't feel stitches."

"You didn't need them."

"I didn't go to a hospital?"

"No. No hospital."

"Then the injury wasn't so bad after all?"

"It could have been your death," he said, "if untended."

She took a moment to reply. "If you hadn't come along with a bandage, you mean?"

Her eyes were pleading with him to lie. She wanted him to laugh and tell her this was all a big joke of the worst kind and that things would be fine now. Of course, he couldn't say any of those things and mean them. Though she had been faced with this situation for only fifty-some hours, she would have to come to terms with what had become her new reality.

"Lucky for you, I did come along," he said.

Kaitlin's shaking intensified, though Michael didn't sense shock setting in, and that was another miracle. Her fragile exterior hid a decent backbone that made her want to try to deal.

"Public places are bad for us," he explained, driven to speech by the intensity of her gaze. "Finding out about what we are would mean the end of many of us. Humans aren't partial to sharing their planet with those who are unlike them. Given that, I couldn't take you to your real home, either."

She didn't immediately press him for more information about that. Her attention moved again to the paper bag in his hand before coming back to his face. When her eyes met his, an electrified shudder passed through him that Michael didn't like at all.

Her bloodless lips parted. "I dreamed that I had a near-death experience. Could that be true?"

"Maybe now isn't the time for details."

"Because you don't have any details?" she challenged.

"Timing is everything, Kaitlin. Those details might hinder the healing process."

Would you want to hear how you nearly bit the big one, and that your life force was drained by a fanged parasite? Or that you now will be initiated into the moon's cult?

He kept those things to himself.

Her gaze remained nearly as steady as his was. "Maybe you'll tell me that I'm going to be a wolf, and that you really are one, too," she said. "Like in my dreams, and according to Rena."

Michael glanced to the corridor before turning back to the bed. Rena had gone, but had obviously spilled some of the dirt he had intended to hold back.

Moving slowly, he stepped inside the apartment and closed the door behind him. "If we're to have a chat, mind if I come in?"

"I thought only vampires had to ask for permission to enter a building."

He smiled. "I was being polite. We have no such rule governing our behavior."

"No. I don't suppose animals have a need for rules," she said.

She was still staring at him, and hadn't moved. Michael didn't attempt another step in her direction.

"Did it really happen?" she asked. "Was I attacked?"

"Yes."

"You helped me?"

He nodded.

"None of it was a dream?"

"Afraid not."

She rubbed her eyes, daring to momentarily take her attention from him, and whispered, "Shit."

"I'm sorry," Michael said.

"For helping me?"

"For how that's going to turn out."

She sat up straighter, resignation in her expression. "Okay. If it wasn't a dream, tell me about what's going on. That's what you meant, isn't it, by withholding details? There's a surprise in store?"

"Truly, now might not be the time for the tough ones."

"Tough for me, or for you?"

"Both of us, actually," Michael said.

She fingered her neck. "Your friend came here to tell me I'm going to become something other than human. Since she was pretty convincing, does that make me crazy if I decide to believe her?"

"Not crazy," Michael said. "Enlightened."

He watched Kaitlin briefly close her eyes and exhale a slow stream of the air that he had helped to preserve by giving her back her life. Thoughts of that rescue brought mixed feelings because of all the unseen consequences. Still, damn it, if he had it to do all over again, he'd have done the same thing.

"You aren't a figment of my imagination?" She asked this seriously.

"No figment, Kaitlin."

She seemed to consider his reply. "If the attack was real, what about the other parts of what I thought was a dream? Did we run through a park?"

"We did. Last night."

"Naked?"

"One of us didn't have many clothes on. Clothes get in the way of a shape-shift."

That shut her up for a long minute. Then she said, "No dream, really? None of it?"

"I'm sorry."

Her eyes were even wider now, and trained on him in a way that made Michael's internal wolf whine. Kaitlin's gray gaze was direct and accusatory. "What is an Alpha?"

Her change in direction didn't throw him, but her use of that word did. Michael promised himself that he would be having some serious words with Rena later on.

"An Alpha is the leader of a pack," he said.

"A pack of wolves."

He nodded, almost able to see the wheels of Kaitlin's mind turning. The scent of her desperation tinged the air, though she was fighting for control over her part of the conversation, knowing its importance had to override her fear levels.

"I've never liked big, scary animals." She said this breathlessly. "And now I'm supposedly going to be one?" Her eyes found his. "Like you? Like what I think I saw you turn into?"

Michael's heart picked up its pace. He had made a vow

never to get this close to a human female under any circumstances and had obliterated that vow with her because... well, again, he wasn't sure why this woman affected him so much.

"Not exactly like me," he replied. "Though you will be something close enough."

Her jaw tensed, sending a spiral of pain through the wound on her neck, pain that Michael also felt. He supposed he was sharing her feelings due to having placed his blood in her veins, and that blood was giving him a heads-up on a few things. But that kind of sharing deepened his determination to stay as far away from Kaitlin Davies as possible in the future, once she knew the score.

"What does *close enough* mean?" she asked.

It seemed they were going to aim for the hard ones after all. This little fireball wasn't about to let him off the hook.

Could he blame her?

"You now have Lycan blood in your veins," he said.

He saw that the word *Lycan* didn't ring a bell.

"Lycans are a very old lineage of shape-shifters," Michael said.

Her head came up.

"Lycans can't replicate themselves exactly, unless two Lycans mate and produce pure-blooded offspring. Because you now have Lycan blood in your veins, you'll be a special combination of wolf and human, two things that can only mix well if the recipient of the blood gift is strong enough to handle their wolf, and pays close attention to the changes."

"Blood gift? Hell, that's what you call it?" Her eyes had gone glassy, though they still maintained focus. "*Lycan* means *wolf*?"

"Yes."

"If this is true, I won't be a real wolf?"

"Half wolf," Michael reiterated. "And half human. *Werewolf.*"

She repeated that term to herself in a whisper, as if trying it on for size, and took time to formulate her next question. "You aren't a werewolf?"

"Lycans are Weres, yes, and yet some older Were families have traits that actually fall under the categorization of shape-shifter. When those like us change, we take on animal form. Wolf form."

None of this appeared to deter Kaitlin from pursuing her agenda of gaining all the information she could.

"What about the monster that attacked me?" she asked.

"Vampire."

She closed her eyes and clasped her knees tighter, as if one of those monsters had gotten into the room. Michael sensed the rise in her blood pressure. There was now a faint tinge of pink in her cheeks.

"That was real." She hung her head. "God. True. There are such things. No joke."

"Hard to believe, I know," Michael said. "For me, it's equally as hard to believe that there are regular old humans that can't change into anything."

He walked to the side of the bed and set the paper bag on the table beside it. Kaitlin glanced up again. Beneath that gaze he felt wrong somehow, and that neither of them deserved the repercussions of what he had set in motion. His blood had bound them together in special ways. Before too long, he would have to break some of those invisible chains he already felt linking to her.

"You chased that vampire away," she said.

"I took care of the problem so that vampire can't hurt others or make more mindless monsters."

"You don't consider yourself a monster?"

"I suppose that's a matter of perspective. But no, I don't."

"Supernatural vigilante, then?" she asked.

"My pack and others like us try to keep the peace. Some of us work behind the scenes to chase the undead away from the human population because only in that way can we, as a Were species, stay safe."

There was more to tell her. Things she needed to know—such as the fact that she had spent one entire day and night in a coma, fighting the transition from human to something else.

He could tell her that he'd never seen a human take such a short time to pass through the first phase of moving toward their half wolf status, and that she was an anomaly.

He could warn Kaitlin that possibly she would hit the next wall in the hours to come, and therefore would need him for a while more, though he dreaded that need for closeness.

He could not bring up the fact that humans, like the one she had been, had hunted and killed his mother for sport.

"Then I should be grateful you were out there." She surprised him again with a complete change of tone. Her voice became softer now, with an almost magical ability to work its way under his tough Were skin. The prickle of anticipation Michael felt when he observed Kaitlin was always unexpected, and wholly unique.

He fended off the desire to shift right there and avoid those gray eyes, the way he had done the night before. But shifting was a private matter, and Kaitlin had already seen him do it twice.

"Thank you for whatever you did to keep me alive, Michael. I mean it."

She was still curled up in a ball, knees drawn tight. "I

didn't want to die and prayed for intervention. So, really, you can be considered an angel. My angel."

Michael counted the passing seconds by his own racing heartbeats, knowing that this was the moment to take his leave. He wanted to argue again that he was the furthest thing possible from an angel. He had lethal teeth, ten razor-sharp claws, and he pretty much adhered to the moon's beck and call. What kind of angel used the moon for their higher power?

He was a tough fighter for the rights of his kind to exist in this world, and yet his reactions to Kaitlin left him feeling fuzzy and ill-defined about the whole human-versus-wolf thing. These feelings were new and unwelcome. They left him feeling vulnerable when that word had never entered his vocabulary. They made him feel guilty about breaking certain vows.

I'm not to be trusted here, Kaitlin, this close to you.

He had to take care of this problem of being attracted to Kaitlin, and quickly. He couldn't afford time away from his hunt for vampires and the protection of his pack.

Now that Rena knew about what he'd done, she could take Kaitlin under her wing. That task would serve Rena right for coming to see Kaitlin uninvited.

He shouldn't linger near Kaitlin Davies for two minutes more. He'd done a good deed, had shared Lycan blood, which was a rare event for any Lycan, and Kaitlin had thanked him. The sun was up. She had made it through the weekend and seemed to be okay.

Damn, though...

Only heartless, soulless vampires left their offspring to fend for themselves. Vamps, and also a new breed of nasty rogue Weres created from the bites of other werewolves bent on passing along that trait to unsuspecting others. He had an obligation here to see Kaitlin through her transition to becoming Were, no matter how attracted to her he was. Three members of his pack had been the recipients of illicit tooth-and-claw encounters. Surely those Weres would understand about Kaitlin needing help, and condone what he had done to save her.

Kaitlin's voice rose again, cutting through Michael's internal chatter. "Why me? If you have a secret to keep, why help me?"

Her beautiful gray eyes reflected the chill of her fear. Kaitlin's sober expression pierced his soul. Hell, this woman made the big bad wolf want to protect her.

"You're young, beautiful and innocent. You have a whole lifetime ahead of you and didn't deserve to die like that," Michael said.

"Does anyone deserve to die?" she asked.

"Yes. The monster that attacked you and dozens of others like it."

"God, there are more of them?"

"A seemingly infinite number," Michael replied.

Kaitlin winced at the pain turning her head caused, and said, "You would have helped anyone out there?"

He had to think about that, and took too long for Kaitlin's current need for answers.

Her eyes were accusatory. "You're telling me the truth? You're some sort of shape-shifter? I wasn't mistaken about what I saw?"

He said, "Beneath a full moon, I change from this shape into another one."

"Only with a full moon? I don't recall seeing one last night."

"I can change other times, as well. Only a few Lycans can do that, and not very many of us."

She fired off another remark. "I'll be a hybrid because I'm also human."

"Because you started out human."

"Why didn't I die, Michael? What about this blood gift you mentioned? How does that work?"

"If you're not born into our species, a transfer of blood is the only way to be initiated. It doesn't take much, and is the only way I know of to heal the damage from a deadly vampire attack."

"But it creates another werewolf."

"Yes," he reluctantly admitted.

Species. Initiated. Heal. Michael wondered how anyone in Kaitlin's situation could possibly comprehend this.

"Would I have become a vampire if the monster's blood had been left inside me?" she asked.

"You would have died and then been reanimated as one of them. Just like them. No heart. No soul. No need for breath. Hungering for blood."

She pried her lips apart. "Maybe you helped me so that you wouldn't have to contend with one more bloodsucker like the one I would have become."

"Being like us seemed the better option, Kaitlin. Our genetics cause us to heal faster than normal, and we recover from injuries cleanly. We can survive a lot of things. With wolf blood in your veins to counteract that vamp's damage, you had a chance. You've made it this far. In another month, that wound will be nothing more than a thin white scar. So I suppose…"

He leaned over her, with his hands on the mattress. "I suppose that though this new turn of events is unbelievable, you can be thankful you're here today."

Staring at Kaitlin, Michael relived how he had breathed life back into her after she had lain on the hard, damp ground. How he had cradled her in his arms and run his fingers over her bloodless face. He, who prided himself on remaining aloof from the human population, had whispered assurances to this woman, though one of her species had destroyed his family and others like his with a spray of silver bullets.

Did helping Kaitlin make him a traitor to his family, or just a bighearted idiot who made a rash decision on the spur of the moment? He felt like a traitor. Hell, saving a life didn't equate to being an angel, and might have been an action he would someday regret.

Yet when Kaitlin broke contact and looked away, he wanted to pull her attention back despite his inner protests about keeping some distance. He wanted to lift her in his arms and trade hot, sultry breaths. Fantasies were appearing about pressing her to a tree in the moonlight, where he'd kiss Kaitlin to within an inch of her life, and revel in each second.

And if he were willing to admit more personal blasphemy, he'd concede the desire to go beyond that kiss-fest and have her in all the ways that counted between a male and a female, while listening to her soft growls of pleasure.

He had to close his eyes to shut those images off.

What had been his motivation for going back on an oath? Kaitlin Davies wasn't human anymore. There was a slight possibility he could have helped her in that park in hopes of just such a situation as this, having been instantly attracted to her, and despite the taboo placed on Lycans mating with human-wolf hybrids of lesser bloodlines.

If that had been the case, though, he didn't recall it. Nor had he stopped to consider that by saving her he would prevent Kaitlin from becoming a vampire. Neither of those thoughts had crossed his mind. All he saw was her, and how badly she was being hurt.

"I think I'm going to be sick, and I think I'd prefer to be sick alone," she announced, bringing him back to the present.

She wasn't looking at him now. He had to go, had to leave her, at least for a while. He also felt sick, confused, sad.

"All right, Kaitlin. I'll go. Things will work out. You'll see."

Promises, little wolf, from what you believe to be a freak of nature, Michael silently added, scanning her profile.

"Werewolves tend to land on our feet, you know," he said aloud.

"Yeah," she agreed in a strangled voice, and with a last stab at defiance. "All four."

Chapter 5

Remember that I gave you a choice.

Michael's words from that night floated through Kaitlin's memory as she looked into the emerald-colored eyes of the man who had uttered them.

Contrary to what he'd just said, Michael hadn't made any effort to leave her apartment. Looking at him, she realized Michael wasn't just handsome, he was extraordinary. Tall, leanly muscled and much too male, he wore a blue long-sleeved T-shirt and faded jeans that fit him like a second skin.

His face was as chiseled as her memory of his abs, and the angularity served up a regal air. Dark hair hung to his chin, straight, shiny, with the slightly mussed look of a man who didn't give a hoot about his appearance.

But his looks were deceiving, because Michael wasn't human, even though he appeared to be at the moment. Something much wilder hid beneath his skin, waiting to get out. She sensed that wildness as if she could taste it.

She had witnessed his shape-shifting firsthand. That wasn't what bothered her at the moment, though. The awful part was the realization that whether or not Michael was a wolf, she was attracted to him. She wanted him in blistering hot, slightly demented ways. Closeness was what she craved...for both Michael and what he kept hidden inside.

Maybe what he'd done to her had caused these feelings. Maybe she was just grateful to him and that was showing up in inappropriate ways. If Michael had turned out to be an emissary from heaven, she would surely have gone to hell for what she wanted to do to him right then and there.

So, it was now official. She might not have died this weekend, but she had gone completely insane.

When Michael moved, Kaitlin wondered if he had felt her attraction to him. Instead of turning for the door, he transferred the paper bag he'd brought from the table to the bedsheets that no longer covered her up.

"You need to eat, Kate."

His voice was hushed, sexy as heck and full of unacknowledged emotion. He'd used the nickname her family used, and made it seem intimate. Beneath his keen green-eyed observation, Kaitlin felt exposed in her old T-shirt, and she was short of breath. The thin, worn fabric covering her was the only thing standing between them, and as a barrier it was a joke.

When Michael's gaze landed on her throat, her neck throbbed mercilessly, as if the injury somehow recognized its savior. Her body lost some of its chill and the room began to spin when his eyes bored into hers in a replay of their connection the night she had nearly died. With that gaze, she remembered the dark fur of the animal he had become.

Needing to think and to decide what to do next, she

looked away. She didn't dare show him how badly she wanted him, or how conflicted she was about feelings that weren't in any way normal reactions to the events preceding this moment.

"Kate. Kaitlin."

He whispered to her in a sensuous, velvety tone—the voice of a wolf prince walking upright on two legs. Lycan. Werewolf. Wolf. She had to look at him. She felt compelled to do as he asked.

His expression was set and sober. His wolfish eyes gleamed. Oh, yes, she wanted him, all right. She could argue all she wanted to, and pass this off as a trip to Neverland, but she couldn't lie about her connection to Michael. As absurd as it seemed, with just one kiss at death's door, he had bound her soul to his.

No dream. No dream at all.

"Kaitlin," he said again.

"If I won't be human anymore, what about my family?" she asked.

"You won't lose them. They don't even really have to know for a while," Michael replied.

"You don't have any idea what they're like, or how close we are."

"We can deal with that later. First, let's tend to you."

What did he see in her? Why had he chosen her to save? She wasn't drop-dead gorgeous, or even close. She didn't stand out in a crowd, dress for success or anyone's approval. In fact, she had always tried to blend in.

Her body was lean and athletic, like a runner's, without accentuated curves and bulging breasts. She had never worn lipstick. Kaitlin Mary Davies was five foot five, and sprang from delicate-boned Irish stock.

She was the eldest of the two Davies siblings and had been taught to question, to test and never to outright rebel.

She had been encouraged to stand on her own two feet, as long as she stood on them in relatively close proximity to her family and her home. And though she had come close on a few occasions, she had never actually slept with a man.

"My father is a judge. Mom is a homemaker." She spoke in a rush. "There are no black sheep in the closet that I know of. It's a sure bet there are no anomalies in my family tree."

Michael let her go on.

"Not only am I getting a PhD in history, you're saying that I've been awarded a degree in animal, and that I now have wolf in my Irish veins. I will be that Davies family anomaly."

Deal, Kaitlin. You have to deal. Slow down. Take this in.

Had he said that to her? His lips hadn't moved and yet she heard those directions as clearly as if he had spoken. Was part of Michael in her mind as well as in her veins?

"Does it hurt?" she asked. "Being a werewolf has to be no picnic. I've seen you shape-shift and it didn't look like fun."

He was using some kind of mesmerizing voodoo to pull her gaze back to his. The jolt of electricity sparking between them was immediate, and like a bolt of lightning stapling her to the bed.

"Yes. It hurts at first, while the body readjusts," he replied. "Then you get used to it, and can look forward to the changes."

She blinked slowly to absorb what Michael said, failing to counter that there was no alternative now, other than getting used to something like that, since the only other option had been taken away. Death.

No, not even death, since she would have come back as one of the undead if Michael hadn't shown up.

"Well," he said. "As much as I'd like to stay, you probably have class today. Go. Getting back into your routine will be good for you."

Stunned by that suggestion, Kaitlin said, "Are you kidding? I go on as if nothing happened, and wait to see if anything will?"

"As much as you can, because that's what life does. It goes on."

"Are you a student?" she asked.

He shook his head. "I'm a carpenter."

"What if I can't act like life goes on? Where will I find you if I need help?" Her voice had grown noticeably quieter.

"Come to the park an hour before nightfall tonight. I'll be there. That's important, Kaitlin. Do you understand? It must be before dark."

"The park? I—"

"You'll be safe, I promise. You can bet that I keep my word."

"Who will I find out there? Man or wolf?"

"Before nightfall, you'll find me. I'll be waiting. After nightfall, you'll find more of your new self, and might not be ready."

Her hands were shaking. Her face again felt cold. As much as she wanted Michael, she also wanted him gone. Yet the prospect of him leaving seemed daunting.

"If there's no full moon?"

"Any moon phase can instigate small changes," he said.

When Michael's lips turned up at the corners, the moment became even more frightening. This was just another day in the life of a werewolf, while for her it was the end of life as she'd always known it.

Afraid to move, Kaitlin watched the thing she hoped for and dreaded all at the same time happen. Michael caught her chin so that she couldn't look away. Then he swore beneath his breath as if trying one last time to fend off his feelings...before his mouth found hers.

The sensation of his slick lips sliding over hers wasn't wholly unexpected. In that intimate act Kaitlin felt the wind in the trees and the dampness of grass beneath her toes. She felt moonlight on her face, and had a sudden urge to sprint through open spaces.

All in his kiss.

Not even a kiss, really. Merely a touch.

However, he soon changed that.

Adding pressure, Michael urged her lips to participate. His warm tongue met hers, sending Kaitlin spinning.

She strained for more of what he had to offer, yearning for a connection that would tame her fears. She grasped at life, seeking to understand what had happened to her, how this man had saved her with his blood and what would become of her now.

She struggled to comprehend the images she'd been shown and the future she would have to come to terms with if any of this could possibly be real.

It was all so damn freaky.

Thoughts fled as Michael's talented mouth conquered hers in a way that left her mindless. His kiss became a deep, devouring act that demanded she respond in kind.

The kiss went on and on as though it might never end, and as if they'd never get enough of each other. Hunger sparked memory. This was what she recalled—Michael's breath in her lungs and his mouth on hers, there at death's door. This was what she needed now in order to get up and go on.

Michael...

As if sensing how desperately she demanded this connection, the pressure of Michael's mouth lightened. His lips left hers to angle across her left cheek, drifting toward her neck in a downward trajectory of kisses. He paused near the band of her T-shirt, took hold of the cotton with both hands and crumpled the fabric in his fist.

He was so damn hot. The room was humid and stifling. Her body was quaking with a longing that had nothing to do with life-altering transitions…unless it was about becoming intimate with a man she really didn't know.

This was body betrayal, big-time, with the hope that Michael would stay and finish what they had started. Maybe then she'd be able to rest. Possibly she'd get over this ridiculous crush if their bodies actually merged.

"Wait."

The command was loud, though it had been whispered through her cracked lips.

God, had she said that?

Michael heeded that command. His head came up. When he looked into her eyes, Kaitlin detected defiance in his gaze, and knew he was scrambling for a hold on his own wayward needs. Still, he was going to do what she asked, no matter what that cost him.

"You're right, of course." His voice emerged as a growl.

She had to say something. "I owe you for saving my life."

"But now isn't the time to repay me, and I wouldn't expect that kind of payment from you anyway, especially when you might not be happy with the way things turn out."

He didn't smile as he went on. "If I go now, you'll settle down. Being near another wolf tends to bring out the wolf in you, and in me. I know that, and I thought…" He let that part dangle, and started again. "Your allure is strong, Kaitlin. I'll admit that."

Michael straightened up before she could reach for him.

He leaned over her once more, with both hands on the bed beside her. Eyes closed, Kaitlin waited for his mouth to betray his words and for Michael to ignore her outburst in spite of what he'd just said.

There was to be no further touch.

She heard the click of a door and opened her eyes to find herself alone. Michael had left her with the tan paper bag.

Her own growl of distress rose in her throat as her stomach again turned over. Giving in to the rush of feeling she'd trapped in her core, Kaitlin tore into the paper bag as though it were made of tissue—ripping it apart, sending pieces of paper flying.

If she couldn't have Michael, she'd at least have this.

She wolfed down the meal as if she hadn't eaten in months instead of days, and with the gusto of someone who might never eat again.

Because you just never knew what could happen from one minute to the next.

Only somewhat satiated, Kaitlin glanced sideways, eyes bleary, startled by her reflection in the mirror. She was on her hands and knees on the bed, bare ass showing from beneath her T-shirt. Barbecue sauce was smeared all over her face and hands, making her look, to her complete dismay, very much the beast she might become.

Staring at that image, she started to cry.

Chapter 6

Sixty-four-thousand-dollar question: How do you cope with life on a Monday when you've almost died over the weekend?

Answer: You either curl up for days on end, or you have a go at what's left.

In the end, Kaitlin had to remember that the Davies family was nothing if not flexible. But she feared that the day stretching ahead would seem like a blur, with life burning like an eternal question mark at the center. Colorless day, colorless surroundings. Heavy books, laptops and ongoing research. Meaningless chitchat. Typical postgraduate stuff.

Because she was no longer herself.

Or so Rena and Michael kept telling her.

Concentrating was difficult when there were monsters all around, and when a person's eternal flame could be choked out so quickly. When this life do-over had turned out to be a doozy.

However bad things were, she was determined to try to cope. She would handle this, because there was no alternative.

Remaining optimistic proved to be tough, though. In the hallway, Kaitlin focused on avoiding others and keeping to the sidelines, not sure she could actually carry on a conversation or if the students she passed would know she was different. Was she different? She had only Michael's and Rena's word for that.

By the time she was halfway through the main university building, odd things were happening. Inexplicable things. Smells, scents and fragrances were suddenly overwhelming and more of an affront to her senses. Polish on the floors gave off a sweet, sticky odor. Scuff marks from black-soled shoes smelled like burned rubber. Paper stuck to bulletin boards made her eyes water.

Crowds of people huddled in the corners, amplifying the odors of damp clothes, hair gel, fabric dyes and perfume. Passing the cafeteria was a big mistake. Although she was hungry again, almost ravenous, the smell of overcooked pizza sickened her.

She wanted to escape, hide, get away, and didn't know where to go or how to outdistance the waves of panic that stuck to her like shadows. She had to wait to see Michael again.

New self. Changes. Don't go out after dark.

She chewed her fingernails in frustration and chose a secluded seat in the back of the library, though she was certain there was no way to work on her thesis. No one gave her a second glance or turned around to stare.

The tick of the wall clock drove her mad. Fighting every agonizingly slow minute, Kaitlin waded through the hours like a sinking swimmer, finding it harder and harder to breathe when beyond the library walls she could feel *him*. Michael. Somewhere close.

Thoughts of Michael made her muscles dance with anticipation. The leftover pressure of his talented mouth brought far too much heat. She looked up werewolves online on her laptop, shuddering as she read lines of a story labeled as myth. She grew more and more restless as the afternoon dragged on. Forgoing her work, she drew pictures of wolves on her notebook and tried to remember the shape of Michael's eyes.

When the clock chimed five, she raced through crowds of students having a normal day, wondering how they could be so oblivious to events unfolding around them. Almost at the exit, she skidded to a stop near a bunch of people gathered outside a closed classroom door. Taped to that door was a note.

"Class canceled due to instructor illness."

Her fear turned major. What if that missing teacher had also been some fanged monster's prey?

Her legs began to shake uncontrollably.

Going to be sick. Need to get out.

Taking in ragged breaths of stale air, Kaitlin slumped against the wall with her head in her hands. After several long minutes she was able to again stand upright, and then only because there were answers to find and truths to sort out.

"Come hell or high water..." She reached for the neck of the sweater that hid what a stranger named Rena had called her "war wound" and finished the statement. "I'm going to find out what the hell is going on."

Michael paced from tree to tree, sure Kaitlin would show up, though he wouldn't have blamed her if she didn't.

He hadn't meant to kiss her. Hadn't realized he was kissing her until she stopped him. Now she'd have the wrong impression of this meeting and what he wanted her to get out of it. She might assume this to be an invitation to a rendezvous. If so, she would be dead wrong.

Kissing wasn't on his agenda.

Touching her was out of the question.

He set that firmly in his mind and stopped pacing twenty feet from the spot where Kaitlin had nearly lost her life, thinking that she would indeed have to be tough to return here so soon.

Making her confront her new direction in life was part of his plan and an important first step in helping her to face the truth. Hopefully, eventually, she would get past being afraid of the unknown.

For the time being, she needed guidance. After tonight, he was determined to turn her over to Rena. Females were so much better than males at dealing with personal issues, whatever species they belonged to. Some kind of innate nurturing thing had been twisted into female DNA.

That's what he told himself, anyway.

Rena wasn't exactly softhearted, but she would step up to the plate if he asked her to. He knew Rena harbored a lust for him that the she-wolf never fully kept hidden, but he considered Rena family. She wasn't the new rusty-haired human-wolf hybrid that his wolf craved in some strange and inexplicable way.

Rena was intuitive. She would see this. Although Rena wouldn't think much of what he'd done to save Kaitlin, the she-wolf would never purposefully harm anyone who didn't deserve it.

So. Hell. Why had he done what he had done, exactly? Why had he helped a human being? Chance? Coincidence? Serendipity?

Humans had not given this same kind of consideration

to his family. After hunting his mother, they shot her, did terrible things to her body and then dragged her off. Illicit game hunters in on the secret existence of werewolves had hoped for a pricey black-market pelt, but hadn't gotten their wish. His mother, also able to shape-shift at will, had robbed them of that last detail.

Michael scanned the lawn. With his sensitive hearing mechanisms on alert, he experienced an anticipatory spike in pulse rate. But it wasn't Kaitlin who approached.

"I get it, Michael." Rena effortlessly covered ground on long, shapely legs.

"What do you get?"

"She's different."

He nodded. "You noticed."

"I wonder what it is, though." Rena stopped beside him with her hands stuffed into the pockets of her jeans, and looked up at him. "What are you going to do with her?"

"I suppose that depends on how she turns out."

"How bad was it for her? I know you wouldn't do this unless it was absolutely necessary."

"There wasn't much to save," he replied.

Rena sniffed the air. "Whatever happened to her happened near here? Some of her scent lingers."

"Rogue vamp," Michael said. "Possibly only days old."

"Damn things are getting bolder. That's the second attack in a week." Rena nailed him with a shrewd stare. "Why did you do it?"

"I suppose I felt sorry for her."

Rena's expression let him know she saw through that answer. She asked, "Is this a new trend?"

"Hopefully not."

Rena looked around. "Is she coming here to meet you?"

"Maybe she'll show. Maybe not."

Michael didn't want to get into this now, since he'd

have to go over it with the rest of the pack tonight. Rena was good at pressing the limits of trespassing on personal space, though. She'd been raised in a family of twelve.

"Oh, she will show, all right. You've mesmerized her," she said.

"She'll get over it. People often idolize their rescuers at first, until that new take on life wears off."

"Yes, but Kaitlin's new take on life won't wear off. She won't be able to go back to her old ways as if nothing happened, will she?"

"I'm hoping you'll help her with her transition to this new life."

"And I hope you're kidding, Michael."

He looked directly at her. "I can't think of anyone better for the task, or that I'd trust with it more."

Rena's eyes were bright with an emotion she almost succeeded in keeping hidden. After helping to raise her numerous siblings, she wasn't going to be amenable to babysitting again.

"Like me, Cade was human until he was bitten," she said. "He's calmer. He'd be a better keeper."

"Cade is all male, as you well know."

"You're suggesting that no male can resist this little human?" Rena fired back.

"I'd rather not deal with having to find out until Kaitlin can make up her own mind about which side she prefers to take."

"In case she wants to hide out among the humans and pretend she's still one of them, you mean," Rena said.

"Like we all do," Michael reminded her.

Rena turned away from him, sniffing at something she perceived in the wind. Michael was way ahead of her and had been monitoring that smell for the past couple of minutes.

"Vampire," Rena growled.

"Two of them," he said. "And I think I might have just broken a promise to our new pack-mate about keeping her safe."

Every nerve in Kaitlin's body screamed bloody murder as she took that first step toward the path to the park. The smell of freshly mowed grass hit her hard. The wide expanse of park grounds ahead of her seemed ominous. However, by the time she'd taken a second step, she was resigned to go through with this meeting.

She just needed a little encouragement.

"One foot in front of the other, that's all."

She marched on, shoulders hunched, her gaze scanning the surroundings. Late-evening light lay in a pink haze on the distant mountain rage. Pastel air dripped through the branches of the trees. Several students milled around near the buildings behind her. No one she knew.

As Kaitlin picked up her pace, she warned herself not to look to the right. Despite herself, she slowed, automatically braking to a stop before reaching the spot where the vamp had accosted her.

She hadn't intended to see this. She didn't want to recall the details of that night, or see if her blood stained the bark of that damn tree.

Don't go any farther. Though inner red flags were waving, the pull of that terrible spot was both a fascination and a horror. Her throat throbbed as if it recognized where they were. This was where she had clung to life.

She stared at the trees without realizing how much time had gone by before her body chilled. A man…no, not really a man, but a creature named Michael, again looking human, caught her wrist in a careful grip. Without speaking a word, he urged her into a jog.

She did not stop to question this, and matched Michael's pace. He led her through another section of the park without communicating to her how different this run was compared to the last one they'd shared. Kaitlin didn't require an explanation, because she sensed trouble in the air. Michael was tense. His grip on her wrist was tight.

They weren't alone. Somehow she was aware of another presence nearby and recognized the scent of Rena's dark jeans. Michael's female pack-mate was somewhere behind them, bringing up the rear.

Was this how it was with werewolves? They possessed an intrinsic sense of each other, aware of Were presence without having to look?

Although the idea was interesting, there was no time to ponder it. Michael ran, and she ran with him—through the park, past the edge of the campus, slowing only when they hit the street. There, they had to walk in order to blend in with the people on the sidewalk.

Once they had cleared the short block leading to the university's athletic grounds, Michael took off again with a speed that was more like flight.

Kaitlin ran like the wind without becoming winded. Cool air on her neck stung. Turning her head made her grimace, but those things weren't half as disconcerting as being mired in the fog of being uninformed. Who the hell were they running from?

Please, don't let it be vampires.

Panic filled her with the thought of fanged monsters. Her pace flagged as the memory of unnatural teeth tearing into her flesh returned, and with it the reminder of there being more kinds of things in this world than anyone knew.

She uttered a sound that made Michael toss her a sideways look. However, he wasn't going to oblige by stopping to answer questions. Instead, he encouraged her on.

They raced around the corner of a small building near the university's farthest fields. Then, slowing so suddenly that she nearly passed him by, Michael whirled and pressed her to the building's brick siding.

"Don't go there," he warned. "Don't think back too hard or too much. To be afraid is to be weak."

"I think I can feel them out there. Vampires."

"They won't get to you. Not with me here and the pack on the prowl."

"It's almost dark, Michael. Don't vampires come out at night? Is that what you were warning me about when you said to come early?"

He nodded. "When darkness comes, we wait for what hides inside it. I wanted you to avoid being caught up in that."

"Who? Who will face those things?"

"I will. My pack will."

Kaitlin refused to address the ringing in her ears that signaled the extent of her panic. She whispered, "I'm not ready."

Warm hands cradled her face. Michael's eyes met hers. "You don't have to see them. No one expects you to. I just wanted you to view the place where you were attacked and accept it. Accept us. Accept me."

Michael drew back after saying that, as if he had just exposed a secret. Did that secret deal with his feelings for her?

"What if…" Her voice faltered, so Kaitlin started again. "What if they hurt you?"

He shook his head. "Not going to happen. Not here, like this. We're fairly fluent in vampire, and these young fledglings have picked up a predictable pattern."

Kaitlin recalled the brute strength of the beast that had trapped her and how she had assumed she would never breathe again. But if darkness was minutes away and Michael's pack would be going after vampires, where did that leave her?

"What do I do?" she asked.

"Go back to your place and wait this out. I was hoping they wouldn't come back so soon. It's unusual they would risk it. I didn't mean for you to go through this again. I'll send someone home with you to—"

"Babysit me? Hold my hand? I don't need that."

Michael held her to the wall with only one hand on her shoulder. Their hips weren't touching. She couldn't feel his breath on her face as he said, "Then it's a good thing you have no say in the matter."

As if their sprint had finally caught up with her need for oxygen, Kaitlin said breathlessly, "Who made you king?"

"Not king. Alpha," he said with a split-second grin that made the rest of the world, as well as thoughts about the monsters occupying space in it, momentarily melt away.

"And as such, you're my responsibility," he added.

Michael's tenseness had returned, which meant that the time for conversation had to be scheduled for a future date. Right on cue with the final nod of his head, the guests he must have been anticipating got nearer, as did nightfall.

Growls rolled from Michael's throat that would have scared the living daylights out of anyone who heard them, and nearly shattered Kaitlin's reach for recovery.

"They're coming," he said. "Lesson one, Kaitlin. Close your eyes and breathe. Inhale and tell me what you find in the wind."

Kaitlin did as she was told. She breathed the night in, coughed, breathed again. Heavy pressure on her nerve endings made her eyes fly open. "Is that the vampires?"

"It's the pack," Michael said. "Some of it, anyway."

The scent accompanying the pressure she perceived

was hard to define and meant more werewolves were coming. Her body responded quickly to this news. Heat closed around her as if a warm breeze had blown in.

Michael said, "Time to go." Then Rena, accompanied by two large men that weren't quite as gorgeous as Michael, but a close second and third, turned the corner of the building…with their eyes trained on her.

Chapter 7

Michael welcomed the members of his pack with genuine gladness.

Cade, with the Danish-born Were's usual levity, called out, "Not exactly the time to get close and personal, boss," noting how close Michael was to Kaitlin.

Rena said, "Two suckers have slunk out of their hidey-holes and are heading for the school."

Kaitlin muttered, "No."

Michael gestured to Cade. "Watch her."

"And miss all the fun?" Cade said, already heading for the new hybrid in their midst. "I assume this is Kaitlin."

Michael nodded. "No time for introductions. Obviously those fanged freaks don't care about anything but finding dinner, and are way too hungry these days."

"Have you ever known them to actually think?" Devlin, their Irish Were, contributed.

"Kaitlin has an apartment," Michael said to Cade. "Can you take her there and wait for us?"

"No problem," Cade returned. "But you owe me."

Michael noted the panic coursing through Kaitlin's body. That panic shuddered within her each time she took a breath.

"A promise is a promise," he said to her. "You can trust Cade to keep the monsters away if any more of them show up while the rest of us deal with the two fledglings on our radar."

Kaitlin was as white as a sheet. He didn't want to leave her, but couldn't send the others to fight in his place. He had told Kaitlin to meet him out here without considering that the vampire attack on her life might have signaled something far worse, like an invasion of the fanged freaks. Before things turned uglier, he'd have to contend with the problem, though tearing himself away from Kaitlin was going to be harder than he could have imagined.

There was no time to whisper assurances to her, touch her or explain why he wanted to do those things.

"Go with Cade, Kate," he said to her. "Trust us."

His heart was pounding twice as fast as usual, announcing his wolf's imminent appearance. Vamp scent was prodding him to act.

The members of his pack all knew what special things he could do with or without a full moon's assistance, and yet Michael had always been uncomfortable shifting back and forth when the rest of his pack had to wait for that one special night per month.

Already, his claws were extending in honor of dealing with old enemies whose presence was a blight on Otherness. His claws were long, curved and lethal. Back when he was a kid, the claws had taken a while to get used to. He had scratched himself more times than he could count. Now, the razor-sharp tips were stained with black vampire blood.

He hid the claws behind his back, out of Kaitlin's sight,

because she was scared enough already and possibly on the verge of being frozen in place.

"Go now," he said, locking eyes with her large grays. "There's no time to waste."

His Lycan power of persuasion helped to make sure she obeyed. They were still connected. His thoughts would become hers if he willed it.

Kaitlin faced Cade, who was three heads taller than she was and twice as broad. Michael understood that she wanted to see the kind of monster that had attacked her so she could truly believe that kind of evil actually existed. But the word *danger* didn't even begin to describe a situation where his pack had to worry about Kaitlin and fight the vamps at the same time.

Kaitlin didn't glance back as she left him. Her spine was rigid and she held her head high. He trusted Cade. Cade was the best of his pack and strong enough to fight his way through a crowd if he had to.

The sandy-haired Dane followed his Alpha's directives without question. Cade had been right, though, to want to question Michael's plan. They were peacekeepers, not babysitters, and the big Were's incredible reflexes would be sorely missed if push came to shove with fledgling bloodsuckers on a bender.

Michael swore beneath his breath for having to make that choice.

"I'll second that unspoken filthy oath you just thought up and raise you one," Rena said, observing him thoughtfully.

Michael tossed her a look.

"Raise you one what?" Devlin asked, glancing after Cade and Kaitlin. "By the way, you do realize that girl is…"

"Is what?" Rena snapped.

"Fragrant," Devlin concluded.

"She's going to be one of us," Rena said.

"Is she, now?" Devlin grinned at Michael.

Vampire presence made the air harder to breathe even for a Were whose system churned oxygen like a well-oiled machine. Michael's wolf pressed against his insides with a desire to be freed. His body wanted to turn itself inside-out and become the thing he harbored.

"Party time," he said as night finally darkened the air, rallying the two Weres. "Under no circumstances can those vampires be allowed to reach the campus."

"Like you have to tell us that," Rena muttered as they all moved toward the spreading blackness that heralded the approach of the undead.

There was no mistaking the stench in the air. The two vampires heading their way moved in unison from shadow to shadow. Although they were youthful in appearance, these vamps were terribly fast, their whereabouts difficult to pinpoint until they passed through a glittering shaft of early moonlight. Then, as if they'd been trapped by a searchlight, both bloodsuckers paused to hiss their displeasure over having any type of light touch their colorless skin.

The moon belonged to the wolves, while vampires were true children of the night—the darker the night, the better. Though Michael didn't know for sure, he supposed that like bats—which were credited as the vamps' distant relatives—bloodsuckers didn't have proper-functioning eyes in bright light, which was why vampires sought out dark spaces and burrowed underground in the daylight hours. The darkness was where nightmare belonged.

The moonlight made these two vamps angry and twice as dangerous. Neither had been undead for long, since both retained some pre-death musculature. Their clothes were in relatively good shape, if the bloodstains were overlooked. However, no one on earth could have believed these creeps were living, breathing humans after a first quick look. No way in hell.

"Ugly bastards," he heard Rena mutter.

One of those bastards heard her and slipped away from the pool of light. Devlin moved after that slinking shadow, leaving tree cover to follow his pasty-skinned prey.

The vamp in the light made a strange keening sound that Michael was afraid might be some sort of signal.

"You're heading the wrong way," he said to it. "This area is protected."

The vamp swelled as if it had swallowed enough air to double its size, though breathing wasn't its forte. It bared its nasty fangs.

"Saw that trick in a circus once," Rena said, unimpressed.

Her remark broke the standoff. The fledgling moved toward Rena without changing its expression, perhaps incorrectly concluding that a female would be the weaker opposing link. At the same time, Devlin gave a shout as the vampire they had lost sight of came rushing at them from the right, with Devlin close on its heels.

Michael had already torn off his shirt to soak up the moonlight. Calling upon the innate strength and reflexes of his Lycan heritage, he had one vampire by the throat before Rena had moved.

There was no time to strip. Michael kicked off his shoes and listened to his worn jeans tear at the seams. Before his next big breath, his continuing morph gave him teeth and jaws to match the claws he had already been wielding.

Loud cracking sounds accompanied the realignment of his shoulders. His spine snapped straight with a shock to the bones. Seconds later, his legs jumped on the band-wagon.

As Rena reached for the vampire in his grip, Michael butted her away, allowing his wolf the room necessary to deal with a creature that had died once already and now needed a reminder that dead was dead.

He howled as he completed his shift. After hitting the ground on his paws, Michael bounded back up to lunge for the vampire's neck. Grabbing hold there with his sharp canine teeth, he shook the bloodsucker so forcefully, the creature shrieked.

Rena wasn't to be left out of this party. She came hurtling back, aiming for the monster's chest with a short, sharp-tipped wooden stake. Putting all her muscle behind the strike, she hit the place in the vamp's chest where a man's heart should have been, and drove the stake deep.

That was all it took to send one unholy bloodsucker back to wherever it went in the hereafter. The creature exploded into a funnel of swirling gray ash.

"Dust to dust," Rena said. "One down."

"Make that two," Devlin announced with a fierce guttural growl as a second explosion came from the area between the trees.

Michael knew they had lucked out with this batch of fledglings.

Silence returned quickly, and as though nothing had happened to disturb it…which was exactly the way Michael had wanted things to turn out. Until, with his extraordinary connection to Kaitlin, he perceived the trouble she was in and whirled on all fours.

The guy beside her was blond, built like a brick house and looked capable enough to handle most of the things life might throw his way. Her new guardian, Cade, was the epitome of a modern-day Viking. Attractive. Make that a real heartthrob. And also a werewolf.

Cade's green eyes, similar in color to both Michael's and Rena's, stared straight ahead, never once veering from the path he led her down. He was concentrating on their surroundings. Kaitlin sensed his reluctance to break their silence.

"Is something there?" she asked.

He held up a hand and shook his head, gestures indicating that speaking wouldn't be a good idea at the moment. There had to be more company up ahead. Dread began to blossom inside Kaitlin over what that company might be.

With a firm hand on her shoulder, Cade urged her to pause. They stood side by side for a minute, listening, waiting. Then Cade stepped in front of her, acting as a protective shield against whatever was going to show up. Because something was.

Kaitlin couldn't see anything past Cade's powerful shoulders and didn't need to. Her neck stung with pain that was like having to suffer through her terrible ordeal all over again. In this case, her wound had become a built-in vamp-o-meter.

Cade spoke to whatever hid in the darkness that lay beyond the meager glow of the closest light pole. "This place isn't for you. Come to think of it, I don't know anywhere that is."

Sounds reminiscent of radio static caused the back of Kaitlin's neck to chill. She froze. Cade tensed.

"I'm sorry." Cade spoke to one particular spot as if he saw something there. "Was that your reply? Maybe fangs hinder speech?"

"Now isn't the time to taunt them." Kaitlin hated every heart-stopping second of this confrontation and formulated a plan to move to another city if she got out of this with her life and limbs intact. She would take her family with her.

Not sure if she could handle another vampire sighting, she made a pact with herself to finish her thesis elsewhere. To hell with it. *To hell with Michael, werewolves and...*

"Vampires," Michael said, finishing her internal remark as he, Rena and the other Were in the pack approached.

Kaitlin spun to look at them with her heart hammering. Cade remained motionless enough to have been turned to stone, his laser-like gaze hovering on that spot in the distance.

"Didn't trust me?" he said to Michael over his shoulder.

"Finished early," Michael returned. "Nothing else to do, so we thought we'd join you."

"Everyone likes company," Cade said.

Kaitlin's attention was on Michael. In human form and completely naked, he was breathtaking. His tarnished bronze skin glowed with a hint of perspiration. He looked like a shaft of moonlight carved into solid form. Without clothes, he seemed not quite as human, and twice as formidable. When confronted with all that pulsing, molded muscle, even she wanted to get out of his way.

More hissing sounds broke up their reunion. The sounds were close. Kaitlin's panic bloomed.

"Five of them," Cade announced.

"Five of them and five of us," Rena noted. "Easy."

Kaitlin felt Michael's attention on her. "Yes, easy," he said.

"Better if there was a full moon tonight," the other male Were added.

"Hell, who needs a fur coat when we have brains?" Rena quipped, raising her wooden stake. "At least more brains than they have."

"Doesn't even seem like a fair fight, really," Cade tossed in.

No one laughed at their restless banter.

Kaitlin was terrified.

"Do you want me to take her away?" Cade asked Michael.

"I'm right here," Kaitlin said, trying not to stare at Michael. "Don't talk as if I wasn't."

"She's not ready for this," Michael said.

She met his gaze. "I'm in the way, but I'm no baby."

"Well, then, Kaitlin," Rena said, stepping forward with a testy come-hither gesture of her hand to urge the vampires closer. "Try not to whine. Vamps like that entirely too much."

There was no time to change her mind about staying. Kaitlin had never seen anything as terrifying as the things that broke through the dark. The night of her attack, she hadn't seen her assailant up close. The pain had sealed her eyes closed.

These creatures were gruesome. Terrifyingly morbid. Their skin was an unhealthy, colorless white. Dark circles ringed black eyes, giving the impression there were no eyes at all, and only deep, empty sockets. They moved like ghosts, hardly touching the ground, their mouths wide-open. They made clicking noises by snapping their fangs together.

Second only to the shock of seeing a vampire was the surprise of watching four werewolves form a line to welcome the creatures. Tall, feral and so visibly alive that Kaitlin's skin buzzed with contagious, keyed-up energy, Michael and his pack stood against the oncoming tide of bloodsuckers like superheroes, with Michael, their Alpha in human form, standing at the forefront.

In place of Rena's wooden stake and Cade's intimidating bulk, Michael sported a set of long, curved claws—the only real visual evidence that the group facing the vampires wasn't entirely human, either.

There was going to be a fight here, too, and she had to either run away or get with the program. With monsters all around, getting with the program seemed the better option. So Kaitlin didn't leave the Weres to handle a fight that was also partially hers. She stood her ground a few steps behind the others with her hands fisted and her stance wide, willing to defend herself this time if she had to.

Inwardly, her new mantra became "If you come at me, I hope to God I can move my feet."

Chapter 8

Michael fought a dark blur, wielding his claws with enough speed and strength to take down two bloodsuckers before the whole fight really got going. Rena toyed with her vampire, faking slashes, feigning to be caught, before finally rallying with a vicious thrust of her wooden stake that struck true and reduced the vamp to ash.

The vampires were fast, but the Weres, even in human form, were stronger. Cade had a bloodsucker on the ground, with both hands around a brittle, bony neck that was ripe for snapping. Devlin fought like a demon with a steel blade he was able to handle only because its hilt was carved out of bone.

Because Weres caved physically to the silvery lure of moonlight but could not touch certain metals in any other form, the glint of Devlin's knife sent shudders through Michael, who had always secretly supposed Devlin actually had a little demon somewhere in his background. Pict ancestors, maybe. Those Celtic blue-faced guys.

He rushed to Devlin and tossed a vamp aside, besting it by twenty pounds of hyper-animated Were muscle. He and his pack had fought vampires multiple times—many of those encounters lately—and knew what it took to eliminate the young ones. But he was concerned. Something was happening in this city, something that had kicked off a new flood of monsters. Kaitlin had been the victim of a fledgling like these five, who were probably no more than a few months old.

Whereas most vamps kept to the fringes of society, where they preyed on the weak and the feeble, this new breed took a bolder tack, slithering through the world as if they belonged there and had every right to hunt. Too many bodies turning up, unexplained, and law enforcement would call in the big dogs of crime fighting. If that happened, everyone Michael knew would be screwed.

By monitoring this area around the college, his pack was doing its part, but Michael feared that the numbers were slowly shifting in vamp favor. Good werewolves didn't create other Weres as a rule, either to support a larger pack or make a point. All it took was one good bite and some dribbled blood into a victim's system, and vampirism could spread like a runaway wildfire.

If these attacks continued and more and more vampires appeared, including some of the older and wiser versions, he'd have no choice but to call in some help of his own. A few choice words to Miami, and his father's formidable friends would hit the trail.

Damn it. He had never seen this many vampires in a single night. Not even in a couple of months.

"Come on, you bastards."

He fought to protect his own secrets, swinging his arms, wielding his claws while in human form. The fighting seemed more personal when meeting these creeps eye to eye. This fight was terribly close to the school. His Weres were growling. The vamps were shrieking. Keeping the Were population out of the limelight was at the highest level of importance, and it suddenly seemed to Michael that the goal was about to get harder.

Weres everywhere knew that rogue vampires were a threat to Were anonymity, and worked to stay steps ahead of the slippery fanged ghosts. His father's pack had done a lot to make Miami safe and keep Florida Weres off human radar. That Miami pack was comprised of some of the toughest werewolves and Lycans Michael had ever seen. He had been raised among most of them and wondered if they were fighting their own battles on a night like this one.

Out of the corner of his eye, he caught sight of Kaitlin. She was leaning over the vampire Cade had trapped on the ground. He found this pretty brave of her, considering… and way too dangerous.

Cade was waiting for her to take a closer look at his captive, perhaps understanding that one of these bloodsuckers had recently changed her fate. Kaitlin gazed at the vampire with a twisted expression on her face and one of her hands was wrapped around her own neck. Michael saw clearly that even as Kaitlin looked at the vampire, the possibility of their existence wasn't sinking in. He supposed it had been like that for him, too, in the beginning, and until he'd actually faced the children of the night in a fight.

"Cade," he said in a cautionary tone.

The big Were nodded and pushed Kaitlin aside. Blocking her view from what he was about to do, Cade delivered that vamp its final death blow with a sharp twist to its neck that was backed by angry, keyed-up muscle. The resulting explosion was the only sound left in the night before both Cade and Kaitlin were covered in a falling cyclone of ash.

Michael sensed how badly Kaitlin wanted to scream,

knowing she would do no such thing. Tonight Kaitlin had taken one more step toward that degree in animal she had mentioned, and he guessed that going backward wasn't in her nature.

"Maybe not so easy," Rena observed, dusting herself off and turning to face the last remaining vampire, which was lunging for her. "Yet doable," she added with a grunt.

Michael watched Kaitlin's gaze shift to Rena and her lethal takedown of that vampire before her wide gray gaze landed back on him. His nakedness made her uncomfortable. She looked only at his face. Her heart was thundering.

For the first time in a very long while, he felt slightly self-conscious.

And then the world again went silent.

Kaitlin broke it. "Thank you," she said to him with a calmness belying the true state of her emotions. She was ready to jump out of her skin if someone said *boo*.

"It's what we do," Michael said. "Because somebody has to."

She kept her gaze level. "They might have made more vampires tonight."

"We take one day at a time to eliminate a few of those possibilities."

"They can't change werewolves? Turn wolves into something else?"

He shook his head. "Our blood is poison to them. They can sense this."

Kaitlin turned to Rena in an obvious attempt to elude the picture he presented without his clothes. He read her thoughts on this easily enough. Kaitlin liked his body. She wanted to go to him, touch him, be held by him. She wanted to...

Hell, he almost blushed, and stopped the mind connection with her in case his body responded to those thoughts of hers and everyone else took note of what his nakedness would not be able to hide.

She spoke to Rena. "Can you teach me how to do that?"

Rena lowered her weapon. "Do what?"

"Fight."

As Rena gave him a sideways look, Michael waited to see how she would reply.

"I guess I could do that," Rena said with a shrug. "In my spare time, and if spare time comes up."

Michael would have smiled if the situation were different. Rena's acquiescence was proof that Kaitlin was going to win Rena over bit by bit. The fact that Kaitlin hadn't run away just now went a long way toward earning Rena's respect. These two females were on the right track, though there was still a long way to go.

Michael nodded his head, thinking the night had ended well, as ash continued to fall like rain.

Kaitlin figured it was a miracle she was still standing after again looking into the face of evil.

Michael's pack formed a circle around her. She wondered if they were waiting for her to faint. She refused to oblige.

She was getting used to being the center of attention, and actually felt like the baby they all probably thought she was. Young. Naive. New to this hidden, underground world, and not yet indoctrinated in the language of claws and sharp wooden stakes.

She hadn't helped them fight, yet she had been willing. And she'd be damned if she'd let these Weres get a whiff of the terror that gripped her.

She squeezed words through a constricted throat. "If this is over, I guess I'd better get going. I need to get some work done on my thesis or I'll never…"

She didn't attempt to finish that statement. After what had happened here, the idea of working on a thesis seemed ludicrous. Staring at a computer would be a letdown, as would escaping to her apartment and leaving this pack to roam the park without her.

More important things than notes and classrooms were happening in the world. People were fighting for their lives and the survival of their species...because there were more types of beings on this planet than anyone would have ever guessed.

White-hot adrenaline was streaking though her. Her heart rate had not slowed. She wanted to make sense of this, when leaving Michael seemed an impossible task.

Moonlight dripped over his body, creating valleys of shadows and light. Michael's eyes were incandescent. His hair, the same color as the darkness around them, gleamed with moon-induced highlights.

All that beauty, and Michael had claws.

In her defense, who wouldn't think themselves idiotic for finding a nonhuman so fascinating? How about for remaining on this spot when vampires were on the loose?

What about believing in the existence of vampires and werewolves in the first place, even after witnessing them firsthand?

Determined to wobble less while in the spotlight, Kaitlin stood straighter. She didn't feel strong. She didn't like fighting. Those things alone made it hard for her to imagine being like one of the people before her.

"I'll walk you home," Michael said, as if nothing extraordinary had happened here, and the fine gray dust sifting down was nothing more than out-of-season snow.

"You'd better not go like that," Cade warned, unbuttoning his shirt before stepping out of his pants. Handing his clothes to Michael, he added, "We'd have people after us for far more ridiculous charges than for being what we are. Indecent exposure springs to mind."

Michael put on the borrowed clothes with a barked "Thanks."

Kaitlin didn't watch him dress. Emotions like lust and fright should have been separated by a vast distance, and weren't. The emotional roller coaster refused to stop and let her off.

"I'd lend you some of my stuff in turn, Cade," Rena said in jest. "But you at least have shorts on. I go commando."

The fourth Were, whose name Kaitlin didn't know, cleared his throat and said with a slight accent she recognized as Irish, "So, we'll be going now, Michael, unless you need us for chaperones, or to have your back on your promenade back to civilization."

Michael sniffed the air before leveling a look at Kaitlin. "Not a vampire around at the moment. I think we'll be okay on our own. What do you think, Kaitlin? Shall we chance it?"

Tired of the hot seat, and though she wasn't sure about letting these werewolves go, Kaitlin nodded. She immediately found herself alone with the handsome shape-shifter, her soul fielding a hunger for Michael that defied rational thought.

When he stepped toward her, she stepped back.

"I'm not the enemy," he said.

Kaitlin looked up at the moon.

"Neither is she," Michael added.

"How can you not think so after what happens to you and the others in that light?" she asked.

He shrugged. "It is what it is."

"Can the rest of this pack fully shape-shift? Become a wolf that looks like a real wolf?"

Michael shook his head. "In this pack, only me."

"Why?"

"It's not in their genetics. At least that's the way it's explained to those of us who can."

She tilted her head, examining the moon beyond the treetops. "Since your blood saved me from death at the hand of one of those monsters, will that change the outcome of my own transformation, if and when it starts?"

"No. Hot blood wins out over cold. Because you didn't die at the hands of that vampire, your human side will have a say in what happens."

"Will I change? For sure?"

"Yes."

"How long until I do?"

"During the next full moon would be my guess."

"You don't know?"

"Everyone is different. Sometimes it takes longer for the wolf to catch up."

She went over his statement in her mind before speaking again. "The next full moon comes the day after tomorrow."

Michael nodded. "Not much time left."

She bit her lip hard to keep from shouting. "Are you *you* when you shift?" she managed to ask.

Michael obviously knew what she meant. "Weres don't lose our minds, like in horror movies. We are aware of everything we do. The wolf isn't another entity taking up space inside us, it is us. The mind still functions properly and remains in charge while in either shape."

"That's something," she muttered.

Michael was close enough to further boost her pulse. Cade's dark blue shirt was a size too large, but suited Michael perfectly. Then again, so would a towel.

Michael was a werewolf, and she knew next to nothing about the reality of that yet, except that Weres were real. They were also brave, bold, exceptional fighters that seemed to be on the right side of the battle against creatures exemplifying the dark side. At least Michael's pack fit that description.

"You scare me a little," she confessed.

"Only a little? I must be losing my touch."

Michael was smiling when she turned back. After reducing vampires to dust, he appeared to have regained his calm. But mind reading went both ways tonight. Kaitlin also knew he wanted more private, personal time with her in spite of his inner protests against that very thing. His hunger for her was an added pressure that topped the winded sensation she already felt by being in the presence of a werewolf.

Michael wasn't only fighting vampires tonight. He was fighting his hunger for her.

The kiss in her apartment proved that Michael wanted her to be more to him than a responsibility. The way he looked at her now proved it.

Michael's undivided attention was hot and untamable. Like his wolf, his needs rode close to the surface of his skin. If he gave in to that hunger, she supposed he'd never stop seeking it. That's what his expression told her, though he wasn't easily giving in. Maybe the big bad wolf was a little bit afraid of her, too.

There might also be other reasons he had to maintain a distance. Possibly Lycans were elitist snobs, due to the strict adherence of his species's undiluted, pure-blood doctrine that Michael had mentioned. No Romeo and Juliet scenario with a half human would be acceptable.

Being off-limits suits me just fine. If I don't have to see you, I won't have to live wholeheartedly in another world.

"Good luck with that," Michael said, the parts of his tattoos that were visible beneath his collarbone rolling with the motion of a gathering storm system.

"You can read my thoughts?" she asked.

"Some of them," he replied.

"The ones that pertain to you?"

He nodded, refusing to explain in more depth. "It's safe now. We can walk."

Possibly it was safe, but her feet wouldn't move. Besides, Kaitlin figured that she had every right to be wary. Michael assumed she was worried about vampires, but with the ability to read her mind, he would know it was both Michael and the moon she feared most at the moment. Michael, because he was Michael. The moon because of all the predictions and insinuations about how that big silver orb was going to affect her in just two days' time.

Michael's eyes were disarmingly wide and green. Being on the receiving end of his intense observation made her dizzy. There was a chance Michael rescued people often with a dose of Lycan blood, and therefore had her reactions mapped out. He wasn't coughing up any useful information about that, though, and only dropping nebulous hints here and there about the murkiness of her future.

"Can't move my legs," she confessed, holding up a hand to ward Michael off in case he had ideas about helping her. "I just need another minute."

She was in turmoil. Could the moon cause that, too, or was this emotional upheaval due to the fact that she had never met a man like Michael in her old world, and didn't trust herself to be in his world now?

"It's okay." His tone was like a brush of silk over her jangling nerves. "A minute more in this place is maybe all we have, though."

His warning was another reminder that there was no use pretending this was a normal meet-and-greet between a man and a woman interested in each other, and that being so close to Michael smacked of danger. That sense of danger charged up her arms like streams of electricity, and tasted like pepper. Her hormones might have been singing, yet not so loudly that she'd let herself lose control, even when Michael didn't take his eyes off her.

She was holding him back. He was needed elsewhere.

A growl of distress rose from deep inside her, and that was as frightening as everything else. In a show of defiance that mocked her lack of moral fortitude, Kaitlin again met Michael's brilliant, forthright gaze.

"You're wrong, you know," she said. "You might be an angel. Having done your good deed in helping me, I hereby release you from any responsibilities you might assume to have over me and my life. You can safely get back to yours, and I'll do the same."

On legs like putty, Kaitlin turned from him and began to walk, still scared out of her mind about what might be hiding in the dark, and needing to lose the moon and that moon's secrets for a while longer.

She didn't get far.

Michael's whisper came in a warm puff of exhaled air on the back of her neck. "It doesn't matter what you say, or how much you protest. I'm here to see this through."

Michael was behind her, close. In spite of his heat, Kaitlin's chill was due to the memory of having his warm breath in her mouth and lungs as it sparked her narrowing life back into existence. Did she owe Michael for that? Did she owe him her blind trust and her future?

"You don't owe me anything," he said. "On the other hand, you do have to trust me."

"Why should I trust you?"

She wasn't going to turn around. That would be a big mistake. Seeing Michael up close made her senses go haywire.

"You've seen me, and what I am. You cannot discredit that or pretend it isn't real, Kaitlin."

"I believe you are what you are, Michael, and that you like it. That doesn't mean I'm going to like it, or accept it as my future lifestyle."

Something sharp scraped along her shoulder blade without tearing her shirt, and Kaitlin knew what that was. Claws. Michael's wolfish claws.

Her muscles shivered in response. Molten balls of fire gathered in her stomach before hurtling toward her throat, burning tissue as they traveled and setting fire to everything in their path. She had to clench her hands to make sure she didn't have claws, too. She felt the tips of her fingers swell.

Hell. Was this reaction caused by lust for Michael, or by a wolf being born inside her?

Kaitlin remained upright by leaning forward on the balls of her feet. Frustration made her groan, and that sound made Michael move.

He wrapped his arms around her, pulled her close, so that she felt every inch of him from his chest to his thighs. His heat scored her back through the loose weave of her sweater. Her breath was as ragged as his was.

"Kaitlin," he said, the word like a further caress. "After I left you this morning, what was your day like?"

"I…" She couldn't get a stream of words out. Heat behind her eyes made her shut them.

She knew what lay beneath Michael's borrowed clothes. She had seen that lovely picture before, just as she had felt the buzz of the nearness of his incredibly honed body.

Would wolf hormones, when added to girl hormones, push her over the edge?

"Your day," he repeated. "What happened? Learn anything you'd care to share? Anything out of the ordinary?"

Michael's tone, and the force behind it, compelled her to answer.

"Yes." She struggled to go on. "I learned that a person can be maimed and nearly murdered, and the world still turns. Vampires and werewolves roam the park around my college, and yet two plus two still equals four. Somehow that just doesn't seem right."

Though she now wanted to look at him, Michael held her tightly. *Go on,* she thought she heard him silently urge.

"I…" she began, again failing to finish the thought.

"Relax," Michael said. "Tensing makes things worse. Listen to me, Kaitlin. Relax. Swallow the fire and put the wolf back in its place. You can do that because it's not time for that wolf's appearance."

"How do you know about the fire?"

"I can feel it roaring through you."

"You said the wolf isn't a separate thing. So how would I put it back in its place? God, Michael, I'd prefer to forget about all of this. Maybe wanting to forget is enough. You also said that being near another wolf might bring out mine. So, what if I don't get near any of you? I've already said thank-you, and meant that sincerely. I owe you my life and won't forget that, but…"

"But what, Kate?"

"You need to tell me everything and get it over with. Tell me now, so I don't have to imagine I'm going nuts, and so that I can prepare."

The night seemed to press in around her. She wasn't sure if she'd ever be able to walk alone on any path through it again.

"You'll feel the fire first," he began. "That's the way the wolf comes into existence, the way the wolf is born. The fire is a sign of internal changes taking place at the cellular level."

She struggled in his arms, but not very hard.

"Once that's finalized, and if you make it through the

next phase, your wolf simply is part of you. Just another piece of Kaitlin Davies, as if it had always been there. It's almost like an emotion rising to the surface at times—a new emotion that rallies and then radicalizes all the other ones."

He had obliged, had told her something, as she'd asked, and now she was sick again.

"*If* I make it?" she said.

"You've already assimilated some of your wolf. I'm not sure how that was accomplished so quickly and your doing so was quite unique. As I said earlier, though, there will be more trials to come."

"I don't want to think about that," Kaitlin argued.

"Unfortunately, that won't stop the progress of what has already begun. It's time to face the facts, Kaitlin. It's time to move on."

Her voice was faint. "I know."

Kaitlin felt her next few questions tank, though she hadn't yet asked one of them. Looking up, wincing with the strain that movement put on her throat, she said, "The damn moon in getting brighter."

Reaching for the collar of her sweater with an action derived from self-preservation, Kaitlin felt for the raw-skinned pucker she'd first found that morning in her room. She ran her fingers over her throat uncertainly, finding that the injury wasn't nearly as sore as it had been.

She almost sat down in the dirt.

Michael tightened his hold on her. "It would be safer for you indoors tonight. You've had enough. You're healing on the outside. The inside takes longer."

Kaitlin teetered again and pointed a finger upward. "Does it burn you? That moon?"

Her lips were trembling. Her hands were clenched so tightly, her forearms had started to cramp. The scent seeping from her pores now smelled like aluminum, the odor of fear. The peppery taste in her mouth had burned away, replaced by the metallic tang of having sucked on tin foil. She feared she might stop breathing altogether if she and Michael stayed here for much longer. Yet she was afraid to move. She was afraid she would throw herself into his arms if he moved.

Glancing at her wrists beyond the cuff of her sweater, she felt…

She felt a kiss of silvery light on her skin that was like the smile of a treacherous lover's lips. Soft, yet demanding. Deceptively light, while at the same time completely deceiving.

An unfamiliar sensation, like roving invisible fingers, worked its way up her legs, her thighs, climbing hand over fist along her vertebrae, one bone at a time. Panic returned. She was panting for breath. "What's happening, Michael?"

"You're feeling the lure." Michael's voice had an edge, as if his explanation merely surrounded a much deeper meaning.

His closeness allowed Kaitlin to keep focus for a while. Michael's arms were supportive. The way his body braced hers gave her some strength. This closeness also sent her mixed messages; sexual signals radioed to her overworked nervous system. Michael's touch was seductive, provocative. By liking this and by translating every meeting of their bodies into sexual terms, Kaitlin wondered who the real animal was.

"You have my blood in your veins," he said. "That's what dictates the way this will go down. With a single drop, you would change, and you've had more than that. You needed more than that."

Dear Lord. Kaitlin kept repeating those words silently as she rocked back and forth on her feet.

"The changes will be noticeable, Kate. Sight, hearing, sense of smell, are enhanced, enlarged, enlivened. Does this sound familiar? Has some of it happened already today?"

"Yes," she replied.

Michael was quiet for a short span of time before continuing. "More small things will shake loose. Barely noticeable things. Longer fingernails. Brighter skin. Hunger."

Hunger.

Inadvertently, Kaitlin again curled and uncurled her hands, already sensing the arrival of more of those changes. The smells at school and the anxiousness over being confined in the library had to be part of the change. The white, haunting reflection in her mirror was part of it, as were the quaking limbs and the sinking sensation in her stomach each time she felt as though the moon was watching her. The treacherous moon that turned humans into wolves.

"Must be hell on clothes," she said, remembering her dream of running barefoot in the grass beside a half-naked Michael, then having him turn up tonight in the buff. She also remembered that in one of those dreams, she had felt light and joyous and had wanted to jump Michael's bones.

"Maybe being a werewolf isn't all bad?" she whispered.

"It can be quite beautiful," Michael said.

She believed him because Michael was beautiful, and nothing that special could step out of a bad reality.

He was smiling sadly when he finally released her and she was able to look at him.

"How many nights, Michael? How many nights will I be affected?"

"Two or three. You'll change as fully as your body determines, and only during the full-moon phase when moonlight touches your skin, though you will be vulnerable to moonlight one day before and one day after that."

There would be a full moon two days from now. Michael said she wouldn't change until then…so why did she feel moonlight sliding down strands of her tangled hair right that moment? Why did her fingers feel strange, as if claws might appear any second?

"The imagination is a strange beast," Michael said, reading her. "You will adjust when the real thing happens."

"I don't want to do this. Be this."

The moonlight was stifling. Chilling. She felt so very cold when the wolf was supposed to be hot.

Her knees buckled without warning. Next thing Kaitlin knew, she was on the ground, head hanging forward, sickness roiling through her.

The hands clamped around her waist were Michael's. With a single heave and the slightest grunt of effort, he had her on her feet, then up in his arms. In a move reminiscent of some distant time when damsels were weak-hearted and repeatedly in distress, he turned, holding her tightly to him, and ran.

Chapter 9

Kaitlin squeezed Michael's shoulders, silently begging him to stop running. They were heading the wrong way. Her apartment was in the opposite direction. Michael was moving fast, as if he was aware of where he was taking her, which turned out to be the closest cover.

Beneath the protection of the roofed park bench, he set her on her feet and waited while she leaned over to wretch, but although her stomach heaved, nothing came up.

"This, too, will pass," Michael said gently. "Fear is making you sick. Nothing else."

Kaitlin wasn't so sure about that. Her blood, as well as her body, had turned icy. She didn't know whether to laugh maniacally or cry, and made a Herculean attempt to stand up straight in spite of quivering abdominal muscles.

"Please, Michael. Make this go away. I'm begging you."

"I'm sorry," he said again, and she recognized his sincerity. He was sorry, and she had to go through this.

"Let's cover you up, and I'll take you back to your place." He was already pulling Cade's shirt over his head without bothering to use the buttons.

Her eyes went to his chest and the scrolling tattoos that left her feeling dizzier. "You said it wasn't going to affect me tonight."

"Hell, Kaitlin. I'm not sure the wolf is doing this. Everything about tonight is strange."

She said, "I can get home on my own." *I'll crawl if I have to.*

But could she get there? Kaitlin gazed out at the darkness with new eyes that were no longer so innocent, and mindful of the danger. Although clouds partially covered the moon, she could feel threads of silver gathering. She smelled change heading her way on the breeze.

"You are a stubborn woman." Michael held out the shirt.

Kaitlin searched the dark, hoping to find different answers than the ones Michael had already given her. *Wolf? Damn.*

"Come," Michael said, offering both the shirt and a hand.

She didn't place her fingers in his. In touching Michael, she'd feel human again and needier than ever, when according to Michael, being human was far from the truth. If her fate was sealed, she had to give in and embrace what Michael and his moon were telling her.

"Cover your head so you won't have to feel the light," he advised. "Maybe that will help to ease your fears."

She shook her head.

"All right." Michael sat down on the bench. "I'll just sit here then, and watch you go."

The idea of leaving the overhang rendered her immobile. Their shelter suddenly seemed to Kaitlin like a tiny ship in a vast sea of uncertainty. Who was she kidding? She wasn't going out there alone. She wasn't really that brave.

"You've scared me, that's all," she said. "This whole night has scared me."

"The vampires are gone, Kaitlin. If you're talking about becoming a werewolf, I honestly thought you'd prefer life over the alternative, no matter where that life led," Michael said. "There are good parts to being what you now are, you know."

"Such as?"

"The park is a great place without the monsters currently tearing it up. The camaraderie of a pack is like nothing else, and almost equals the sensation of moonlight on your skin. My world is sensuous and beautiful beyond the top layer that other people see. And due to our added strength, we don't have to be afraid of much."

"Beneath that top layer is a fur coat," Kaitlin said.

"True. Yet after a while, even those who weren't born to the wolf begin to like it."

She faced the park. "If I'm already feeling odd, and it's not just sickness, what will happen to me if I step out there? What if I feel the moon already?"

"It can't be the moon."

"Okay. I'm going to find out," she whispered, with an added inward *maybe*. If she took a giant step, she'd know for sure if what she was feeling was fear or something else. Something worse than fear.

With her eyes closed, she slid a sandaled toe forward, allowing two inches of skin to meet that damn mystical lure Michael had mentioned, hoping for the best, praying for a miracle.

* * *

The look Kaitlin gave him when she turned her head was one of a sorely wounded soul in search of enlightenment. Anger was in that look, and condemnation.

Could he blame her?

Nothing happened when she stuck out her foot, though it was clear that she had anticipated a reaction.

Michael shot to his feet, anxious about this whole deal, and was beside her in a flash. Kaitlin's eyes were glassy, her face pale enough to belong to the undead. She was looking at him without seeing him. Looking through him.

Muttering an inward curse, he reached out to her. Kaitlin shied away, leaving the shelter of the overhang by taking several steps into the night. Standing in the open, with a mixture of moonlight and darkness crossing her features, she gazed up at the sky as if tempting the moon to strike. *Here I am*, he wouldn't have been surprised to hear her say.

But she remained silent.

"Talk to me," he said quietly to the woman who single-handedly obliterated what he'd come to expect as the usual process of transitioning from human to Other. It was clear to him that she was feeling something.

He had never seen this kind of recovery or the arrival of her current level of awareness, and wasn't sure how to proceed. His plan to hand her over to Rena might have backfired because he wasn't certain Rena would understand the complexity of this particular case, either.

What was she seeing, standing there?

What was she feeling?

He closed his eyes and looked into her mind.

"Kaitlin," he said, able to feel the stirring, faint movement of the wolf tucked deep inside her as easily as if his own wolf was doing the fidgeting.

He cut off a rising growl. Kaitlin's wolf was waking

before the rest of her could catch up. The moon was calling to her early, and that just wasn't right.

She wasn't Lycan. There wasn't one real wolf bone in her body. A possible explanation for her reaction to wolf blood was that he had given her too much of it and her system was in a state of confusion. He really didn't know what to expect. Although Kaitlin wasn't the first human he had protected from fanged demons, she was the first human he had shared his life force with. The first person he'd wanted to share himself with. Rescuing her had felt personal.

"Kaitlin." He called to her again, moving to within touching range without actually making contact. "Tell me what's going on."

"I see things. Valleys and hills." Her voice was distant, as if she was relating part of another dream. Michael figured she was hallucinating, since there were no hills or valleys surrounding the college, and they were standing on flat, grassy ground.

He wondered if Kaitlin wouldn't be able to handle her transition, if he had merely extended her life by hours, instead of years, before that inner bonfire took her down. She looked otherworldly as she stood there, and more transparent than solid. Paler. Slighter than ever.

When she spoke again, his heart fluttered.

"More of them." Her gray eyes flashed as she struggled to focus.

"More of what, Kaitlin?"

"Vampires."

"Damn it all to hell!" Michael didn't question her perception. He put his fingers in his mouth to whistle, knowing the pack would still be relatively close and patrolling the area, and that they would hear his call.

"These damn bloodsuckers just aren't going to give up,"

he said with his senses on full peripheral scan. "I don't know why so many of them are coming out tonight. There must be a reason."

As he looked at Kaitlin, Michael began to consider whether this new wave of bloodsuckers had something to do with her. Was Kaitlin some kind of vampire magnet?

Insane idea. He shrugged it off. Vampires didn't plan, or have specific goals for taking revenge on their enemies. Vampires only wanted one thing, and that was to feed. Their entire existence depended on finding humans to feed on. Yet they were coming to this area as if he, Kaitlin and this damn park were ground zero for an undead rally.

"I have to get you home." He waved the blue shirt at her and stressed the word. "Now."

Seeming to comprehend the problem, she nodded. Instead of coming to him, though, she spun on her heels and took off at a run in the opposite direction…like a damn little half-human fool who hadn't believed a word he'd said.

Kaitlin couldn't breathe but refused to stop running, sure that if she kept going she could outdistance the nightmares that felt like her past, present and future all rolled into one big terrible tangle.

She felt much too vulnerable near Michael, possibly because she actually was. He held all the cards. He was the keeper of Lycan secrets. Michael wanted her to be strong, while also fostering her need for him. He would gladly have carted her home, and then what?

She was alive, and riddled with guilt about that. Michael belonged with his pack. If his pack were to accept her, and that was what she ended up wanting, she'd have to get Michael to sever whatever ties bound them together so that he could do what he needed to do without worrying about her.

So she ran away from him, dreading every yard of ground she covered that created more distance and lamenting her need for space. She needed to be on her own to think. Michael needed to be with his pack. She would face this werewolf prognosis head-on as soon as her emotions caught up.

She ran without assistance or support, not looking at the moon. Her legs were strong enough to carry her over grass and concrete, and those things kicked up familiar, comforting smells in a world that had first spun her around and then dumped her on her ass.

She didn't feel like a werewolf, despite the sickness inside her. Her legs were her legs. Her chest heaved with a need for oxygen like any human's lungs did while sprinting. Still, if being a werewolf meant she'd stop being afraid of every damn shadow, maybe that was a good thing.

"I'm still Kaitlin!" she shouted to the moon that was supposedly going to help change her.

What she wasn't, she quickly found out, was fast enough to outdistance a vampire.

Michael moved so fast, his surroundings seemed to have liquefied. Kaitlin didn't know how to truly perceive the dead, and she was heading toward one of them.

He ran for only a short time before allowing his wolf to take over. Arms, legs, feet, torso began to morph in record time. With one good leap into the air as a man, he landed as a wolf and bounded forward with the kind of speed only an animal could utilize.

With the sound of cars in the distance and civilization too close to put him at ease, he became aware of Kaitlin's racing heartbeats before seeing her. In his wolf vision, she was a heat source.

He also detected that vampire slithering through the dark on a parallel path to the one she had taken.

He caught up to her in seconds. Hurtling past Kaitlin with a fury inside him that bordered on insanity, Michael lunged at the vampire, meeting it in a tremendous body slam that sent shock waves through the air.

They fell and rolled over in the grass, tumbling body over body until Michael came out on top. Without hesitation, he bit down on the vamp's neck, severing ligaments and everything else in his way, until the vamp's head rolled away from its emaciated body.

Done deal. The undead could survive a lot of damage, but not without a head. He had to assume that the person that vampire had once been would have thanked him for putting him out of his afterlife misery.

The whole thing took less than a minute. When he looked up with his muzzle dripping vampire blood, he was afraid of the picture he presented to Kaitlin.

She wasn't there.

Without the ability to speak, he was momentarily at a loss. He backed up, searching the area, convinced that he had to be mistaken, and that she had to be hiding nearby.

He heard the pack coming. They were running full tilt, cutting through the night like well-aimed arrows homing in on a target. As for himself, shifting back and forth from his wolf form so many times in a short period had left him lacking in sustainable energy and panting with the effort to maintain his current shape.

Wanting to run, to find Kaitlin and chase more vampire prey, Michael waited for the pack to arrive. Rena was in front, and slid to a stop beside him. All four Weres wrinkled their human noses. Four menacing human growls of disgust rumbled in the dark.

Rena said, "Where's Kaitlin?"

Michael growled a reply.

"Shit," Rena said, already sniffing for clues as to the direction Kaitlin had taken. "There's something chasing her."

The others nodded in agreement.

Michael was already gathering to move.

"Michael." Rena again faced him. "Though I don't condone what might happen, it would end your responsibility where she is concerned if you let her be. Like she wants you to."

Yeah. That's not going to happen.

Michael leaped ahead, tearing through the night, pounding the ground, swallowing the dark breeze as he followed Kaitlin's trail like a wolf possessed.

Old thoughts reemerged as he raced on; bits of remembered remarks and phrases from his youth.

There are some good humans, Michael, but it's not worth risking our species to seek them out.

People have always shunned what they know to be different, and that fact will never change.

Your mother didn't stand a chance against silver bullets specifically designed to take down our kind, from the weapon of a hunter because of greed and a hatred for what he could not understand.

No one came to your mother's aid. None of us were near.

I'm sorry, son. I will always regret having to tell you that your mother is not coming back.

He heard those words often enough to be able to see his father's lips moving. His dislike of getting close to humans had grown from that moment. He had vowed never to interfere where he didn't belong. And then he had helped a human named Kaitlin without thinking, feeling her pain and picturing his mother alone and dying. Wondering what would have happened if someone had kicked that wolf hunter to kingdom come and helped his mom get home.

He had broken a deep-seated personal vow. Now he knew he had imprinted with a human whether or not he had meant to. For a werewolf, imprinting was an unbreakable union, and lifelong.

Kaitlin must have felt this, too. She had been chained to him by his actions. Though she wanted to be fiercely independent, that wasn't going to be the direction of her future.

Hell.

He loped faster, glad that Kaitlin had sensed the monsters on the loose tonight and had the wits to run. She was heading back toward the college. In a night of missteps, moving toward a crowd might be one small thing in Kaitlin's favor.

He ran faster.

She had veered toward a building that used to be the main college library. While the building wasn't empty or derelict, and still housed some collections, it was no longer the gathering place for most of the university's student population, by the looks of things on a Monday night.

His hopes slid a little. The fact that the building wasn't empty was a worrisome detail that had to be carefully considered. Who wouldn't notice a large wolf shadowing a woman through corridors and half-empty shelves?

Kaitlin? Michael sent a silent call. *Hold on. I'm coming.*

He had promised she would be safe tonight, and that promise had been broken. Would she believe anything he said after this?

A rain of dark, foul-smelling ash struck his muzzle, but Michael kept running. A vampire had perished here just moments ago. Who had seen to that if his pack was behind him?

He was accosted by another strange scent that he almost recognized until something deferred his attention from it.

His head came up. His ears pricked forward.

Bless her pale, shapely hide. Across that chain binding them together, Kaitlin had heard him and was answering his silent call.

Chapter 10

The beast on her tail was closing in.

Kaitlin tore through the hallway like a winged demon, knowing this old library better than most people, having spent a year doing research here before the newer building opened. She hoped that fact would help her now.

She moved right, turned left down a long corridor, not sure if she should shout for help or lead the monster away from the few other people occupying this building. She wasn't sure she could handle this new threat, or even face it.

To say that this had been a long day was an understatement. She had set her studies aside in order to learn something entirely new that would help to guide her future. The scent of vampire was one of those things. And though that putrid odor would be forever embedded in her lungs, it didn't mesh with the unusual smell of the thing chasing her.

Were there different smells for different vampires?

Were there different *kinds* of vampires?

Guilt about running away from Michael was an added pain to the pressure in her lungs, but she couldn't have this both ways. Either she wanted him with his pack, or with her.

Still, facts were facts. She was a hindrance to his pack when dealing with these monstrous fanged creeps. Her family's credo had been about keeping out of trouble by not standing out. By blending in. Following their lead, while at times resisting her rise of inner rebelliousness had been her daily quest.

She ran as fast as she could, energized by fear. Nerves were firing. Adrenaline was dumping into an overwrought system.

Without having to look, Kaitlin knew the beast was right behind her. Maybe running turned vampires on. Possibly their minds had been left for dead, while the rest of them worked off the smell of terror. Being near other people didn't seem to deter this particular monster. Neither did racing through enclosed, lighted hallways.

Her pursuer's presence was like a dark, unshakable shadow. A reminder she didn't need about the things vampires were capable of. Yet there was also a familiar pressure in the air that sliced through the rest of this sensory bullshit. Wolf.

One more right turn brought her to the staircase leading to the mezzanine overlooking the main library floor. Circumventing a few people by managing to remain just out of sight, Kaitlin groped for an idea about what to do next. Although she didn't want to call Michael again, she whispered his name.

The irony of sprinting through a research facility when she couldn't stop to learn more about what was chasing her stayed with Kaitlin as she raced through another row of mostly empty shelves. There were only so many places to get away from this thing.

Damn it. I'm screwed.

Kaitlin? Hold on. I am coming.

Michael's words buzzed through her with a crackle of electricity. In the midst of a high-speed chase probably not destined to end well, his effect on her continued to exemplify the word *seductive*.

Running from Michael had been a stupid move. She saw that now. She kept moving, dodging shelves, breathing through her mouth. Though Michael wasn't here in person, she knew he soon would be. All she had to do was hang on and take this monster on an extended tour of the stacks.

Kaitlin hoped to God she could do that, because it was going to take a miracle to pull off. Then again, she had already experienced one miracle, care of Michael, and was exhaling the breath to prove it.

"Hurry, Michael," she whispered, resigned to be a damsel this one last time, and swearing a solemn oath not to make it a habit.

Hurry, Michael.

Kaitlin's shout reverberated inside Michael's skull leaving a long, lingering echo.

When he reached the entrance to the library building, he knew he'd have to lose the fur. Problem was, beneath that fur he was naked, which would no doubt cause quite a stir in university hallways, especially since the days of thrill-seeking streakers were over.

He had to get as far as he could on all fours first.

He loped through the open doors and down the first corridor, sensing Kaitlin's presence as if she'd magically appear if he looked hard enough. If she had been there, he would have pushed her against a wall and kissed her stupid for taking so many chances with a precious life that had been given a second chance.

He would also have done more than that.

Michael! Panic laced Kaitlin's call.

He pushed through an office door, scaring an elderly woman who was leaving. He spied a desk and a man's jacket hanging on the back of a chair.

Ignoring the woman, who had quickly exited, probably to call the police or animal control, he morphed back to a more acceptable shape, sweating, breathing harder than usual. His internal heat level was at a record high and left the wolf, safely tucked inside again, whining to again be free.

Grabbing the coat, shoving his arms into the sleeves, Michael raced back to the hallway figuring that being half dressed was the only option open to him and better than nothing when a life was at stake.

He lucked out again. A forgotten backpack leaned against a wall beneath a bulletin-board. He snatched it as he ran, finding a pair of jeans rolled up inside. Pausing only seconds, he pulled them on.

Kaitlin. I'm on my way.

I'm sorry were the words she sent back that stoked the fires allowing him to pick up more speed.

He found the stairs Kaitlin had used. Following her scent, grimacing over the odor of what was chasing her, Michael took those stairs three at a time.

Kaitlin was leading her shadow on a crooked path with hopes of ditching the beast, oblivious to the scent of the creep's bloodlust that saturated the slightly stale library air. Michael found it hard to believe that a bloodsucker had dared to enter this building. Did that mean bloodsuckers were evolving?

He could not allow this one to be seen. He had to kill it. End it.

Hold tight, Kate.

He had said those words to her before, on that first night, wondering if she would survive. Michael repeated them again now, as much for his own peace of mind as for hers.

Hold tight, little wolf.

He reached the mezzanine without drawing too much attention to himself. Luckily, this old library didn't have many students lingering at its scattered desks. The few who were present were deep in their studies.

Kaitlin's scent grew stronger as Michael rushed toward the shelves leading to a back wall, where the stink of what was chasing her hovered. He nearly stopped to consider the shock of that smell.

The thing pursuing her wasn't a vampire.

He saw her. Kaitlin's fear got stronger with each step the thing that chased her took, and yet that fear hadn't crippled her. He was moved by that show of bravery.

The thing focusing on Kaitlin hadn't expected him, and didn't bother to turn as Michael approached from behind. Taking hold of the creature's shirt, he spun the short, tightly muscled body around with a twitch of his arm and stared into a dark, expressionless face.

It was a Were he held onto. A Were in man form that carried in its scent the foul odors of a bloodsucker because it was covered in ash.

There was no time to deal with the ramifications of that.

"Out of your league, my furry friend," he said with a harsh half growl. "And much too far from whatever hole you crawled out of."

Without struggling too much, the Were hissed one word, "Her," with a breath that smelled of dead fish.

Since the Were's gaze was glued to Kaitlin, there was no doubt about who the beast meant. *Her.* Michael didn't like this. What was a lone wolf doing in Clement? Why hadn't his pack gotten wind of it before this? Why hadn't he?

The creature's response left him with the sinking feeling that it had one specific goal tonight, and that goal was Kaitlin Davies. No one else. Just Kaitlin. He had thought the same thing about the vampires.

Why would that be true, if it were?

"Who are you? Who sent you? Plenty of others weren't lucky tonight when they faced us," he said.

The Were didn't even pretend to fight Michael's hold. It stood there with its red-rimmed eyes locked on Kaitlin as if mesmerized by her.

This was both creepy and surreal. If this creature was crazed, the scents drifting upward from those students had to be working on the demented Were's mind. Yet it didn't seem to notice.

"Leave this Were to me," he said to Kaitlin. "Go now. Wait for me in the hallway. Don't go outside alone in case there are more of these guys."

Bless her, she nodded and said, "Should I get the other people out? There aren't many students here."

"Can you do that?"

"There's a fire alarm on every floor."

He nodded. "Use one."

When she turned, the Were in his grip began to struggle. It wanted to go after Kaitlin. The short male Were was strong, but unsteady on its feet, as if weakened by sickness. Sweat gleamed on a face that was as pale as a vampire's. Muscles that should have been taut quivered. This Were might have wanted to hurt someone tonight, yet wasn't strong enough to best an Alpha who had made Kaitlin's safety a personal mission.

Kaitlin didn't take long to find that fire alarm. The shrill sound streaked through the building like the roar of a tweaked nerve. He heard students leave their seats and head for the door, grumbling about being disturbed by what could have been an overused prank.

The Were in his grasp strained against Michael's hold, snapping its human teeth the way vampires snapped theirs, possibly recognizing what the alarm bell meant. No one liked fire. However, this Were's mind had to be severely muddled for it to believe there was a fire without scenting a single wisp of smoke.

Michael had to try to get this wolf out of the building and into the open, where he could explore the reason for its unannounced presence. But the Were twisted suddenly as if just regaining its wits, and was stronger than it looked.

Michael had never enjoyed fighting. He detested unnecessary violence. His family had been decimated by his mother's murder. Nevertheless, keeping secrets was paramount, so getting this Were out, and away from humans, was at the top of his list.

He tried to drag the flailing werewolf to the stairs. The Were had a punch like a prize fighter, and several of those punches in a row threatened to knock the wind out of Michael. He tasted blood, ditched the idea of getting this guy out of the building peacefully and rallied with a right cross of his own that managed to stop the Were long enough to try to get a better look at him.

The rogue wasn't going to submit to closer observation or be taken anywhere. The eyes were black, wide, wild. There wasn't much human left in that face, though the Were could not transition inside the building or outside without a full moon. Nevertheless, this guy's body was trying to do just that, and trapped in the inferno of mutating cells.

The fire alarm had been going off for a few minutes too long already. There would be a response soon. They had to get out.

"Why?" Michael asked, managing to pin the Were's arms to its sides after receiving another blow to the stomach that temporarily turned his vision red.

The Were spat in Michael's face and again tried to bite.

"I don't know what you're thinking, my friend." Michael wrestled with the beast. "Or what you've done to smell so bad, and what you're up to."

He tried again to drag the Were to the stairs. The wolf shook him off, jumped over the railing and hit the floor below with an audible crack to several leg bones. The maimed creature howled as it lunged through a window, breaking the glass, spreading shards in all directions.

Michael stared, too surprised to move.

"Michael?"

His attention snapped back to the floor beneath the mezzanine. Cade was there, looking up.

"You might want to come down here," Cade said. "Pronto."

Damn it. There were so many reasons why he didn't like that remark.

Kaitlin watched the few people in the library leave. She stayed just inside the door in the shadows, hoping she wouldn't be seen.

In spite of the fear and the anger she was feeling, she was determined to remain human, even though her body was telling her it wanted to change. Energy was sparking within her, as if her nerves had become live wires. She flinched with each inaudible zap of white-hot electricity, shocked by those sensations, feeling as though she had been electrocuted.

Half her body was chilled. The other half was extremely hot. There seemed to be a line down the center of her body to separate the two temperatures, just as there were going to be two sides of her physically when the full moon showed up.

Light-headedness was a side effect for having passed in and out of shock for the past few days, she supposed. The miracle was that she no longer felt sick to her stomach.

Her skin was twitchy. Her scalp tingled. She imagined moonlight playing on her skin, though she was indoors. None of those reactions hurt her. They were scary, new, weird.

Although Michael had encouraged her to wait for him, Kaitlin wasn't sure she should. She would be relatively safe in a crowd and there were plenty of students and university staff members surrounding her. When those people dispersed, she would have to find someplace safe to hide from both vampires and wolves until she got her wits back.

Peace was what she craved. Peace, quiet and everything having to do with the term *normal*. In her mind were echoes of explosions that had been vampires turned to ash. If that wasn't incredible enough, her mind also churned up an image of one central figure standing in all that ash like a mythical phoenix rising from the flames.

Guess who.

Michael's presence always gave her a whole new series of shudders and quakes, followed by an unusual pressure on her eardrums. He was now her Alpha. What kind of power did Alphas actually wield over their packs? Maybe her attraction to him was part of that.

Michael wasn't much older than the other Weres she had seen tonight. Cade was larger. Rena was sassier. Together, they formed a tight family unit that seemed to easily read each other, and willingly traded verbal barbs and clothes. This was going to be her new second family. She would graduate from the university with an advanced degree soon, and then what? Would she leave this pack behind? Did that happen?

Damn it. Explaining these new connections to the family she already had was going to be a bitch.

Obviously, some Weres weren't as nice as Michael's pack. Case in point, the Were in the library that had tried to kill her.

Sirens in the distance were getting closer, the sound underscored by the ongoing shriek of the fire alarm.

After discovering this alarm was false, firemen would depart and everyone would go back to their routines. Everything would be *as usual*, with the exception of the possible broken chairs and shelves on the mezzanine, the result of Michael dealing with a beast that was like him on the outside, but seemed to be very different on the inside.

Michael hadn't reappeared. She'd heard something break on the mezzanine when she took the stairs to the main floor. Who would explain the destruction in this building if there was any? Who was going to question it?

She couldn't wait around to see. With the building clearing out, she had to appear to be as surprised as anyone else by the sound of the alarm. She had to go outside, but she wouldn't go far.

The night assailed Kaitlin when she marched tentatively down the steps. Onlookers had gathered on the lawn to see what had happened. Kaitlin walked through them, catching sight of a gleam of black hair in the lights. Her heart sputtered, though she reasoned this wasn't Michael, because she had left him behind.

It was Rena.

"Brava, Kaitlin." Rena stepped forward to meet her. "If your hand tripped that alarm, you're fairly wily."

"I feel like hell," Kaitlin confessed, looking over her shoulder for Michael.

"Welcome to the club. I feel that way half the time I'm awake," Rena said.

"Really?"

"Nope. That's just my first and maybe final attempt to bond with a new pack-mate."

Kaitlin took a moment before speaking again, wanting her voice to be steady, refusing to show the extent of her frustration with tonight's events to a wolf who possibly wouldn't have the same take on things.

"What now? Can I go home? Is it safe?" She didn't see anything in this crowd that resembled a raving lunatic. What she needed right then was a hot shower and her bed. She was going to cover her head with as many blankets as possible and hope the world would go away.

"If he thinks it's safe," Rena replied.

"And if he doesn't?"

"Then Michael will try to pawn you off on me, me being the only other female in this pack."

"I'd be sorry to put you out."

Rena tilted her head. "Really?"

"No. Just trying to bond with a potential pack-mate."

Rena's bark of laughter ended with a smile. No blood stained the she-wolf's clothes. There was no ash in her hair or other evidence of having fought vampires tonight. Rena looked calm on the surface, though Kaitlin doubted this female ever embodied the word *calm*.

She wondered what they all did when they weren't prowling for bad guys. Fight each other for sport?

As Rena's eyes slid past Kaitlin, the she-wolf's smile faded. "The king approaches," she said. "Prepare to bow."

Chapter 11

A heat wave preceded Michael, the kind of warmth that combated the chills icing half of Kaitlin's spine.

Being in close proximity to Michael meant moving toward his species one internal trick at a time. Refusing to look at him was not an option, though. The sheer magnificence of Michael striding toward them stirred up feelings that moved Kaitlin way down deep.

Even after being chased by vampires and fighting off round after round of chills caused by the threat of gaining a whole new identity, Kaitlin wanted Michael. Badly.

Michael's eyes were on her as he came up alongside. Those eyes were like green flames. Concern for her registered within his gaze, and also something of a deeper, more personal nature. Whatever it was elicited tingling sensations on the back of her neck. Every glance, look, gaze, snapped their bond tighter.

"Good play with the alarm." He spoke without turn-

ing his fiery gaze down a notch, and in a voice that resonated as half gravel, half growl. Kaitlin wanted to return
that growl, and choked off the sound by closing a hand
around her throat.

"You sent that vampire back to whatever the opposite
of heaven's pearly gates might be?" Rena asked, interrupting the shared heat of the moment.

"This wasn't a vampire." Michael's tone was tentative
and thoughtful.

"What?" Rena asked, as if she hadn't heard that right.

"Wolf," Michael said. "And he got away."

Cade, standing quietly behind Michael, spoke. "That
might explain what I wanted you to see. You do see it—
the thing that I see?"

Michael said, "Yes. Beyond the trees."

"Oh." Kaitlin groaned, sure more bloodsuckers were
showing up and that there was going to be an endless supply of them before she noticed that the Weres were purposefully avoiding staring directly at those trees. They had
not locked on to that spot the way she'd seen them lock on
to vampires. Their wolf radar was humming.

"Trespasser," Rena muttered. "Is that the one that got
away, Michael?"

He shook his head. "That sucker was a mindless beast."

"This one's Lycan," Cade said. "I can feel the vibe from
here. He feels a lot like you, Michael."

"Friend or foe, that wolf should know better than to
show up unannounced," Rena remarked.

Wolf. They were talking about a wolf, not a vampire,
and the Weres' apprehension was contagious. It had been
a rogue wolf chasing her into a corner in the library. These
Weres called all unwelcome, unexpected guests rogues.
Mindless beasts, Michael had said.

She was about to look for the source of their newest concern when Michael laid a hand on her arm without addressing her.

"Cade," he said to the big Were.

"I'll watch her," Cade was quick to reply, possibly hearing Michael's silent command.

"I'm going with you." Rena took a step in the direction of the trees after Michael did.

Michael gestured for Rena to wait. "This is my job. If that wolf has bad intentions, we would have known by now. Besides, he smells good. How many bad guys can you say that about?"

Michael's levity didn't lighten the mood. Kaitlin got it—the fact that wolves didn't cross another pack's boundaries without permission, and that more than one of them had obviously done so tonight. She was learning the rules one at a time.

When Michael strode toward the trees, Cade's hand replaced Michael's on her arm. "Pack business," he said.

"Really bad timing," Rena added. "The area still reeks of vampire dust, and now this."

"There aren't any other packs around here?" Kaitlin looked from Cade to Rena.

"None close," another as yet nameless Were said, coming through the crowd to stop in front of Kaitlin. "Name's Devlin."

He eyed her rudely. Nearly as tall as Michael, and leaner than either Michael or Cade, this Were had straight chin-length brown hair that hid half his face. He was dressed like the others in jeans and a long-sleeved shirt. Unlike the others, he wasn't tidy. His shirttail was out, and he had missed a few buttons. Bits of ash clung to his right shoulder—the remains of the vampires, singular or plural, that he had slain tonight.

"Now isn't the time to flirt," Rena chastised. "Get a grip on your libido, Dev. Strange shit is coming down."

Devlin ignored her. "I'm Irish. You're Irish," he said to Kaitlin, leaning closer to her, invading her personal space. "Right?"

Kaitlin threw Rena another quick glance before replying. "My family was from Kerry, yes. Way back."

"Magical place, Kerry." When Devlin's lips upturned at the corners, Kaitlin wasn't sure she liked the wryness of that grin.

"What is it with the Irish?" Rena snapped without taking her eyes from Michael's retreating backside. "You act like other Irish people are all long lost friends."

Devlin shrugged. "Ireland is a small country."

"You can always go back there," Rena suggested.

"Why bother, when everyone has come here?" Devlin's grin widened. His rapt attention made Kaitlin more nervous than she already was. Even though these wolves were protecting her, she felt caged. She felt trapped by the thought of what might happen in two days' time when the moon was full. She now had vampires *and* rogue werewolves after her. How unlucky could a girl get?

Cade wasn't going to let her go anywhere without a chaperone, and she knew better than to try to shake these Weres again. Doing so might prove to be a suicidal move with so many alternate species hiding in the dark. In this case, werewolves were the safer bet.

Looking at Michael left her feeling uneasy. Like the physical war going on in her body between fever and ice, she faced another kind of quandary. She wanted to stay away from Michael to avoid the emergence of her wolf, while at the same time she mourned his departure.

* * *

Lycan was a distinct scent that most Weres recognized long before seeing the bearer of that scent. Actually, it was more like blood calling to blood, and a vibration that came off as a smell.

Michael's awareness told him this now as he filed details about this newcomer near the trees in his data banks.

Lycan. Capable. Expensive clothes. Radiating a kind of power that depicts a position of authority.

"Hello, Michael," the Were said when Michael got within ten feet.

This Lycan had a voice that matched his strong Were vibe.

"You know me?" Michael paused to get a look at the stranger.

"From a long time ago," the Lycan said. "Your father told me to look you up when I got here."

"You know my father?"

"I know Anderson Hunter well."

"Yet you came here unannounced."

The Were nodded. "That couldn't be helped. We tracked our prey to this location and have just arrived in Clement. When I heard the alarm in the building over there, I came to investigate and saw you. I waited for you to approach so that I could introduce myself and apologize for intruding."

Michael said, "And you are?"

"Dylan."

"From?"

"Miami."

Michael's memory churned up a name. "Judge Landau's son?"

"In the flesh, and sorry to have to reintroduce myself in this way."

Michael nodded. "I remember you."

"I was hoping you would. That makes things a whole hell of a lot easier."

The newcomer was tall, fair-complexioned and would be considered incredibly handsome by most of the women on the face of the earth, Michael had to admit after careful scrutiny. Dylan had long blond hair, very light in color, that would have hung to his shoulders if not tied back. Dressed in jeans, a black long-sleeve shirt and black boots, Dylan Landau gave an impression of being human at first glance, while probably not so completely human after a second look from someone who knew better. A hint of wolf was there, etched on Dylan's face, sculpting his appearance.

Michael did remember this guy. Dylan Landau was the pure-blooded offspring of the big Miami pack's Alpha, a Were Michael's father often associated with. Though Dylan was a few years older than Michael's twenty-five, Michael recalled visiting the exclusive Landau compound on occasion and watching Dylan and his friends.

"You chased prey here?" Michael asked.

Dylan stepped forward. "I've been helping some friends track a rogue."

Michal wondered if Dylan's rogue might be the same rogue he'd fought in the library, and waited to ask about that.

"We're three hours from Miami. That's a long chase across many pack lines," he said.

Dylan shrugged. "This is personal for my friends, and therefore personal for me. Do you give us permission to be here?"

Michael nodded. "Do you hunt a werewolf, or a vampire?"

"Wolf."

"You know that wolf is here?" Michael asked.

"Yes. He's a fast, slippery sucker," Dylan said. "This is

someone you wouldn't want to meet face-to-face or have hanging around. That alone warranted trespassing in your territory without advance notice."

Damn it, Michael silently swore. This was more bad news on a night already full of it.

"I might have just seen that rogue. We need this right now about as much as we need a hole in the head, Dylan. We have had sudden vamp problems. They've appeared out of nowhere in numbers that, if tonight was an indication, are almost more than we can handle with a small pack like ours. And then a sick Were appears in a room full of people."

Dylan said, "Sick Were, you say? Probably wouldn't be our guy, then."

"So we now have two strange Weres loose in Clement? Hell, what are the odds? Have you tracked your rogue to one place in particular?"

"Somewhere in there." Dylan waved at the closest buildings.

"We just cleared out the old brick building. That rogue got away, injured."

"It's as we feared, then," Dylan said. "Our prey already has made some friends."

Michael ran a hand over his hair. "Who is this wolf you're after?"

"Name's Chavez. He's been caught several times on our home turf, only to manage to get away. The last time he fled, he ate his shirt in the back of a police car to get rid of evidence. He's so slippery, nothing sticks."

Michael tried not to show too much concern with news that was so much worse than bad. "I've heard the name. Chavez makes the underground fight rings and creates his own little Were armies that kill cops."

"That's the guy," Dylan said. "A bad wolf that keeps on ticking."

"Who came with you on this hunt? Did you bring your own pack to try to catch the bastard?"

"I came with two Weres directly connected to one of those fight rings. The first goes by the name of Scott. Adam Scott. Miami cop, and pack-mate. The second is a talented she-wolf whose brother was murdered by one of Chavez's anti-cop fight-and-bite parties."

The news left Michael queasy.

"Old grudges run deep," Dylan went on. "The two wolves I travel with have scores to settle, which as we both know makes them twice as dangerous to an adversary, even if it is a notorious killer like Chavez. We got word that Chavez was heading this way and decided to do something to contain the problem."

Michael glanced around. Now that students were dispersing from the lawn by the library, he had a clear picture in his mind of the other visiting Weres in Dylan's group. Besides Dylan, the she-wolf he'd mentioned was also a full-blooded Lycan. Adam Scott wasn't.

He caught no hint of Chavez or the rogue that had escaped from the library. If they were hiding, it was in a safe place.

"Your friends are waiting by the side of the building," he said.

"Yes. We're biding time until the people clear out."

"Just so you know, there are plenty of vampires willing to get in the way of anything you might do."

"So we trade," Dylan suggested. "You help us and we help you."

Michael considered that suggestion. He wasn't naive. His pack was comprised of a few strong Weres. Beside Dylan and his big-city friends, however, some of whom were cops and detectives in their day jobs, his own pack-mates were babes. Relative to the world of hardened super-naturally gifted criminals like this Chavez character, his pack would have to be doubly on guard and in top form.

Then there was Kaitlin, the little rebel who refused to follow directions or stay put. Who knew what kind of trouble Kaitlin would get into with the full moon only two nights away? Chances were good that she'd need help with her transformation, and he wanted to be there for her.

Luck hadn't exactly come his way lately. He had thought about calling Miami for help with the onslaught of blood-suckers, and now he didn't need to. Help had just dropped into his backyard. The negative here was that the new Weres had brought a couple of bad guys with them. The worst sort of bad guys, as he'd just seen. And Chavez was rumored to be bad wolf number one for the creation of more dangerous rogue werewolves than anyone Michael had ever heard rumor of.

"Michael?"

Dylan was waiting for a reply to his question about working together and trading aid, and there was only one answer. For some reason trouble had picked quiet, rural Clement, Florida, for its next stomping ground. And that was just too damn bad for everybody.

"Deal," Michael said, seeing no viable alternative.

"Wolves."

Rena had said something but Kaitlin still couldn't focus properly. The landscape around her had again fuzzed over, blurring her surroundings, needling her awareness with a message she couldn't grasp. The moon was affecting her, too, though the rules werewolves went by told her that wasn't possible.

At least she was no longer the center of attention.

Most of the students and library staff had gone. Only a handful of people milled around by the old building. The area wasn't as empty as it seemed, though. Smells were magnified to form solid objects that she remembered from the dreams. The greenery of the trees. The dampness of grass. Everything the wind carried.

There were ghosts. Things she could sense without seeing. Michael had gone to meet one of these formless entities and Kaitlin restlessly watched.

The tension of the Weres beside her hadn't eased. She wondered if they also just sensed the ghosts, or if they knew what was going on. Cade's hand, on her arm, wasn't motionless. Rena shifted her weight from foot to foot as if she was trying to make up her mind about what to do.

The fact that there were no vampires present at the moment seemed like a gift from someone keeping tabs on her ability to handle things. Surely wolves knew how to deal with other wolves? Michael had done so in the library.

"Good guys have arrived," Devlin said, as if he knew that for sure.

"I certainly hope so," Rena remarked, "since something is going down."

Kaitlin's vision cleared somewhat as a figure walked toward them. Her heart skipped ahead several beats when she saw Michael.

He wasn't alone, and even she, new to this game, recognized the power hidden behind the outline of the Were following him.

Michael didn't look happy.

"Dylan," Michael said when he and the visitor reached the pack, "meet Rena, Devlin, Cade and… Kaitlin."

The fair-haired Were nodded to each of them in turn. His gaze hesitated on her a few seconds too long before he acknowledged Kaitlin with a slight inclination of his head.

Though this new Were's handsome face registered no reason for the hesitation, Kaitlin felt as though she had set off an internal alarm in the guy's mind. Could every Were tell she wasn't quite up to speed? Maybe he was wondering why she'd been included in this evening tête-à-tête. *That makes two of us*, she wanted to shout.

"Dylan is from the Miami pack, and therefore to be considered family," Michael said. "He brought friends."

Call her paranoid… Kaitlin felt Dylan's attention on her when he wasn't looking her way, as if Dylan possessed the ability to scan her mind without her permission and was seeking something none of the others gathered here had noticed. Possibly he was deciding if she could be trusted. Maybe he didn't like hybrids.

Her chills returned as his scrutiny kicked up the detritus of more memory data. From deep in those memories, she heard an issued threat.

It's a damn shame that if you live and decide to threaten or expose my kind, it will be my job to kill you. Saving your life tonight would have been for nothing.

The night she had been attacked, Michael had spoken those words. And Michael was looking at her now because he knew what she was thinking.

Chapter 12

Only Kaitlin's heartbeats, registering inside his own chest, filled the silence inside Michael's mind.

She was remembering the threat he should never have spoken aloud while assuming she was in a state that made hearing him impossible. He felt her trust begin to dissipate as if being swept away with the breeze.

The situation was precarious.

His thoughts locked on to hers.

You can trust me, he sent to Kaitlin, careful to put up mental barriers that no one else in their present company could get past. Those words were for her. He offered them sincerely.

She wouldn't make eye contact. That kind of rejection felt bad on a night when the term *bad* had morphed into something inconceivable. His pack was faced with a dire situation, and their Alpha could not tear his thoughts away from the latest addition to the group.

He shook his head to clear Kaitlin from it.

The escaped criminal Dylan and his friends hunted was a serious transgressor. It was said that Chavez bit every bad guy in his path. In this wolf's gruesome underground bite rings, he pitted handcuffed cops against the worst were-wolves in his pack, most of those wolves career criminals with no love for law enforcement. Most of them harboring grudges like the ones Dylan had spoken of in his brief explanations about why his traveling companions were on this hunting expedition.

Many that Chavez had bitten were continuously drugged and half-crazed like the Were in the library, so it was said. New understanding of what he had fought in that building took an ugly shape. He felt bad for letting that one get away.

Werewolves had far-reaching memories, and grudges were part of that. In his dreams Michael saw himself running through valleys that time had not discovered or named. He wished he could go back to those times now. The future didn't look quite so rosy with a new caliber of monsters interloping.

Weres and vampires had always been at war. Their animosity was nothing new. The distaste werewolves had for vampires stemmed from medieval days when knights were somehow transformed into immortal guardians and after that, things went wrong. There had been a slip of the fang from a rogue immortal as far back as that, which created a whole new species living outside the rules in the golden rule book.

Michael had heard of good vamps, and was almost sure there had to be some, since part of an afterlife personality had to do with the former life and soul, but he had yet to find one. And those original knights hadn't been heard of for centuries.

Again, his thoughts turned to Kaitlin, who seemed to attract both vampires and Weres, himself included. He wasn't so blind as to have missed Dylan's half-hidden scrutiny of the pack's new addition. Dylan had been drawn to Kaitlin, perhaps for the same reasons everyone else was, with the exception of the ever-skeptical Rena.

Something else. Tonight, while in a daze, Kaitlin had spoken of those same hills and valleys he had seen in his mind as if she possessed wolfish memories she had no right to. Only Lycans belonged to the past and the years before the Flood. No other Weres could go back so far, see things so distant or past their own recent initiation into the wolf clan.

Kaitlin had shared his visions, though. She had felt what he had felt in that moment—the spontaneous wildness, and his desire for the simplicity of an existence long past. For this to happen, their bond had to have been sealed tight, just as he had predicted.

"Are you going to tell us what's going on?" Rena, first to break the quiet, asked.

Michael heard Dylan answer Rena's question as if the conversation was taking place in the distance and didn't include him. Kaitlin was tuning in to his thoughts, as he tuned into hers. Her face, so white and beautiful, reflected her unease. How different was she, and what did that mean? He wondered if he had overlooked something important, due to their closeness.

You have no choice really but to trust me, trust us, he sent to her. *I'm sorry that seems so hard.*

She responded aloud. "There must be someplace you can put me, send me, while I wait to see what the moon will do. Or, hell, why don't you use me as bait to catch your rogues, since I seem to be the draw for most of the monsters around here?"

The conversation around them ceased. Michael shook himself back to the present, enough to realize that he had taken several steps forward and now stood nearly chest to chest with Kaitlin. She was the only wolf here who wasn't looking at him, and hers was the attention Michael wanted the most.

"Don't be ridiculous," he said to her. "We have promised you protection, not to dangle you like a carrot."

"What about Michael, Rena?" he heard Devlin ask. "Aren't you going to make a comment about his libido?"

"It's none of our business," Cade said, quelling that joke.

Dylan cleared his throat to regain their focus. Although this truly wasn't any of his business, he said to Michael in a steady voice, "She has Lycan blood."

Michael said, "Yes." *So sue me.*

Dylan didn't need to ask how that happened, or whose blood Kaitlin's veins contained. That had become obvious from Michael's behavior so far.

In a lowered voice, Dylan said, "Was she entirely human to begin with? I hope you realize what you've done."

Michael tore his attention from Kaitlin as she said to Dylan, "What are you talking about?"

"I tried to tell you," Devlin said to him.

"I hope you're going to tell us what that other thing is," Rena said to Devlin. "Otherwise, we're wasting time by standing here."

"The Irish sometimes possess other qualities if their families go back far enough," Devlin said. "And Kaitlin's family is Irish."

Kaitlin stared at Devlin as if he had suddenly gone mad. Michael knew she wouldn't show more signs of vulnerability now, in this crowd. She had mentioned hating the limelight and that she never wanted to stand out. This conversation was testing those issues.

Bless her, she had proved herself tough enough to handle what came her way tonight, making some headway into being accepted by his pack. Vampires in the park. The werewolf in the library. She wasn't used to being half wolf, and now there was a suggestion she might not fit the half human part of the equation.

None of that mattered here, he supposed. He had to get the heat off Kaitlin and allow her some breathing room. Everything else could be handled in private. There was a criminal to catch. Everyone here was at risk.

The arrival of Dylan's friends was both a relief and a distraction. The two Miami wolves heading their way garnered everyone's attention.

"Tory and Adam," Dylan said by way of introduction.

It didn't take Michael long to observe the details of what amounted to a super team of hunters. These Miami Weres radiated strength and power. Existing in a big city like Miami would mean they were tough, resilient and experienced.

Tory, the Lycan female, was a stunner with long, curly red hair and perfectly white, flawless skin. In spite of the balmy night, she was dressed in leather.

Her light-colored eyes gave him the impression she had seen a lot, been through a lot. In that gleam lay the hint of a world filled with pleasure and pain in equal doses. Her serious expression revealed a depth of sadness that didn't quite eclipse the tension she tucked inside her deceptively svelte body.

The other Were was male, tall, well-built, with a dangerous aura most career cops had. Adam Scott had dark hair and a tan complexion marred by a scar that ran down the left side of his face. He carried a gun, and was too far out of his jurisdiction to exhibit a badge. That scar would have proved he wasn't a Lycan if his scent hadn't. If he'd been

Lycan, no evidence of past battles would have remained for public viewing. And that gun he carried had to have been modified for a Were's aversion to metal.

Miami had sent an A-team after Chavez.

Still, something else about this pair needled at Michael's mind before he figured out what that was. The red wolf and the cop were a pair. A couple. The fact that they had imprinted was written all over them, from the way the cop let Tory take the lead, to the way her expression eased when she looked at Adam Scott. They were lovers. Mates.

Michael looked to Kaitlin and back to the pair, wanting to question the validity of his perceptions. These two, from different backgrounds, had imprinted and had been accepted into Judge Landau's Miami pack. Lycan rules about preserving undiluted Lycan blood had been broken with this pairing, and no one seemed to care.

"What about the rogue I saw?" Michael asked Dylan, getting back to the situation confronting them and the reason for their visit.

"It's likely that one was created recently, which is why we have to find Chavez as soon as possible. We don't have long until the full moon," Dylan said.

"Clement is a small city. There's no room to hide a force like Chavez and his gang. If there were to be a bite club, it would be big news."

"That's why we need to catch him here, before he moves on to a larger city. There are fewer places to hide here, and as you say, a population this small would notice a missing person or two."

"Hell," Michael muttered. "Clement wouldn't know what hit it."

"Let's hope Clement doesn't have to," Dylan said.

Kaitlin retreated several paces. Michael felt her fatigue

and flagging energy, a state made worse by the reminder of how close the next full moon was.

He wanted to hold her, and couldn't do that. Being Alpha of his pack and acting like one had to take precedence over his emotions.

"What else am I?" Kaitlin addressed Dylan, interrupting with wide, innocent eyes. "If you know so much, maybe you can tell me that."

Dylan Landau turned his light eyes her way. "I really don't know. I have met only one other female who had a vibe similar to yours."

"What was she?" Kaitlin pressed.

"Something dark," Dylan replied. "Though it turned out okay."

Kaitlin faced Devlin. "What were you suggesting I might be, with your Irish remarks?"

Devlin shrugged. "It's not for me to say."

"That would be a first," Rena quipped wryly.

The importance of catching a fiend like Chavez took a momentary backseat to the female Michael called his little wolf, and who two Weres had just insinuated might turn out to be so much more than that.

Not for the first time, he wondered what the hell was going on.

Nothing Dylan had said about her made sense, Kaitlin thought. She was as human as anyone else in Clement. At least she had been until last Friday night.

Had everyone gone crazy?

Had she?

Scanning the faces in this circle of Weres, she couldn't read any of their expressions. She did sense the emotional turmoil under the surface that no one was showing up front.

"So," she finally said, refusing to let this go when it was so damn important. "If that's true, and you all think I'm something else, as yet undefined…what would that do to the half human, half wolf classification this pack has already given me?"

No one seemed to be able to answer to that, or dared to give an answer a shot. Kaitlin again looked to Devlin. "Why don't you give it a go, since you brought it up in the first place?"

"Well," he said. "I suppose the rest would depend on what percentage that other part might be."

"Which is what we all picked up on without understanding why," Rena said, catching on. "And again, can we get on with the creeps who have invaded out town?"

"Yes," Michael agreed. "Kaitlin's heritage isn't our problem. Mad werewolves who chew on others for sport are."

Tory, the Lycan female, spoke up. "I'm guessing more than one of these buildings has a basement, and that Chavez would pick a place like that to hide in."

"He'd have to share it with vampires," Rena said.

Adam Scott had a deep, authoritative voice. "That means we either do a sweep, building by building, and preferably after everyone in those buildings has gone home for the night, or we wait until the next moon and watch the fireworks as Chavez reappears with whomever he has bitten between now and then."

"Hell, how many wolves could that be?" Michael asked.

"You don't even want to know," Adam replied.

Kaitlin zeroed in on the scar on Adam Scott's face, then touched her neck to finger what remained of the injury that would also leave a mark like that. She wondered what had caused Adam's wound, and if it had been an injury on his day job or the antics of a crazy werewolf like the one that had cornered her in the library. Was Adam here for retribution?

Cade spoke. "In the meantime, we potentially face a slew of vampires in each of those places, all of them up and kicking in the dark."

Kaitlin searched the faces in the circle, not certain where things would head next. Night air sparked with the power of the combined presence of these Weres. She should have been proud to be one of them, and accepted by them. At the moment, and with all the cryptic insinuations about her possible heritage, she would have preferred to stick to the part human, part wolf description...with no room for housing anything potentially far worse.

"What do you think, Kaitlin?" Dylan was asking her.

"What do you mean?" she returned.

"Can you venture a guess as to where the rogues might be? Or where they won't be because of a nest of vampires?"

She was shoulder to shoulder with Michael. His tension increased with Dylan's question.

"You think I'd know that?" she said.

"Didn't a vampire hurt you?" Dylan asked.

Her hand was on her throat, which meant that Dylan didn't miss much.

"If one did, you might be able to sense them better than we can," Dylan continued. "From farther away."

She thought back. It was true that she had sensed vampires tonight and had warned Michael, but how she had done that was a mystery. Fear of being out of her league among these experienced Weres kept her from speaking. Michael was looking at her. They all were.

"It can't hurt to try to locate them," Dylan suggested. "Maybe part of you understands how to do that."

"Why would it?" Michael's voice registered his uneasiness with this line of questioning.

"Because she has been up close with one in a different way," Dylan said.

Hell, could everyone read her mind? Did all of these Weres know what had happened to her?

"Sorry," Kaitlin said, frustrated, scared all over again by Dylan's reminder of that vampire attacker's foul breath and how close she had come to dying. "I don't see how I can know their location when I barely know the direction of my apartment."

Michael moved. Turning slowly, he spoke to everyone. "Let it go. We can start the search and do one building at a time if we have to."

As all eyes shifted to him, Kaitlin swayed. The ground was moving, and a quick look at the others told her no one else had noticed. More outside pressure came, as if the night again was closing in. Piled on top of the internal pressure threatening to make her shout, she caught a new scent that was similar to the sharp odor of rotting wood.

She widened her stance. Raising her face to the sky, Kaitlin drew in a breath of night air that might have carried a message of sorts if she could figure out how to access it. Both the earth and the wind were trying to communicate with her, and that notion was bizarre. Still, she had a feeling their message was important.

Was it a warning? A signal to be wary?

Why did she think the wind could speak her language? Who would believe it?

Michael felt the direction Kaitlin's mind had taken. Before he had a chance to explore further, she slammed a mental door in his face. He didn't know how she did that, because it was a barrier he could not scale.

Before long the others would notice how Kaitlin had frozen in place. They would note the ashen pallor of her face. Getting her out of there was crucial. She wouldn't want them to discover the reason for her sudden color loss. Sooner or later, they would pick up with greater detail the new thing blossoming inside her.

The rapid growth of the wolf inside Kaitlin was like nothing he had ever encountered. He couldn't wrap his senses around the reason for its early intensity, or comprehend why it was happening to her at all…unless Dylan and Devlin were right, and she wasn't quite human to begin with. Perhaps they were nearer to the truth than he had been because he was close to her on a level that extended far beyond their brief acquaintance with her.

Imprinting with Kaitlin was no joke. Lust and attraction and cravings were all part of that. Longings to be near her, to touch and smell her, had been magnified to alarming proportions. Because of that, it was entirely possible that he had missed something important.

Hell…maybe he hadn't felt sorry for her that fateful night and some kind of magic had been at work the whole time, directing his actions where Kaitlin was concerned. Maybe she had lured him there.

Her aliveness was expanding. The thing centered at her core had picked up a glow, as if an internal lantern had been lit. She had wavered in and out of transparency prior to this, or so he'd thought, convinced at those times that he had made those things up.

He wasn't so convinced about his imagination now.

Dylan had been wrong in assuming what Kaitlin hid was dark, though. If this other side of her carried dark traits, it did a damn fine job of faking the opposite. Michael was afraid that if she stood here much longer, that internal light might shine from her pores, becoming a beacon for every living thing in their surroundings.

Light was the essential element that vampires and rogue

Weres lacked, the element that species clinging to the dark left behind, along with their former lives. That had to be why they were attracted to her.

He also wanted to melt into that inner light, and into her. Kaitlin Davies was some kind of unidentifiable spirit, and this first inkling of what that spirit looked like would have surprised everyone here. Even Kaitlin didn't know this. Whatever had been hidden inside her must have been dormant before tonight.

As her gaze gravitated to him, the wind picked up. For a moment, Michael believed she had conjured it. But it was an ill wind that Kaitlin was showing him, and tucked inside it wafted the unmistakable odor of several bad things.

Chapter 13

Rena was the first to speak. "Hey, are you all right?"

Michael shook off the spell he'd been under and barked, "Fine," then pointed to Dylan. "There's a nest in the building beside the athletic field." He inhaled deeply, finding images in the wind. "More unwelcome guests are being housed in a warehouse beside the dorms."

No one asked how he had managed to pinpoint the intruders so quickly, and he wouldn't have told them anyway. Kaitlin's secret rogue-honing ability was safe with him for the time being, despite Dylan questioning her about it. While he had a feeling she had called up the wind blowing through the circle, he was the one putting names to the evil nestled inside it.

At the moment, Kaitlin didn't look well. Possibly she was wondering the same thing about calling up that wind, and recognizing the hints of what it carried.

"I'll take Kaitlin home first, and then we can rendezvous at the field," he said. "She's not up for the kind of guests we're expecting."

Kaitlin didn't argue with that. No one else did, either.

Michael felt some semblance of relief. Her unusual fast track toward her wolf had shifted from his shoulders to those of her parents. He had nothing to do with this other side of Kaitlin. Family secrets were always a burden, but her family obviously had not told her about theirs.

Relief was quickly replaced with empathy. How could her family have hidden a secret like this? Or did her family even know about her, if Kaitlin didn't?

Had she heard those comments? Damn it, he'd forgotten to seal them off. Stiff, and as white as a ghost, Kaitlin whispered, "Please help me."

And that was exactly what he was going to do.

Taking her hand, Michael nodded to the others and headed for the trees with the knowledge that Kaitlin wasn't up to chasing after more turmoil.

Hell, neither was he.

War raged inside Kaitlin. She hadn't been able to duck fast enough to avoid all the bad information flooding her mind. The world had changed one too many times and she was having a hard time keeping up. If her DNA carried something that was other than human, and also other than the new infusion of wolf, she'd have a lot to confront her family about. The family she had always trusted and loved.

Did this make the other members of her family different, too?

How different?

The answer, whenever it decided to show up, made family decisions and directions about not standing out in a crowd doubly dubious. Was the fact that they didn't want to stand out because the Davies clan was something *Other*?

The opposing factions inside her didn't know how to respond to the latest round of news. One side wanted her to growl in distress. The other wanted her to disappear.

Beyond her thunderous heartbeats the night had become a symphony of sounds that were like nature's music. Night birds sang in the distance. Grass rustled as she and Michael walked.

Leaves swayed and crinkled over their heads. Branches rubbed together. This stuff had nothing to do with the moon that peeked out from behind overhead clouds. She had heard this kind of music only once before, in a recent dream.

"Do you have any idea what that secret is?" Michael asked as they walked briskly toward the street. "The one someone in your family might have kept from you?"

Kaitlin shook her head.

"You need to talk to me, Kate. Tell me what I can do to make this easier for you."

"Michael." The word was special, safe, and made her feel better. But it was only his name, not a talisman or an answer to Michael's questions.

"I only have an inkling of what you're going through," he said. "It's very different in my case, since I knew from the start what my family was, and what I was. No secrets there."

Michael was taking her home, doing his best to help and honestly trying to understand the situation. She loved him for that.

"I'm scared." She tugged on Michael's hand to make sure the bond was tight, wishing some of his incredible strength and confidence would rub off on her. "And I'm sick of being afraid."

She remembered saying this same thing to Michael before. How long ago had that been? Hours? Days? She had lost track of time. God, could it have been only that morning? Was this the same damn day that she had awakened screaming?

"You haven't noticed the moonlight for a while," he observed.

"I do feel it. I had made up my mind to give in before…" Before what? Before two werewolves she didn't know had pegged her as being different? Before a beast these guys called a rogue tried to make her his dinner?

Had Dylan's and Devlin's attention been the initial spark that started the ball rolling on that new Otherness inside her? Was the wind to blame? The wind that turned the movement of branches into voices that sang of starlight, escape and freedom?

She feared she might have a nervous breakdown trying to piece this together before they reached the street.

"How could you know where the monsters were hiding when the rest of us couldn't?" Michael asked.

"I saw a picture in my mind."

"Like the hills and valleys you spoke of earlier?"

"Yes. Like that. Just a picture I was able to decode." She glanced at Michael. "Maybe those pictures will go away if I don't concentrate on them."

"Would you like them to go away?"

"Yes." She tested his grip again and found it secure. "There's more."

"Like what?" Michael asked, slowing their pace.

"Something very dark is nearby, coating whatever light remains in this place."

Michael eyed her again. "In the park, you mean?"

"This darkness covers more area than that. When I first sensed it tonight, I thought I might be the cause, because of what Dylan and Devlin had said. I don't think I am. I don't feel darkness inside me. I'm not like the other anomaly Dylan mentioned, am I?"

"I'm not sure what Dylan was talking about, and am pretty sure you'd know if you had darkness inside you," Michael replied. "More than that, I'm sure I would have noticed."

"I can't be a vampire. You told me that. Yet I can sense them."

"No vampire. I promise you that. You did not die by a vamp's hand, and death is how their poison is passed along. Wolf and vampire can't exist in the same body. And all Weres can sense vampires at times. This wouldn't be news for your wolf."

Maybe it was nothing new, Kaitlin thought, and yet Michael was thinking about the crazy werewolf in the library that had nearly completely covered its wolfish odor with that of its vampire kill, mixing up scents and causing confusion.

"In any case, that has nothing to do with you," Michael said, aware that she probed his thoughts.

They paused near the street across from her apartment. She hadn't been there since heading out to meet Michael earlier. Windows were dark, making the place that had been her haven seem uninviting. Traffic in front of the building was light, since most students near the campus walked or rode bicycles. She had no idea what time it was.

Michael had somewhere else to be, and they both resented that. He didn't want to leave her any more than she wanted him to. Was she supposed to curl up in a chair and wait for any news they would eventually bring her if the pack survived finding nests of vampires and an escaped convict with an army of criminal-minded werewolves?

"That werewolf came after me tonight," she said. "You believe that might not have been a coincidence."

Michael's scrutiny intensified. "That rogue, if it had anything to do with Chavez—the wolf Dylan and his friends are chasing—could just as easily have gone after any woman who was out here and alone."

"Do some Weres do that? Chase humans?"

"Bad ones might."

"What about the vampire attacks? So many of them?"

Michael's green eyes were bright under the streetlights. "We are going to find out about that. I am going to find out."

He stepped off the curb, pulling her along with him. He would leave her soon, and the thought of Michael fighting a wolf so bad that Miami Weres had chased it here, and that he might be hurt in that fight, was almost too much for Kaitlin to bear.

"You'll have to," he said.

She glanced at him.

"You will have to stay here this time, Kaitlin. You have to promise me you'll do that."

The energy sparking between them was exquisite and addictive. Kaitlin didn't want to promise Michael anything that had to do with being separated from him. Though she was scared when she was with him, being without him seemed a terrifying idea. He hadn't gone anywhere yet and her longing for him had already tripled in scope. The very thing that had been her first inconceivable anomaly had now become her safety net.

She found herself again chest to chest with Michael, not sure who had made the first move. His body heat was scalding. The sexy Alpha's breath was rich.

Kaitlin cursed the night, the visitors and everything else that stood in the way of her having Michael to herself, including the guilt she harbored for being so selfish. Each second ticking by felt like an incredible gift, and also a monstrous mistake.

"All right, Michael," she said. *If I lie, you will know it.*

"Let me hear you say it." He whispered this to her, leaning down to capture her gaze. "Say the words, Kaitlin."

"I promise to stay put."

His lips brushed her forehead, setting off small internal explosions that mirrored the rocking ground beneath her feet. She wrapped her arms around Michael's waist, frightened that this might be the last time to indulge in a stolen embrace, and that the danger tonight was too terrifyingly grim for any semblance of normalcy to return afterward.

"This isn't wise." His lips rested on her temple. She heard his intake of breath.

"No." Kaitlin closed her eyes to absorb the riotous sensations he caused in her body by placing one brief kiss in the wrong place. "Probably not."

But it is glorious, she silently added, slipping her hands beneath the hem of his jacket. *You are glorious.*

Michael wore no shirt beneath the borrowed tweed coat. He shuddered when her fingertips danced over him.

The jacket was too small to contain Michael. His wide shoulders stretched the seams. When his arms encircled her, the coat rode up his back.

Testing the limits of her craving for him and pushing thoughts of guilt and danger aside, Kaitlin pressed her palms to his warm flesh. She moved her hands upward, over his waist and abs, acutely aware of each inch she traveled and awaiting his response.

It wasn't the response she had expected.

He released her, caught her wrists in a viselike grip and sucked in a breath. But she wasn't going to let him off that easily. What she wanted from him wouldn't take up much precious time.

She waited out the few seconds it took for Michael to loosen his hold on her wrist. When he did, he gathered her closer.

His kiss was a feverish devouring that captured her completely from the first touch of their lips. No light thing, and an action without warning, this kiss threatened to fade the rest of the world out of existence.

Lips. Tongue. Teeth. This was why Michael was so dangerous. He was a talented warrior for justice and sublime as a lover. She was going down in flames, craving him, wanting him, needing him, in spite of the dangers the night had brought. Their mouths were merging in an endless, mindless seduction of every other part of her.

Deep within her body, shocked by this kiss, Kaitlin felt her wolf stirring. The sensation was indefinable and disturbing, as if she had swallowed an animal whole and it was still alive.

Barreling upward, this inner wolf clawed its way to her throat, where it made a rumbling sound that resembled a groan of pleasure.

Michael echoed that sound.

She climbed up his body by wrapping her legs around Michael's hips. She clung hard to his shoulders as the kiss went on and on in a more provocative version of the first time Michael had placed his mouth on hers…in darkness, at death's door.

They were on the street, at the curb, and his hands tore at her clothes without a care for who might be watching. Hell, she didn't have to worry. No observer would have recognized shy, quiet Kaitlin Davies.

When Michael backed away from the street, she was sure they were going to finish this without a bed and four walls, and in this one case, the darkness might be a friend.

* * *

In the back of Michael's mind, a warning light flashed. Time was short. Others were waiting, depending on him to join the hunt. He just couldn't stop kissing Kaitlin. Everything he had always wanted was centered in her fragile, misunderstood body.

He liked to think that on some level he knew what he was doing, and that following his instincts about being physical with Kaitlin would turn out all right. He had never been delusional.

He could have taken her to her apartment, one rationalizing flash told him, but if he was late to the hunting party, Rena might come calling and break down the door. Instead, he carried her, with her legs around his waist, to the trees bordering the park; merely a few yards of backpedaling from the rest of civilization. He wanted her all to himself and was breathing hard. But then Kaitlin had always taken his breath away.

She was perfectly positioned to rub him the right way. Against the jeans he had nabbed from a student's backpack, the space between her jean-clad thighs created enough friction to heat the planet. The only question left was how he was going to get her out of those pants in a semipublic place, in order to explore what she was offering.

They were hungry, unashamed, wanting.

He didn't plan on being disturbed.

There wasn't time to treat this right, treat Kaitlin properly, and he hated that. However, her plans were crystal clear. She dug into his shoulders with her fingers. Her tongue danced with his. She was clinging to him as if her life depended on it, and he didn't slow down long enough to tell her it didn't.

As for himself... Michael Hunter enjoyed his reputation as a badass Alpha who had never been tamed, and didn't want to be domesticated now, no matter how much he wanted Kaitlin. Those warning lights in his mind told him that if he and Kaitlin followed through with a physical merging, they'd have to deal with the repercussions of a hasty, spur-of-the-moment hookup for days to come. After imprinting with her, having sex would seal the contract their bodies had made.

Hell. He was damned if he did, and damned if he didn't do what any normal male would have done to the female pressed tightly to him. Kaitlin being part wolf just made the decision easier. Wolves were all about action and satisfaction. Animals didn't consider consequences.

He was hard, and aching. His wolf was cheering him on, pushing him, roaring internally with a desire for him to consummate this union and get it over with. Kaitlin eased back far enough to look him in the eyes. Maybe she saw his misgivings in the dim light.

"Now who is afraid?" she asked huskily.

Damn it, she was right. He was afraid…of himself and the magnitude of his needs. He was afraid of the female in his arms that he craved desperately in the middle of a crisis. Nothing else seemed to matter, except her, and this.

"Do it," she whispered between deep, fevered kisses. "Let me see where this leads. I can't stand not knowing what it's going to be like. Hurry, Michael. The others will come for you, and I will have this before they do."

His mind blurred as his hands moved over her firm backside, tugging her free of her attachment to him. Before her feet hit the ground, he had torn her sweater over her head.

She wore thin, see-through lace over her small rounded breasts. The lace was a very pale, very feminine shade of blue.

He heard the fragile thing tear in his hands; heard it

float to the grass as softly as if it were a leaf falling from a branch over their heads. The softness of Kaitlin's skin made him feel clumsy by comparison. The fragility of her bone structure was a turn-on. The big bad wolf had become mesmerized by Little Red Riding Hood. So, how would this new take on the story end?

Her body was just as he had imagined it would be—tight, compact and beautiful, with balanced shoulders, a narrow waist and slim, sensuous hips. Her clothes hid strings of lean muscle that he hadn't allowed himself to look at the night she'd been mauled by the bloodsucker. On that night, he had covered her with a blanket and warmed up her struggle back to life. There had only been an inkling of this attachment to her. He recalled questioning his objectives even then.

Now, Kaitlin, his half wolf protégée, was offering herself to him, not out of duty to an Alpha, but because she needed to either put her lust out of its misery or pile on the flames. The next few moments were going to decide that for her.

"All right, Kate," he growled, reaching for her zipper.

Chapter 14

The sexy sound of her zipper sliding down overpowered the erratic, audible pounding of Kaitlin's pulse.

She caught a breath as Michael's fiery fingers slid into her panties, heading for the moist spot between her thighs that awaited him. This was no-man's land. But Michael wasn't really a man, as far as definitions went, and he had already captured her mouth again with a muted growl of ecstasy.

Her shoes were off. She had dropped them when he carried her. Michael's free hand rested on the sensitive skin of her lower back. When his fingers reached that special spot she wanted desperately for him to find, Kaitlin gasped. The moment was hedonistic, and magical.

She stood within the circle of Michael's strong arms, completely naked from the waist up, and Kaitlin didn't give a damn. Michael's wolf voodoo was heady enough for her to see this through. His inner fires were all-consuming.

She was ravenous for him. Wild inside.

He didn't undress. There was hardly time to breathe, let alone master more details like that. When he lifted her again, it was to place her over the hardness tucked inside his jeans. This hardness was for her, and Michael's erection had to be as glorious as the rest of him. The questions left unanswered, as well as the holes in her life story, were about to be filled by someone with secrets of his own. They were two of a kind, really. They had secrets in common.

Michael...

His kisses never stopped, and his lips had a direct link to her soul. Kaitlin wanted inside his jeans, remembering clearly how buff and beautiful his body was. She might even tear his jeans apart with her teeth. Another minute without having him inside her would be an unacceptable eternity.

This wildness was new, and so strange, she didn't recognize herself. When Michael's mouth finally left hers, Kaitlin growled menacingly and leaned closer, already mourning the loss. The bruised ache of her quivering lips was nothing when the look in Michael's eyes promised there was more pleasure to come.

With a graceful move and very little effort, Michael took her to the ground. Stretched out beneath him on the grass, Kaitlin's body buzzed with anticipation. The electrical connection they had threatened to bring up a shout.

Her arms were pinned over her head. Michael's mouth hovered above hers as he searched her face.

What are you looking for, king of the pack?

His mouth was millimeters away from hers. His wolf-green eyes blinked, and the memory of when she had first seen them returned, along with a swell of internal heat.

Her pulse drummed, kicked. She ached in places so deep, her entire body throbbed.

Bite. Kick. Scratch. Take him. Have him.

Those weren't proper things for a nice girl to think. With his weight holding her down she couldn't move her legs or make room for him to slide between them. Michael's longings echoed hers. His body quaked with need and his arms were corded with tension. If he'd freed her hands, she would have ripped into him, raking his back with her nails, pulling his hair.

When she arched her back and raised her hips, he let a hot breath escape that was the equivalent of a whispered curse. He ground himself against her as if he was ready to get to the good part of this union.

The wildness inside Kaitlin was growing to alarming proportions. Each nip of his teeth drew whatever the thing was that she possessed closer to the surface. That thing swam upward through her bloodstream, through her muscles, pushing against her organs and expanding outward.

Michael let go of one of her hands to run his fingers over her face, her throat, her neck, with a touch like velvet. The musky scent of his arousal was like perfume and told her that Michael was ready to consummate.

Her eyes closed as she waited for what was to come next. It was all she could do to count the seconds until then.

His mouth slid downward over her neck and chest. A damp lap of his tongue over her right breast made her insides spasm. He circled her raised bud slowly, taking time they didn't have.

She bucked beneath him, wanting more, wanting everything. But his mouth returned to hers with another mind-numbing kiss that threatened to rob her of all remaining breath. And then his kiss became softer, lighter, until Michael's wonderful manipulations ceased so abruptly, her eyes flew open.

He blinked slowly with his gaze riveted to hers as if he

wasn't sure what had happened, or what had interrupted the act they both wanted so desperately. But something had.

He released her, backed up and got to his knees so quickly, the motion left her winded. He stood up, reached down to grab her by the waist and pulled her up beside him, silently warning her not to speak, protest or argue by giving her a worried look.

Freed from his spell, breathing hard and fast, Kaitlin easily discovered what had separated them. There wasn't just a new scent in the air. What rode the wind was a malignant stench that could mean only one thing.

Company.

Michael sent her a glance that could have been perceived as an apology, and didn't waste any more time. Swooping down to gather her sweater, he said, "Change of plans." He helped her to dress, and led her away from that spot, adding, "Christ, I should have known."

With a cautious glance over her shoulder, Kaitlin saw shadows gathering on that street that must not have belonged to the good guys—which meant that hiding out in her apartment was no longer an option. Like it or not, she had to go along for the pack's next shadow-busting session and hope she had the nerve to see it through. She and Michael had to place their needs on hold in order to set wrongs to rights.

Maybe the interruption had been a good thing, she now thought, because as she tried to probe Michael for information on what they were running from this time, she felt him raise a mental wall that couldn't be broken down, even when she tried really hard.

"Where are the others?" Michael asked as Rena and Devlin approached at a jog. He scanned the area with his senses wide-open, noting two other Weres in the distance, within a tight radius of where the rest of them were standing.

"The Miami crew are nearby," Rena replied. "Those Weres are serious hunters and kind of spooky."

"They have good reason to be good at what they do," Michael said. "Imagine how many bad guys migrate to Miami for the weather alone, not to mention the fact that a city that size makes it a hell of a lot easier for Others to find hiding places."

"As well as victims," Devlin said.

Rena turned to Kaitlin. "Bad night for anyone's initiation. Tough luck, Kate."

Michael sent Kaitlin a warning not to pursue that thought. Rena was riled up, and the kind of wolf who thrived on danger. She would have been a good addition to a pack like Dylan's, where the concepts of daring and danger were interchangeable. His fear had always been that Rena might desire wider pastures someday.

Everyone present felt the evil vibes of the bearers of the unique scent Michael had pinpointed by the street. Rena and Devlin faced the trees, on edge and on guard. Devlin's expression had morphed into a rare seriousness.

Michael pointed toward the building in the distance that housed English lit classes, its upper floors rising over the treetops. "Is Cade there?"

"He's with Dylan," Devlin replied. "They started toward the old library, tracking the wolf that got away."

"Then they're looking in the wrong direction." Michael glanced east. "Because whatever they're looking for might have found us first."

Kaitlin was the first to spin around, following the odor that had gotten stronger in the past few seconds. Michael supposed her racing pulse was an indicator of Kaitlin realizing she hadn't yet passed the strength, speed and agility tests necessary for getting a Were through trying times like these. Anxiety was visible on her pretty face.

Again, his heart went out to her.

Like a wave siphoned from a dark ocean, the stench of malicious malignancy rolled toward where they stood, getting stronger with each beat of Michael's heart. Any Were worth his salt could have perceived that it wasn't vampires causing this particular wave, but entities whose blood ran as hot as his pack's did.

This trouble came from werewolves like the one he had encountered in the old library, whose disappearing humanity had been replaced with insanity. These Weres were unwashed, unkempt followers of the master criminal that had made them into what they now were. Beasts.

The air was charged. The situation was deadly. For whatever reason, Chavez had chosen to infiltrate a college town and had brought along friends crazier than he was, who had no doubt been created by a few savage bites. Chavez chose men who were bad to begin with and made them worse with an infusion of a tainted wolf virus that had been diluted over and over again until hardly resembling the original thing.

Hopefully, Chavez hadn't brought along too many.

If Dylan, Tory and Adam Scott hadn't arrived tonight, Michael dreaded the thought of what might have happened when Chavez loosed his henchmen. Michael went so far as to consider Dylan's showing up nothing less than divine intervention.

Time was up for thanking his lucky stars, however.

"Ready?" he asked his two pack-mates. He had to protect all of his pack, to the best of his ability, and leaving Kaitlin somewhere on her own was not going to happen. She'd have to come along.

He heard the sound of someone running. Dylan appeared wearing a grim expression. "That big wolf of yours."

Michael stared, trying to make sense of what Dylan was saying.

Rena stepped forward. "Cade?"

"I think they have him," Dylan said, relaying a message that struck terror in them all.

Shivering, Kaitlin took an involuntary step back, rocked by Dylan's dreadful announcement. Cade had protected her. He was a good guy, strong and intuitive. How was it possible he'd been captured?

"Are you sure?" Michael demanded.

"He went into the old library and didn't come out. I tracked him there and lost his scent. I came to tell you." Dylan paused, then turned on his heels as if he'd seen something beyond the trees. "Damn it, it's impossible for this town to be infested so quickly, and a damn good thing there's no full moon tonight."

Michael's pack-mates were already running toward the old library, driven by their love for Cade. Michael, with his hand on hers, followed. Dylan sprinted ahead.

Kaitlin knew enough about rescues to understand that there had to be a plan, and that there wasn't one in this instance. This didn't look good or feel good, but she was now invested in the welfare of this pack enough to take Cade's abduction as personally as the rest of them did.

Anger made a comeback. As they ran, her lungs felt near to bursting. She heard every footfall, experienced each movement of her muscles as if her body worked independently from her mind. Running felt good to her, even though it had been stimulated by the wrong reasons. Somehow they would find Cade and set him free. She'd never had real friends in Clement, or anyone concerned about her well-being until lately. Cade was part of that new existence.

Michael was silent beside her, his face a mask of anger and resentment over what was happening in his town.

"If you let go of me, you can get there faster," she shouted.

If he transformed now, Michael would become an even bigger force to be reckoned with. She pulled her hand from his and said, "Go!"

He didn't look at her.

"Go, Michael," she repeated. "I'll be all right. I swear I won't take any chances."

No one else was paying attention to their struggle to remain connected physically, and the extent of needs that required them to touch. But she saw that Michael realized the truth of the freedom she had just offered him. Since the rogue werewolves couldn't morph without the help of a full moon, Michael might hold the advantage when dealing with them.

"Your connection to Cade is older and takes precedence," she said.

With a long look at her and a silent message that said *Stay close, stay safe, or nothing will be worth this*, Michael began to tear off his clothes.

It was when he had shifted that Kaitlin's steps faltered. The ground that had moved and rocked earlier that night was tripping her up. She stumbled, cussed and grabbed for the gnarly bark of a tree, which didn't save her from a fall because her fingers seemed to go right through the trunk, as if she had imagined it.

The darkness surrounding her lightened to a dull gray. She caught the wink of stars overhead as Michael's moon broke free of the clouds, not quite full. Not yet.

It was in that instant, between one breath and the next, and as her heart continued to pound, that she felt Kaitlin Davies's outer semblance begin to dissolve.

Chapter 15

Red-orange flames of anger and anxiousness burned in Michael's gut. He had never felt stronger, and at the same time less like himself.

He passed Rena and Devlin in his race to the library, seeing only Dylan ahead. Dylan's vibe was also red-hot, his wolf churning up energy on a nuclear level. None of the Landau clan Michael knew of could shift at will. He wondered what Dylan would think of his ability to do so.

He and Dylan approached the steps to the old library building together. Dylan didn't comment about Michael's new shape, knowing better than to divert energy from the search for Cade. It was also likely that Dylan had seen this kind of special ability before.

There were no signs of students or staff near the doors. After the fake alarm Kaitlin had set off earlier, most of the people had finished up and moved on. One or two were left, and Michael's impression was of aged humans closing up shop.

He and the Weres had to be wary of being seen. Those two people in the building had no idea what kind of evil their library might house beneath its brick walls, if Cade had been taken there. And that seemed likely.

The foreign wolf's odorous trail was easy to follow. Dylan responded to Michael's soft growl with a nod of his fair-haired head. The scent was so strongly wrong here, it seemed the damn wolves had left a trail of breadcrumbs behind.

Might be a trap.

"Correct," Dylan agreed, hearing Michael's wariness. "This is much too easy. Any creature with a sense of smell would be able to follow this trail."

Michael watched Dylan check to make sure the hallway beyond the doors was clear, hoping the two people in the building were out of sight.

"Stairs leading down," Dylan said. "Just inside this hallway. Chavez is never this easy to track, so the ease of this discovery has to be a trick. We're being manipulated, Michael, and they're using Cade as bait."

Michael anticipated what Dylan would say next, allowing him to say it.

"If we bust down those doors leading to their den, they might be waiting. We don't have any idea how many there will be."

Dylan sniffed the stale air in the corridor before continuing. "I'm guessing more than one Were, and that their ringmaster won't be in residence. Chavez's MO is to let his wolves do the dirty work for him."

Killing Clement's pack was the dirty work Dylan was alluding to. Yet with his own pack and the Weres Dylan had brought with him, there was a good chance of stopping this criminal before it was too late.

Nevertheless, Michael's senses were sending up red

alerts. His senses detected vampires. The odor of rotting flesh overrode the harsh wolf scent pervading the hallway. He knew for a fact that the two opposing kinds of creatures would never have joined forces. The world of Otherness didn't work that way. So, why were both scents leading them deeper into this library, each of those odors as strong as the other?

Has to be that these rogues have taken over the old location of a nest, he said silently to Dylan.

"Or obliterated that nest," Dylan said as Rena and Devlin arrived.

Rena wrinkled her nose. "The place reeks."

"Why are the doors still open?" Devlin asked. "Shouldn't this building have closed up some time ago?"

"Yes," Adam Scott replied, striding in on long, muscular, jean-clad legs. "It should have been closed up tight, which doesn't bode well for any humans left inside."

Michael was glad to be in wolf form so he didn't have to elaborate on the sickening ideas taking shape in his mind about what would soon happen to any unsuspecting humans there were. Rena's expression registered her disgust over the same idea.

He looked past Rena for Kaitlin and didn't see her. He didn't sense her closeness when she had promised to keep up.

"We can't just waltz in there," Devlin said.

"And we can't leave Cade," Rena countered.

Dylan nodded. "We can't all go in there. Some of us have to remain here in case more beasts decide to cruise by." He looked to Michael. "Do you agree, Alpha?"

Michael growled and tossed his head toward the doorway behind them, ready to get on with this and get Cade back.

"Which of us has to remain?" Rena asked Michael. "Please say that isn't going to be me. Cade is my friend."

Of course, Rena already knew that staying put was the case, and she also knew why. He had asked her to take over Kaitlin's care if anything should happen to him, and there was a decent chance something would. Though Rena hadn't agreed to this scenario, she wouldn't cross the wishes of an Alpha who was supposed to take care of them all, but who suddenly harbored doubts about his ability to do that.

Rena's face colored. "Shit. Kaitlin must be outside."

Kaitlin wasn't outside, though. She wasn't even nearby. Growling his displeasure, Michael gathered himself to go and find her.

Dylan stopped him, speaking softly to keep the echo in the empty corridor to a minimum. "You're needed here, Michael. Let's break down some doors. Tory is outside. She'll watch Kaitlin."

Michael growled again and showed his teeth, seeing no need to shift back and speak for himself. After seeing his canines, the pack would get the picture that he was torn between wanting to find Kaitlin and needing to rescue Cade, and that one of those two victims was a hell of a lot weaker than the other.

"Michael?" Dylan said. "This is your ball game. Your call."

Swallowing needs that had curdled in his throat, Michael turned from the doorway. They had to save Cade, and his heart hurt over having to make that choice. He was counting on Dylan being right about Tory watching over Kaitlin.

They headed for the stairs leading to the basement in single file, with Michael in front, silent on his lethally clawed paws.

* * *

Kaitlin could no longer feel her body. She was as light as the air she breathed. Walking was impossible when standing required effort to keep rooted to the ground. Eventually she got to her feet and teetered, unable to regain any real sensation in her legs.

She was scared, and alone. She had promised Michael to keep up and was paying for that breach of promise. Detouring off course hadn't been her plan. It had been automatic, as if she'd been lured away from the pack by a power outside herself that was too compelling to resist.

That wayward power didn't seem to be wolfish, or fanged. Werewolves were muscular and heavier than she felt at the moment. Without a full moon overhead, the things she was feeling couldn't be blamed on that. She felt odd, and as though the slightest breeze might blow her away.

The taste in her mouth was no longer connected to Michael's breath, and more like licking starlight. Her insides had cooled. Some new thing was vying for space in an already overcrowded body.

Her vision sharpened. The grass she stood on was bright green, when at this time of night that grass should have been as colorless as everything else cloaked by darkness. Shadows glittered beside her, revealing their secrets and letting her know that no vampires hovered.

Crazed werewolves had apparently gone elsewhere, too. For that, she was truly lucky…if anyone could have called a person who was now half wolf and possibly also partially something else beyond that, lucky.

So, what other thing would show up to complete the assault on her humanity? Besides werewolf and vampire species, what else was there? She hated to think there could be anything more.

Do I feel like a wolf, at all?

Maybe she was beginning to. She had growled when Michael rolled her in the grass. The scope of her senses was widening. Those things left little doubt that when Michael had given her his blood, he had also transferred some of his specialized wolf particles.

As for this new thing inside her...

Would that negate her place in the pack if and when it showed up? What the hell else was left for her to be? Another kind of animal?

Her vision, so clear at the moment, showed several footprints lingering in the grass. The trail Michael and the rest of the Weres had taken lit up with a phosphorescent glow in the infrared spectrum. Birds in the branches watched her. Bugs flitted soundlessly through the leaves.

None of that erased the drive to follow Michael. Tasting starlight couldn't overpower the strength of her need for him. She had to man up and face this next challenge. She had to confront the future while accepting that life was leading her on a new path, wherever that path led.

Ignoring the other tug on her attention, and on legs that felt as though they belonged to someone else, she started after the Weres, hoping it wasn't too late.

The stairs led to a lower floor of offices, continuing to a subterranean level filled with machines and air-conditioning units. Some of those machines were on, and the noise was deafening to Michael's sensitive wolf ears.

The floor was damp. Like most old building basements in Florida, where sweltering weather often caused a buildup of moisture between walls and in enclosed spaces, this basement was particularly rank with mold and mildew. This kind of pollution was likely part of the reason for needing a new library on the other side of the university's campus. If mold seeped into the ventilation system, those spores would affect the longevity of books and the health of the people reading them.

The Weres couldn't cover their noses. Scent was what had led them here and what would hopefully allow them to perceive an attack before one actually happened.

Other Weres had been here, all right. Several of them. Buried deep in this maze of machines was Cade's familiar scent, as well. They were close to where the big wolf was being held. Michael's fur ruffled with tension.

There wasn't enough room for the pack to travel through the rows of machines shoulder to shoulder, which would have been the optimal formation for confronting an attack. But if Michael's instincts were correct, two or three of Chavez's wolves were all that called this place their temporary home. He sensed no big attack about to happen. Nothing jumped out of corners with knives or razor-sharp teeth.

Put more at ease by what his nerves were telling him, Michael rushed ahead with a harrowing howl that seemed to echo for miles. The battle calls of his pack added to the eeriness.

The room they were seeking sat at the end of a long tunnel of overhead pipes. The stench of that doorless room's inhabitants added to the foulness of the rest of the place, causing an instantaneous gag reflex. Adam Scott shoved past Michael with his weapon drawn and aimed. The Miami cop stopped just across the threshold, and lowered his gun.

Cade was there, and standing. Slightly bloodied and covered in filth, the Were Michael had long called his friend turned to face them with a wicked smile on his face. At his feet lay two of the Weres that had helped to capture him. Both of them were dead.

Michael downshifted back to his human shape with a sound of crackling bones and grinding body gears. As he stood upright on two legs, Rena broke the silence. "We should have known you could handle this, Cade."

Cade's smile showed a chipped front tooth. "Piece of cake."

Dylan asked the next question, backtracking to the door to peer into the gloom beyond. "Is this all of them?"

"Here, yes," Cade replied. "Their chatter told me they aren't alone in Clement, and that there are at least four more."

Rena asked with relief in her tone, "Only two of them took you?"

"Sorry to be a disappointment on that score," Cade said.

"Why did they take you?" Michael asked. "You don't fit their profile. They like bad guys."

"I hate to say this," Dylan remarked thoughtfully. "Can we entertain the possibility that these Weres went out on their own, without Chavez's blessing? Or that Cade might have been a decoy for some other action?"

Michael spun in place, understanding what Dylan had been getting at and not liking it one bit. He was out the door before anyone had time to question why, running on human feet, scaling the steps when he reached them in leaps and bounds while sending silent messages to Kaitlin that he hoped she could hear. *Watch out for Weres you haven't already met. Bad news is on the prowl.*

Racing out of the building and across the grassy quad, Michael encountered no one. He was thinking with a one-track mind. Abducting Cade could indeed have been meant to throw them off the scent of the real reason for that pathetic abduction. One such reason could be tied to Kaitlin.

If Kaitlin was the goal and more crazed wolves caught up with her, he'd go ballistic and hunt them all down, to the ends of the earth if necessary. He would dedicate the rest of his life to the task of finding them if they hurt her.

The park was empty, its long swathes of grass lit by the moon. Tonight, for the first time since he'd been patrolling here, the place felt eerie and unfamiliar. The scent of wolf was everywhere and nowhere, pervasive in spots, merely a hint in other places.

When the scent became strongest, it was a fragrance he recognized. Female. Pure-blooded Lycan. He hadn't met many Lycan she-wolves, since they were rare and scarce in the States. Teams went in search of them all across Europe to bring back, in order to facilitate imprinting and the continuation of Lycan family bloodlines.

Dylan's friend Tory stepped into his path, blocking him from moving past her with a sparkle in her eye and a halting hand gesture. The lithe leather-clad redhead didn't speak and shook her head to make sure he didn't speak, either, using her expression to encourage his silence. Seeing that he got this and would comply, she sent him a message. *Follow me.*

In stealth mode, they moved forward. Without his special abilities, Michael wondered if he would have seen Tory out here. Her black leather outfit blended with the night's shadows that moonlight didn't reach. Only her flaming mane of bloodred hair stood out when he looked really hard past the darkness.

Tory wanted to show him something and didn't have to point out what that was. He scented Kaitlin easily. And Dylan had been right about Tory watching over Kaitlin in his absence.

Grateful, he sent to her. This was one good thing in a night of missteps.

He would have felt Kaitlin's closeness in a crowd of Weres.

Erecting a mental barrier to temporarily seal himself off from her, Michael waited beside Tory for whatever she was going to show him. He was to be an observer on this occasion, and not the wolf who wanted very badly to be Kaitlin's lover. Holding himself back from rushing to gather Kate into his arms was added to the growing list of the toughest challenges he had ever faced.

Seconds, he told himself. *Just wait for a few more seconds. Another Lycan has suggested that I see this.*

Kaitlin stood with her back to a tree. Her hands were on her face, hiding her eyes. Though she was shaded from the moonlight by the canopy of leaves and branches, light shot through her as if she had been pierced by that light. As if she had swallowed it and the moonlight shone from her pores.

He didn't realize he had moved until Tory's hand stopped him. Michael stared at Kaitlin, wondering, not for the first time, what the hell was going on. His little wolf began to look transparent. She glowed now with the refracted colors of a crystal, dispersing light from no visible, perceivable light source. For a full minute, he didn't realize that she was that source.

Did you know about this? Tory silently asked him.

Michael shook his head without asking the question faltering on his lips. *What are we seeing?*

I've never found anything like this, Tory said. *Nor, I gather, have you?*

He could not reply. Michael was sure what they were facing had nothing to do with Kaitlin becoming a wolf.

It's beautiful, Tory said. *She's beautiful.*

Yes. Kaitlin, like this, was a beautiful surprise. A stunning surprise.

What was happening to Kaitlin here was no wolfish reaction. She looked to have swallowed a star.

He tried hard to remain calm, and was failing miserably. Michael groped for answers for this new turn of events without finding any.

The way she looked. That light shining through her wasn't like any wolf transition he'd ever seen or heard of. Kaitlin exhibited none of the pain of a body's rearranging molecules—things all Weres had to go through. Earlier, he had chalked that up to being merely strangely inexplicable.

Who was he to argue with details about the birth of a wolf inside a possible nonhuman species he wasn't familiar with?

What was absolutely clear to him and the she-wolf standing beside him was that Kaitlin Davies had truly been special from the start, and that specialness was making itself known here, perhaps with very bad timing.

She wasn't just different. She was an enigma. And he, along with a host of others passing her in school hallways and issuing grades for however many years now, had been fooled.

She is what she is, and also wolf, Tory said.

Yes, was all that Michael was able to reply.

Kaitlin isn't like the other one that came through Landau's gates a while ago. The light she shines isn't meant to delude others into thinking she is something she's not. It's pure, and feels airy. Her brightness hurts my eyes.

She doesn't know, Michael explained. *Kaitlin has to be as surprised by this as we are.*

Tory nodded. *She will need protection until she figures it out. Even I am attracted to whatever she is. No wonder you've had a rush of vampire problems.*

A vamp invasion that I might only right now be comprehending, Michael confessed. *It has to be the light. Her light. They can't resist it.*

May I make a suggestion, Michael?

He waited for Tory to go on. His nerves were jittery.

Bring her to Miami. She will be safe there for as long as she needs to be. Or until...

Michael glanced sideways. *Until what?*

Until her people come for her.

Michael's stomach turned over its nonexistent contents. He began to ache inside. He wanted to howl at the thought of Kaitlin hiding behind Landau's carefully guarded Miami gates. He refused to think about Tory's other statement.

He hadn't stopped to consider the ramifications of Kaitlin's other half being so Other, beyond how special she already was to him. As he observed her, sadness filled him.

That other wolf hybrid you and Dylan mentioned, he said to Tory. *What was it? What did that turn out to be?*

Banshee. Rosalind was a wolf and banshee mix, through no fault of her own. Her bloodline carried the secret for centuries. She was a dark soul able to mimic whoever she was with, and whatever species faced her. It was an incredible thing. A dark miracle.

She. Another female had appeared in Miami, with a unique side.

Banshees were dark spirits that announced death. Celtic spirits. Devlin has spoken of such things on occasion, he said.

Jesus. Did he want to think of Kaitlin like that, or know more? He rushed on.

How well did that pairing work out for this dark hybrid, if in fact it could? Spirit and wolf? I can't begin to imagine that, Tory.

And yet it worked out well in the end, or as well as could be expected. She helped our pack get rid of a savage nest of vampires, and in doing so, found her mate.

Michael didn't want to ask the big question eating him

up, and had to. *Did her kind come for her? Was she taken away at some point?*

Tory shook her head. *Rosalind took herself away, knowing what she was and how others would react to her. Her mate went with her into isolation, and was happy to do so, since he was unique, as well. It was a happy ending to a very weird tale.*

Your pack helped her, in turn?

All decent wolves are welcome in our pack, and Rosalind was both wolf born and the lover of a very good Lycan.

Michael didn't have time to consider her words further. Kaitlin, finally sensing company, turned toward where he and Tory stood. Her hands no longer covered her face. The light they had witnessed had faded and was rapidly disappearing, leaving a stunned little half wolf, half something else, standing on wobbling legs.

Chapter 16

Sensing movement around her, Kaitlin dropped to a crouch, remembering seeing Michael doing the same thing once or twice before.

Night sounds had not ceased. Birds, crickets and rustlings from overhead formed a symphony that filled her with a different sort of longing than the one ready to take her over. But Michael was nearby, and what she felt for him each time they were together was highly charged. Those feelings prevented her from spinning out.

Her body vibrated with the need to get closer to him, this latest round of emotion spawned by nothing more than a few minutes of alone time. She'd growl in a minute, speak his language, encourage Michael to take her someplace private where passions could be explored and put to rest… at least until she could breathe without thinking of him.

Until she could forget what had just happened to her, here.

In the midst of all the bad stuff, longing for sex with

her Alpha should have brought shame. Instead, the picture of what a session like that would be like revved her up. She had become someone else altogether; someone with little regard for the plight of others. Someone self-serving and greedy.

But she cared about what happened to Rena and Devlin and Cade after having just met them. So she wasn't so bad. Her morals weren't pushing her in a new physical direction, her treacherous body was. That and the desire, the need, to not focus on the rest of what was going on.

She scented Michael's approach, able to smell the wolf in him and the woman he was with. Seconds after discovering him, Michael was by her side.

Her legs gave out. She sank to her knees.

"It's all right, Kate," Michael soothed, crouching down to look into her eyes. "I was worried. I'm relieved to find you unharmed, and can't even begin to explain how scared I was."

"Cade?" she managed to say.

"He's all right. Cade took care of himself."

Her relief over that news was like a sweeping tide of joy. She had been right in letting Michael fight for his pack.

He was looking at her strangely.

"What is happening to me?" Her throat was tight.

"What does it feel like?"

"It feels like a wolf is holding me hostage, and if it weren't for that, I might fade away."

"What do you mean by *fade*?"

"Lose myself altogether. Lose what's left of me."

She watched pain contort Michael's beautiful face as he asked, "Have you experienced this before?"

"Not like this. Never like this. Before, I merely wanted to hide from others."

Michael was silent for a few beats, probably thinking over what she had said. Kaitlin glanced to the female Lycan with the wild red curls. Tory was her name. "You saw this. You witnessed what was going on with me. I felt you nearby."

"Yes," Tory replied. "I was here."

"Can you tell me what it is? Give me a clue?"

"I've never seen anything quite like what happened. I've suggested that Michael bring you to Miami once the situation here eases, so that the Elders can try to answer your questions. Would you like that, Kaitlin?"

"I'm not sure I can get through two more nights, let alone plan for the future." Her teeth were chattering from a buildup of fear.

"Nothing about this night is usual." Michael captured her attention again with his liquid green gaze. "We'll get through it."

He was sincere, and trying to help. Kaitlin just wasn't sure anyone could help her if wolf turned out not to be her dominant half. She was beginning to doubt that it was.

"I'm not following the usual going-to-be-a-werewolf routine, by the looks on your faces," Kaitlin said, positive that she was right about this one thing. "If you can't tell what I am—this other part of me you know isn't human—then maybe you can tell me why the monsters are behaving as if they have the answer we lack."

"It's your scent." Tory's voice dragged Kaitlin's attention away from Michael. "There's no night in it. Not like ours. You have wolf in you, and therefore should smell like one. You don't."

Kaitlin tossed her head to try to relax her rigid neck muscles, and found that moving did no good. Stress was mounting. A scream was imminent.

"What do I smell like to you, Tory?"

The she-wolf didn't hesitate to answer that question. "Grass. And trees."

"Because I've been standing here, beneath the branches?"

"No. Those things are separate and familiar smells. What you are is altogether new to me and wouldn't be of too much concern except for the fact that you're being chased by two different species, one of which is a dreadful offshoot of mine," Tory said. "Because of that, you need help, and helping others with wolf in their blood is what we do for each other."

"What you do in order to protect your secrets."

"In order to welcome new Weres into the fold," Tory clarified.

"Even part Weres housing an unfamiliar other part?"

"You'd be surprised if Tory answered that," Michael said. "Miami isn't Clement. Things aren't as simple there."

"I was under the impression things weren't simple here," Kaitlin said earnestly.

Michael got to his feet. "Until we do know what's happening, it might be best if we keep you out of range of anyone else who might come along thinking they know something we don't."

She looked up at him with wide eyes. "Is there a place where they won't be able to find me?"

"Yes. My place."

Images of a brown comforter with white stitching appeared in Kaitlin's mind. In memory she heard Michael say, *You're in my room. In truth, taking you anywhere else might have been bad for both of us.*

She now understood that a hospital would have found the anomaly in her blood if she had been taken there and treated. What form would that anomaly take? Did it have the characteristics of a virus? She would have become a freak show.

She was going to be stashed away so the monsters

couldn't find her. She would go along with this so that Michael and the others could get on with their search for a killer.

After that, how normal could things be?

Like kids who were adopted and spent lifetimes searching for their real parents, needing to connect those dots and yearning to understand their genetics, she also would want to find out what else swam in her DNA.

Michael's expression mirrored what she was sure showed in hers. Lust and need and fear were all there, pasted onto the beautifully crafted, chiseled features that had caused her to believe Michael was an angel.

His bronze skin was flushed from running and shifting. His muscles quivered and danced with telling signals she could only interpret as passion held in check, because her muscles were doing the same thing.

They were like two pieces of the same puzzle, in need of uniting in order to present a unified whole. When they were together, the pull to merge was overpowering. If they followed through on those needs, would that union be as dangerous as everything else going on in Clement?

"I'm here, Kaitlin," he said, reading her thoughts, wanting to reassure her.

Michael's concern for her was evident. He would override his duties if she were to crawl into his lap. If she didn't watch out, if she wasn't careful, Kaitlin Davies could prove to be the ruination of his pack.

"That won't happen," he said. "I won't let it."

A flush of heat crept up her neck. He read her so easily.

"Why wouldn't they find me at your place?" she asked him.

"Special walls and scent-proof insulation. I did the renovation myself."

He had told her he was a carpenter. She remembered

that, though thoughts of day jobs and thesis preparation had no place in what was transpiring.

"Smart move to do that," Tory said. "We've done the same thing, mostly rebuilding from the ground up. It gives us a sense of isolation and peace in a world where there isn't much chance of either."

Kaitlin took the hand Michael offered, and stood up, no longer surprised by the electrical charge skimming the surface of her palm as it met with his.

"You think I'll be safer there?" she asked him.

"For a while," Michael replied. "Until this mess clears up."

"And if I don't want to be left behind?"

"You'll have to trust me. Until we know the reason for monsters invading Clement, and what else your body is trying to tell us, we have to take you out of the picture."

She got that, and found the truth depressing. If she was something new, that thing came with the title of *hindrance*.

"Will I be there alone? In your home?" She dreaded that scenario.

Michael nodded. "Are you going to be all right with that?"

"Yes," she replied, lying through clenched teeth, wondering how many other eyes peered at them from the shadows.

She didn't perceive anything else out there in the dark at the moment. Michael's vibe was too heady, too strong, to look beyond. Tory's presence was nearly as bold. Both Lycans stood out from their surroundings as if they'd been pasted onto the landscape.

How werewolves had come into being was anyone's guess, and the stuff of mythology and legend. She wanted to ask if Weres knew the history of their species. If some kind of spell had caused this man-wolf union.

She had a lot to learn, and wasn't going to do so by touching Michael. If her hand lingered in his, the balance would shift from a reassuring caress to their passion making an appearance. She had no doubts about that. Since Michael had arrived, things had started to tumble inside her, growing claws, creating waves of pain.

She looked away from Michael, wondering how she could have made it this far, this long, without figuring out about the inhuman part. Without being shaken from a sleepy state by Lycan blood, another side of her might never have appeared.

Michael was zoning in on her, trying to look past her skin and see what she was hiding. She wished he'd tell her what he found. She wished somebody would.

At that moment, her quaking muscles had nothing to do with species frustration. These quakes were precursors, premonitions, forebodings, foreshadows, pointing to what lay ahead.

"I'll take Kaitlin to my house, and then join you," Michael was saying to Tory. "Hopefully the others will have picked up Chavez's trail by now, and the chaos will soon end."

When Tory smiled, Kaitlin noticed that her teeth were very white against her pale, flawless Lycan skin. Tory's face was equally as perfect. Kaitlin experienced a pang of jealousy that made her stomach flutter. This Miami she-wolf was like Michael. Tory was of his kind, and there had to be countless others like Tory more suited to a union with this Alpha than she was.

Maybe my fading away would be a good thing. The best thing.

She blinked slowly. When she opened her eyes, Tory was gone. She was pressed to the tree and Michael's face was close to hers.

"Don't even consider fading away, whatever that means," he advised huskily. "I read you like a book and I'm going to stay one step ahead of you. You're not going anywhere, except to safety."

"We don't belong together." Kaitlin heard the pleading quality in her tone.

"Who says we're together?"

In the midst of all the chaos and uncertainty, the hint of a smile lifted the corners of Michael's lips. This was a glimpse of the Michael she didn't really know, and hadn't yet met. This was what Michael was like in better times, and to his friends.

She wanted to know that guy, see that grinning expression on his face often, directed at her. She wanted all this to be over so there was a chance that could happen.

Michael was in balance. He was man and wolf in a mixture that didn't rule him or make him immune to the problems of others. She wrapped her arms around him, unable to resist the power of his allure.

"You're needed elsewhere," she said breathlessly.

"I also need to know you won't do anything stupid while I attend to those other problems."

"I'm one of those problems."

"No. Never."

"A liability."

"Someone who simply needs to be safeguarded for a while," he said. "Is that going to be a problem for you, Kate?"

"Yes, if it takes your attention away from others who need it."

"Will it help if I ask you to get over that and comply just this once? Listen this one time?"

When she shook her head, her cheek brushed his. Kaitlin's breath caught. She was sure that her inner wolf twisted. She wasn't the only one craving what this magnificent male had to offer. The beast her body was creating desired him, too. At least that much was clear.

Michael didn't escape the rawness of the emotions she was radiating. Like her, he was caught in an inexplicable craving for a female who was, in reality, a stranger, and who obviously had her own special power. The power to attract others.

His muscles flexed as if they realized that what he wanted to do to her, with her, wasn't a good thing. But he rested his mouth on hers anyway.

The night itself seemed to hold its breath. A surge of electricity sparked as his lips moved over hers...and then the other thing—that uncertain, nebulous something else—took hold of her, wrangling her desires into submission and blinding Michael with the force of its unexpected appearance.

Chapter 17

Michael stepped back as if he'd been struck by a bolt of lightning. The shock was severe, jamming his senses, firing up all of his nerves at once.

His head swung from side to side to negate the onslaught. His muscles convulsed, shaking him up, slowing his thinking. Kaitlin was doing this, and probably didn't know how, or why.

Once he had broken contact, the surges careening through him ceased. His wolf pounded at his insides, stimulated by the sudden rush of adrenaline coursing through his body, but he reined that wolf in.

The first thing that went through his mind was that he'd lost his mind. He perceived a rift in the atmosphere. That rift hung between the trees, reaching from the lowest branches to the ground like a shimmering curtain—black as the night and moving with an action that reminded Michael of disturbed pond water.

Kaitlin saw it, as well.

"Kate," Michael said, at a loss for words.

Her eyes came back to him, their color changed. No longer gray, those enormous eyes were now a tarnished gold.

That wasn't all. The harder he looked, the more changes Michael found. Gray eyes that had turned golden then became green—the brilliant green of a Were's eyes. Kaitlin's lips parted for a growl that was low, guttural, and the sound resonated in Michael's bones, dispersing more inner vibrations that caused his claws to pop like spring-loaded blades.

"Kate." He hid his hands and worked to get a grip on his own physical changes. "Are you all right?"

She didn't reply…at least in any humanistic way, with a voice, words and sentences. As a flurry of leaves fell from over their heads, she responded in an entirely different manner.

She began to undress.

Her sweater again came over her head and was tossed aside. Moonlight streaked her shoulders with a golden glow that matched the flare in her eyes.

Michael withheld a growl, needing to stop this, while at the same time his body was responding physically to the sensations flooding him.

The scene was strangely seductive, and inappropriate as hell. The situation in Clement was bad at the moment, and Kaitlin behaving as if she'd had a complete personality reboot was highly suspect.

"Kate. Let's go," Michael said, wishing times were different and he could take her up on whatever this offer was going to turn out to be. Any other time, and with any other woman, he wouldn't have hesitated. But a wayward premonition pummeled him.

When she dropped her jeans to her ankles, his wolf

strained at its leash. She kicked the pants off, along with her shoes, and wore nothing now except a pair of blue lace underwear.

Slender arms beckoned to him with a provocative slide down her sides. Her every move was sensual and extremely erotic. And still, that premonition floated around, as yet unformed, kicking brutally at Michael's mind.

What are you up to, Kate?

Damn it, she really didn't seem to know.

And then, as if his own inner light had flashed, Michael understood what was happening. This wasn't just a strip-tease in his honor. It was much more than that. She was shedding her outer layer in preparation for a big reveal, whatever the hell that might be.

"No." His whisper was soft and unheeded.

One minute Kaitlin was there, standing, flashing her tricolor eyes and moonlit skin. Then she was falling to her hands and knees, fighting for each ragged breath.

Before Michael could catch her, whatever spell she was under expanded and Kaitlin looked up at him, having morphed seamlessly into the furred-up shape of a copper-colored wolf.

He froze for what seemed like an eternity, the oaths he wanted to use lost behind his heart's frantic beats.

"This is impossible," he muttered. Because it was impossible. Kaitlin wasn't full-blooded Lycan, nor was she a shape-shifter. Here she was, though, on all fours, her red-brown fur still ruffling from her transformation. A full transformation.

"Don't be afraid," he said, as much for himself as for the new apparition beside him. "It's okay. We can handle whatever this is."

In agitation, he raked his thigh with five of his razor-sharp claws. Kaitlin's wolfish gaze went to the blood seeping from his self-inflicted wound. The fur on her back stood up.

"No. Kaitlin, don't be afraid. Just wait for another minute and maybe the reason for this shift will come."

Hell, what good would waiting do? Michael reasoned. Who was going to explain this? He couldn't believe his eyes.

There was a new heaviness in the air, and movement that hadn't come from anything containing blood in its veins. This heaviness was created by the wavelike undulation of the nebulous black curtain, the rift in the atmosphere strung between the trees.

What the hell was that? Where had it come from?

Beneath a shiny muzzle, Kaitlin's mouth opened for a speech she couldn't make. What emerged from her throat was a harrowing howl that touched Michael's soul.

There was no time to worry about the strange rift beside them. Kaitlin's wolfish vocalization drew him into yet another shape-shift. With a power reminiscent of the moon, and overriding his own desire to keep the wolf at bay, Kaitlin pulled his wolf into shape.

The going was slow and like wading through mud. He tore off his clothes as his body eventually shivered into its alternate form. Kaitlin's wind whipped his fur and the fires raging inside him until, as a wolf, Michael stared back.

Their muzzles touched. Lightning-like nerve fire struck Michael. Then the damn curtain moved again. When he looked around, Kaitlin had left him. She was sprinting toward that rift in the night as if she had to find out what lay beyond the eerie onyx shimmer.

Michael loped after her. He caught her by the back of her neck and clamped down with his teeth before she reached the strange, rippling veil. Planting his paws, he dragged her to a stop. Though Kaitlin struggled and roared, he held fast, wary of that wavering incongruity, not liking how frightened he was.

Whatever lay beyond this thing had to be calling to Kaitlin, the way the moon called to him.

With a growl of his own, Michael tugged Kaitlin with him to what he hoped was a safer distance. Eventually, her struggles ceased and she collapsed in the grass with one last gut-wrenching whine.

Yes, Kate. It has been one hell of a night, Michael agreed.

She was instantly a woman again, and his transformation matched hers. With human lips, he found the nape of her neck, the little hollow that was damp from the heat of her transitions and smelled like heaven.

She turned, pressed herself closer to him, nipped his chin with her small human teeth. Her hands slipped around to his back and slid over his bare buttocks. She was riled up, fiery and in need of something only he had to offer, no matter where they were.

The eroticism of the danger of this moment was unnaturally exquisite. He knew better than to keep this going, but ignored the warnings. Kaitlin's breasts, against his chest, were hard and straining. She moved with animal instincts, finding the places on his body that responded the most to her touch. In this moment, they were animals in human form, caught up in a desire running rampantly out of control.

Kaitlin wouldn't understand the urgency of the need to mate that all wolves experienced after a shift. He had mastered those desires in the past only with practice and concerted effort. He had only dated human women to avoid this very thing, and having to settle down.

But as she continued to press against him suggestively, his mind lagged behind the impulses of his body. He, too, had shifted too many times tonight. His body needed release.

Resisting Kaitlin, who held so many fascinating feminine secrets, was not possible. A man, Were or not, had only so much control. And damn it, his was gone.

He took her mouth savagely beside that damn alien curtain. To anyone who might have been watching, and if he had been able to speak, his message would have been... *I hope you enjoy the show.*

He wasn't the only savage here. The animals beneath the surface of their skin were letting their wishes be known by demanding satisfaction the hard way, with teeth and nails. Kaitlin's wolf was as tempestuous as his was.

He had Kaitlin in his arms before she could utter a protest. Feeling strong now, he strode through the park, reaching his house long before their passion had waned.

He laid her on his bed and listened to her growl of pleasure. His kissed her again, then slid a hand between her silky feverish thighs. What he found between those thighs was petal-soft and worth the howl he choked back.

"Kate..." He spoke her name with his lips on hers, punctuating the word with a meeting of their tongues.

Her response was to kiss him back with her moist, plush mouth, and with enough fervor to melt away what remained of his forced resistance. With her arms wrapped around his shoulders and her nails digging into his tense, corded muscle, she was daring him to stop this, while letting him know that wouldn't be allowed.

With shaky fingers, he opened her. The shaking was strange. His mind had never interfered with his sexual conquests, the way it was nagging at him now. He hadn't cared for those other women the way he cared for Kaitlin. None of the others had been potential mates.

He could not stop this. The momentum of these kisses

were sweeping him away from rationality. Doing what they were about to do would cement their pairing and complicate their lives. What male wanted his preferences to be dictated by a force beyond his control? By a she-wolf giving him the come-hither?

His hips were pressed tightly to hers, pinning the hand that still covered her most private of places. He had to have her, and that was that. Denial and regret would have to wait their turn.

He slid the tip of one finger inside her, finding more heat and a waiting, willing dampness. Kaitlin was not only allowing this, she was actively encouraging him. She had become a seductress, with a lure that rivaled the moon's.

Her body was hot, but Kaitlin, inside, was volcanic. A storm had been unleashed and she was riding the crest of the wave that would carry them both away.

His cock was hard, throbbing. The effort to hold back was making him sweat.

She moved against him, thrusting her hips upward in a way that left him no other option but to take possession. After one more sharp breath, he eased into her with his eyes shut, soaking up the incredible molten lushness that paved the way to Kaitlin's core, resisting the urge to strike fast and true.

Restraint was not an option. He wanted to move, dive, take, possess and mark Kaitlin as his so that every other wolf on the planet would keep their distance. Wolves sensed possession. Good ones accepted it.

He pressed his hard length into her slick waiting womb, thinking he might go mad if they were interrupted. Man to woman and wolf to wolf was the way this was going down. There was no room for anyone or anything else. All problems seemed distant.

Drawing back slightly, feeling her nails rake his lower

back in protest of his withdrawal, and scenting the iron-like odor of the blood she'd drawn across his skin, Michael pressed more of himself inside her, shuddering, struggling with himself to give Kaitlin a few more seconds of breathing room before fully filling her depths.

When she gasped with pleasure—this time a soft, sighing sound—he began to stroke her, moving slowly in and out, fearing that time was almost up on the limit of his patience.

He stroked Kaitlin smoothly again and again, moving his hips to meet each answering thrust of her hips. Chanting warnings that made no sense and didn't suit him, Michael built up a rhythm and held steady to it with his pulse pounding in his ears.

Each thrust he made now deepened their connection and led them closer to the apex of sexual gratification. Kaitlin's insides tightened around him, massaged him, held him captive with a sweet, creamy allure. She was willing to take all of what he had to give. She was gloriously tight. Instinctively, she did all the right things.

Christ, Kaitlin...

They were going to reach that climax together, and Michael didn't want this to end. He didn't want to see the look in Kaitlin's eyes when she opened them. That look would either be accepting, or one of horror and regret.

Her next move refocused his attention. He hadn't realized he had slowed down until her long, sleek legs locked him in place to ensure that he took her up on the release of the last bit of barrier left between them. Her heat was the equivalent of lightning.

Michael suppressed a roar.

All right.

Okay.

Gripping her hips with his hands, he drove himself into

her with a force that left them both breathless. The world around him began to beat in sync with his heart. His pulse rocketed, echoed by Kaitlin's.

Thunder rolled inside her. Kaitlin's body quaked beneath his. He reached her core, filled her completely and held himself there. Her climax burst, carrying him along with it. That blast of pleasure was like swallowing a shooting star.

The world exploded into prisms of color. And as that moment engulfed them, Kaitlin spoke, whispering a series of syllables that he couldn't understand. And then she went limp in his arms.

Chapter 18

Michael looked at Kaitlin lying on his bed. Her hair fanned out across his pillow in an auburn tangle. He wanted to touch her, yet didn't, afraid of his need for a rematch. If he had his way he wanted to always watch her like this.

Hoping Kaitlin could hear the senseless things he muttered to her that were meant to put her mind at ease, his mind churned out wishful scenarios where Clement was at peace and there was time to indulge in his fantasies. That was what imprinting did. It made slaves of the Weres snared by the ancient spell and to the physicality of love.

Michael felt some discomfort over what had happened between Kaitlin and himself. He had taken advantage of her moment of weakness. Consummating this relationship with her meant that they now actually had a deeper bond. Their connection had been completed, instead of being severed, as he had originally planned. Now that Kaitlin had shifted and they had shared an incredible intimacy, their future was set in stone.

They had no say about this. But honestly, he wouldn't have complained, even though he heard the binding chains rattling. The change taking place inside him would ensure a future of cravings. A few minutes inside her had to have been worth the lifetime of rule-breaking credits that stretched ahead of them, but Michael wasn't sure he could stand wanting Kaitlin any more than he already did.

Right now, while she was out cold, her body beckoned to him. And that wasn't the biggest part of his current dilemma. The thing that puzzled him most was how she had shape-shifted on her own, when that was unfeasible.

"Will you do it again?" he asked her sleeping form.

After bringing her home, he hadn't left her side. Couldn't have left her. An hour had gone by and he had not rejoined the pack. Feeling guilty about this, Michael sent a message to his pack-mates that something had needed his immediate attention and was the reason for his delay. Rena sent back that they hadn't found Chavez, and the hunt was almost over for tonight.

The pack was safe. Kaitlin was safe.

He stretched out a hand to touch her, then let that hand fall to the bed. The time had come for him to leave Kaitlin and he dreaded the fact that duty eventually demanded a separation. No matter how much he wanted to stay with Kaitlin, as the Alpha here, he had to show his face, help with his pack's search for intruders in the last couple of hours before the sun came up. Leaving them on their own had been a massive breach of his power.

Common courtesy demanded that he make sure their out-of-town guests had a place to stay and were comfortable while they hunted in Clement, and his own digs couldn't be ruled out because of the delicate bundle breathing softly on his bed.

He lamented this disturbance, wanting to possess Kaitlin in every room of this house, and on every surface.

"I have to leave you."

Would she be here when he returned? Cuffing her to the bedpost would have been cruel and unusual punishment, even to address her unpredictable behavior...though the Were cop, Adam Scott, had probably brought along a pair.

He smiled wickedly at the thought. Some Alpha he was. He should turn in his claws.

Kaitlin didn't move, and didn't seem to be breathing. Michael leaned over her with his own breath held, and found his hand on her shoulder without being conscious of putting it there.

The room was saturated with her sweet, addictive fragrance. There hadn't been any further sign of her wolf.

He had to speak again, afraid he'd kiss the shoulder that lay beneath his hand. "What was behind that curtain in the park? Do you have any idea? Did that dark spot in the park have anything to do with your shape-shift?"

She didn't stir.

He hadn't expected her to.

"How did you do that, Kaitlin Davies?" He had sent her so many silent directives to sleep, there was no chance she would have been able to answer him. Stiff from sitting, Michael reluctantly drew back his hand, stood and stretched. He needed a shower and couldn't afford the time. He had to show his face to the others, who, despite his message, would want the truth of what had happened tonight.

That truth was that Kaitlin had blown all Were rules apart by shifting before her first full moon. Without a full moon. Into a four-legged wolf. Oh, yes...and he hadn't kept his pants zipped.

Dressed in fresh clothes, he leaned over Kaitlin's sleeping form one more time. "In a life filled with surprises, you take the cake, Kate."

She hadn't opened her eyes once. Not even a flutter of her long lashes.

"Will your eyes be gray when you open them?"

I'd like them to be gray, he said silently.

"We have a phrase for all of this," Michael said with his mouth close to her ear. "Learn and burn. It's not very pretty, is it?"

As long as she couldn't hear him, Michael offered her a confession that he hadn't dared to acknowledge until this second. "I am used to fighting for justice, but I'm a newcomer in the fight for love. All I have to offer you at the moment is the use of my home and my protection. Will that be enough?"

His lips rested on her earlobe. "A second touch, just this once."

He kissed her cheek, without lingering. Kaitlin's skin retained its warmth, though her inner fires had faded. He covered her with a sheet and whispered, "I wonder what other surprises the future might bring."

Slowly, he backed away from the bed, fighting with himself all the way. "Wait for me," he said to her from the doorway, praying that he spoke the truth when he promised, "I won't be long."

But Michael had to wonder what he'd find on that bed when he returned, and if it would in any way resemble the woman he had fallen so hard for, in so short a time. The woman who had chained herself to an Alpha, through no choice of her own, and who, while lingering in the throes of passion, and after shifting back and forth into the shape of a wolf, had spoken in a language that Michael feared didn't have anything to do with the terms *wolf* or *human*.

* * *

"The warrior returns." Rena strode forward to greet Michael across the street from his home. Cade, Devlin and Dylan were with her. Though Cade looked slightly worse for wear, he wore his bruises well.

None of these Weres looked as tired as Michael felt. They had been up all night without wasting energy on shifting back and forth so many times that Michael lost count. Their minds weren't ablaze with questions. They didn't have to calculate possible personal future outcomes.

Finding them near his house meant that the pack still hadn't found Chavez or stumbled upon more of Chavez's savages. He felt some relief over that, still overly conscious of having been elsewhere when he could have been needed.

"No sign of them at all?" he asked Dylan.

"Found more vampires," Dylan said.

"They're dust," Rena explained.

"You were right," Dylan continued. "These vamps were new to the bloodsucker game. And since Chavez could not have created monsters with fangs, it's a cinch that Clement has another kind of master on the loose."

Michael winced. "I should have been with you."

"Don't worry. You weren't missed much," Devlin teased. "All in all, the night was fairly quiet after that first round of bloodsuckers showed their pretty faces early on, and Cade kicked some beastly ass."

Rena cuffed Devlin on the shoulder.

Dylan said, "We believe Chavez has holed up on the south end of town. We need to check that out tomorrow. Right now, I think you know that everyone here needs rest."

After a careful scan of Michael's tired face, Dylan added, "You included."

"We need dinner. Or is it time for breakfast? I can't remember the last time I ate," Cade said. His wounds were superficial, and had already started to fade.

Michael spoke to Dylan. "You're welcome at my house. Adam and Tory, as well."

"Won't it be a bit crowded?" Rena quipped with a lilt of well-aimed sarcasm in her tone.

Michael tossed a mental coin about whether to tell these Weres what had happened to Kaitlin tonight now, or just show them that eerie dark spot that had appeared in the park from out of nowhere, and leave Kaitlin's unbelievable wolf morph out of it. The coin came up tails.

"Before we disperse, I'd like to show you what I found out here, and why I didn't join you," he said.

"Lead the way," Dylan said with a wave of his hand. "I have another half hour of energy left before I start eating this grass. Adam and Tory will find us soon with a final report on what else they've learned. Our trail will be easy for them to follow."

"Do you Miami Weres have some Sherlock Holmes capabilities?" Rena asked Dylan.

"Just a damn good sense of smell," Dylan replied. "They stayed behind because they're hungry for a Chavez sighting, and anxious to get this over with."

"Is it payback?" Michael asked.

"Let's just say that Adam thinks so, since he knows firsthand what Chavez's fight clubs can do."

Michael recalled the scar on Adam Scott's face, deducing that the cop must have gotten that scar by being up close and personal with Chavez. A testament to Adam's toughness would be that he had survived such a meeting. The scar remained visible because Adam hadn't been Were when he received the injury.

The Chavez mess in Miami again made Michael think that dealing with a fledgling vamp or two seemed lightweight, when in actuality vampires were no joke and a threat to everyone.

Add to that problem the sudden appearance of a black wavering mass of unknown origin and a female who had shape-shifted without a full moon or Lycan lineage…and maybe Clement's problems were catching up with those burdening the larger cities.

"What I want to show you isn't far," Michael said as they all walked across the still-dark, empty campus grounds. He was confident that though these Weres had had their share of trouble in the past, none of them had encountered the likes of that unusual glimmering curtain.

He was right, and thanked his lucky stars that the strange thing hadn't disappeared by the time the pack got there to see it. They all stared at the peculiar spot as if not quite believing what they were seeing.

Rena rubbed her eyes and asked, "What the hell is that?"

Dylan's expression was reflective, though he didn't venture an opinion. It was Dev who seemed to have one.

"It's a portal. That's what you would call it. We'd know it as a veil."

"Who is *we*?" Rena asked.

"Those of us who grew up with stories about this kind of thing," Devlin replied.

"You mean Irish people," Rena said.

Devlin stepped closer to the dark spot and lifted one hand.

"Don't!" Rena insisted. "Don't touch it. We like you in spite of your faults."

"What kind of a veil?" Michael queried.

"A veil between worlds. A doorway that leads to somewhere else."

"Where does it lead?"

Devlin chewed on his lip, possibly, Michael thought, in an attempt to keep from answering that question.

Michael tried again. "Dev? That thing leads where?"

"Fairyland," Devlin said. "Though it's actually the land of the Fey, where no one can trespass without being invited, and safety is an issue even then."

Rena let out a bark of laughter. Cade smiled. Dylan passed a look to Michael that made Michael uncomfortable.

"It's magical?" Michael asked.

"Not to those who live behind it," Dev said.

"Why would such a thing appear in the States, and Florida in particular?" Dylan asked.

"And tonight," Michael added.

Devlin shrugged his big shoulders. "Likely because she's here, and they know it."

"Kaitlin, you mean." Dylan glanced again at Michael.

"That's the only explanation I can come up with," Devlin said. "These things don't appear without a reason. It's not an invitation to test the validity of those old stories."

Michael blinked slowly to ease the ache behind his eyes. Staring at the wavering curtain had a dizzying effect.

"You've seen one of these before, Dev?" he asked.

Devlin shook his head. "I've only heard the tales."

"Yet you believe this might be connected to Kaitlin in some way?"

Michael hated that he tended to believe Devlin's explanation when he didn't want to. He sensed rightness in it because of what he had seen. There was a chance that Tory, having witnessed Kaitlin shining like a lighted crystal near here, might have believed it also, if she had been present.

Michael heard himself ask, "If it followed Kaitlin here, what does that make her?"

He really did not want to hear Devlin's take on the answer, though that answer was crucial. The nonsensical syllables Kaitlin had spoken rang in his ears as if she had just uttered them. Were those the syllables of another species?

"It makes her one of them, or did until we woifcd her up," Devlin answered. "I suppose the appearance of this portal, so close to where she is, would suggest that Kaitlin either is, or has something to do with the Fey."

It was clear that no one besides Devlin had any idea what that might mean. Their worried gazes moved back and forth between Dev and the ominous onyx sheet in front of them.

"A fairy?" Rena said, clearly having none of this. "You're saying that Kaitlin is a fairy?"

"Fey," Devlin corrected. "Believe me, Rena, that's a whole different thing from the image in your mind."

"How so?" That was Dylan.

"The Fey are nothing like the little twinkly things with wings in children's books. In fact, they are life-size, and can be quite aggressive and dangerous when crossed."

"And you know this from rumors?" Rena pressed.

Devlin took offense at Rena's skepticism, though he said calmly enough, "Stories handed down through the years are different than rumors. Most of them have real starting points, like the old tales about werewolf sightings that no one here would laugh at."

"So," Cade said. "If Kaitlin is Fey and that thing in front of us is of Fey origin, does it mean Kaitlin can use this fluttering doorway to leave us? Where would she end up if she did?"

Devlin turned to Cade. "She'd end up someplace else. I suppose the Fey exist in a place that's like another layer of the world that no one, other than them, can access. How else could these doorways just show up? Why wouldn't we be able to see what lies beyond them?"

"That's convenient," Rena remarked archly. "You just create a doorway and use it to avoid air travel. Anyone care to try their luck with this portal?"

Devlin offered Rena a dare. "I'd like to see you try."

Michael was feeling sick to his stomach. This portal, doorway, veil, gave him the creeps, the way other things that hid in the shadows often did.

"How can you be sure about this?" He directed the question to Devlin.

"I can't be sure of anything," Devlin admitted. "Do any of you have a better explanation that we'd rather go with?"

The area fell silent, due to the fact that no one could come up with a better explanation for that bizarre anomaly. Rena, Michael noticed, did not advance on it, despite Dev's dare.

"I wonder how long it will stay here," Cade mused.

"Maybe we should get in touch with Kaitlin's family. Maybe she should," Rena suggested. "Her family would have to know about this. Right? If that thing is connected to her?"

"Yes," Devlin was quick to say. "They would have to know. Fey don't just happen, like a human bitten by a wolf and then becoming Were. You can't accidentally become Fey. The stories say they can take human form if they want to and walk among us, but they are always Fey on the inside, and they carry those characteristics with them."

"What characteristics?" Michael asked.

Devlin shook his head. "I suppose we'll find out."

The problem was, Michael thought, he had already seen some of what that Fey blood could do. It could leap over the rules governing the parameters of another species. It could bring a wolf to life in a person when a wolf wasn't due, and make a woman shine with the light of a star, attracting the interest of both Weres and the undead.

It could very well be the reason Kaitlin seemed to be a vamp delicacy. And why he had noticed her in the first place. It was one answer to ponder, anyway.

"And so," Rena said without looking at Michael, "we just happened to have given one of those creatures a little something extra to kick around in her system. I wonder how Dev's Fey will appreciate that, not to mention any relatives Kaitlin might have over there."

Devlin glanced from the spot between the trees to Michael. With a sober expression on his face, he said, "I'm thinking this can't be good."

Chapter 19

Kaitlin stirred on the soft surface, uncurling her body and opening her eyes. Details filled in swiftly this time. This was Michael's house. His bedroom.

Lights were on. There were voices inside her head, threatening to drive her mad, and she couldn't silence them. She heard her name spoken and covered her ears, trying to concentrate on something outside herself so she could make sense of things.

The room was a cool ocean blue, immaculately maintained and sparsely decorated. Michael's taste ran to dark colors and carved oak furniture that he might have crafted for himself as a carpenter. By the looks of things, he was talented in his day job. She ran an appreciative hand over the headboard behind her.

Only one picture hung on the wall by the bed—a framed watercolor of hills and valleys similar to what she had seen in her visions. The reminder made her turn inward again to a place she didn't want to go…and to what had transpired between Michael and herself—the cause of the aches she felt each time she moved.

She hurt all over. Every bone pulsed, as if each of them had been broken and too quickly mended. And she knew why. She had lost her shape tonight. She'd lost Kaitlin, for a time, and without fading away completely had returned to have mind-blowing sex with Michael.

The growl she felt rising wasn't her stomach calling for fuel; it was a sound that got stuck in her throat—a response to the aftermath of having real sex for the first time. They had shared a kind of intimacy that affects the soul, and she had become a wolf when she wasn't supposed to.

Full-on sex.

Full-on wolf.

Heaven help me.

The fact that this room smelled like Michael made all those recollections worse. His delicious masculine scent filled the air and clung to the pillow, making her want to accept being like him. Making her consider stopping the fight against the aftereffects of a crazy major body re-alignment that seemed impossible, but obviously wasn't.

She was alive. She was here, and Michael had seen to that. He truly was her guardian angel in a world that had tilted off balance. He was a beast with a heart.

"My guardian Were."

Speaking felt strange. Her throat was raw on the inside.

She studied her hands. Her fingers were fingers. Not paws. Her face felt like her face when she examined it, with no elongated muzzle. Arms, legs, were all there and looking human. Between her legs a deep-seated soreness pulsed that had nothing to do with being a wolf and everything to do with Michael's talent as a lover.

She remembered it all, though the wink of a reality-check light warned that she wasn't fully ready for any of this.

She didn't look forward to finding out what the needling insistence in the back of her mind might be—that urge to find those hills and valleys she had seen images of.

She sat up.

Michael's voice lingered in her mind like an echo, but so did those other voices she could not place. One thing was for sure. She had kissed *normal* goodbye in a really big way, and there were consequences for that.

The creak of floorboards focused her attention on what might lie on the other side of the closed bedroom door. Was this a house? An apartment? Did Michael live here alone? She wondered who else might come through that doorway.

She didn't know much about Michael. Not even his last name. The other time she had been here was only a vague recollection. She didn't remember much about how she had gotten here tonight. Her mind was overtaxed and sluggish. She now swore she heard muffled voices when a search of the room proved she was alone.

Had someone whispered her name?

Chills began to ice her skin…skin covered by an unfamiliar, shapeless T-shirt dipped in Michael's scent. His smell contained male pheromones that made her feel braver than she actually was.

She got up, searched for the rest of her clothes on chairs and the floor without finding them, wondering if Michael had brought her from the park bare-ass naked.

Damn it. She was sure she heard her name this time, and glanced to the door to see the knob turn. When that door opened, she sat down on the bed, waiting for the next ax to fall.

A figure stood in the doorway, backlit by a light in the hallway that didn't allow her to see anything other than that person's silhouette. The tall, slender outline could have belonged to either male or female. The newcomer didn't speak.

"Who are you?" Kaitlin's overworked nerves fired up another warning.

Although the windows in Michael's room were closed, a breeze ruffled Kaitlin's tangled hair. The back of her neck began to tingle. She hoped to God this wasn't a type of vampire her senses didn't fully comprehend yet. Some bloodsucker sneaking under the radar when Michael had told her his place was safe.

"Answer me, please," she insisted. "I've had enough surprises tonight to last me a lifetime."

It was clear by then that whoever this was wanted to remain an enigma, and that seemed ominous.

"Damn it. Speak up, or get the hell out."

The vehemence in her tone didn't scare the person whose features were hidden from her. Kaitlin felt the coolness of this person's attention. The light behind him or her got brighter the longer that maddeningly mute person stood there.

"Then get out," she said, hoping this intruder would obey without a fuss, since she had exceeded her tolerance level by miles and didn't have the energy or know-how to back up a threat.

The figure in the doorway complied with her demand by backing up. Her visitor then disappeared without closing the door. Kaitlin was on her feet before her next ten heartbeats had pounded out a further warning, and chasing after whoever it was.

Michael's head came up. Kaitlin was moving, and sending warm vibes up and down his spinal column. He couldn't concentrate on that at the moment, though.

Devlin sidled over to him and lowered his voice. "The awkward thing about a veil like this one is that the passage leads both ways."

Michael stiffened. "You mean other things can access it to come here?"

Don't you dare leave, he sent to Kaitlin, picturing her wandering through the rooms in his cottage.

He addressed the next question to Devlin as if they all truly believed Dev's monologue about suddenly appearing shimmering veils being a bridge between worlds.

"Who would come out of there, if the Fey did cross over?"

"I've never seen one of them," Dev admitted.

"Then you don't actually know they exist," Rena argued. "Aside from your comments about stories having a basis in reality."

"If they don't, we're back to trying to decide what that thing is," Dylan pointed out.

"So, do we sit here and guard our park from what might come out of there, or get some much-needed rest?" Cade asked. "Say the word, Michael."

"I'll stay," Michael volunteered. "The rest of you can go home. Some of you have nine-to-fives and will be on your feet again before you want to, and tomorrow brings us not only closer to a mad Were and his henchmen, but also one step closer to the full moon."

He perceived Dylan's discomfort with that reminder of Chavez being at his nastiest as a werewolf under a full moon. As the pack exchanged looks, Michael weighed his options. He would get home as soon as the sun rose to check on Kaitlin. At most, there were two more hours until the new day dawned.

In their favor was the fact that few vampires chanced being caught above ground with a margin that narrow. And

Tory and Adam were monitoring the location they believed might be Chavez's temporary digs for signs of trespassing Weres coming and going. In terms of concern, that just left this freaky portal to the Fey as a potential problem. Vamps and Weres were at least partially predictable. Who the hell knew what the Faerie folk could do?

He was tired. Spent. And he was facing another strange anomaly in a night overflowing with them.

"Dylan," he said. "Cade will show you how to get to my house. Make yourself at home. There's food in the kitchen and blankets in the closet. I have one favor to ask of you."

"Ask," Dylan said.

"Will you stay close to Kaitlin until daybreak? I'll be back by then. We probably won't be able to see this thing after the sun comes up anyway."

He waved at the spot that stubbornly refused to disappear, and looked to Devlin. "If it's here tomorrow, what will it look like?"

"Not sure, boss."

"Oh, goody," Rena said. "That thing might pick up the sunlight and be invisible?"

Devlin shrugged. "You now know all I know about it."

Which wasn't very much, Michael thought. He considered the ramifications of there being another species with the power to create a doorway in and out of the damn park he was supposed to patrol. And that species might believe Kaitlin to be one of their own.

He eyed the curtain.

Was this to be a Fey rescue mission? Was he nuts for believing Dev, and his own eyes?

"Seriously?" he said to Dev. "You don't know anything else?"

Devlin shook his head.

It was nothing really to go by. Not enough to bring enlightenment. The word *Fey* conjured no images in Michael's mind, other than the one Devlin had opposed about tiny beings with wings. He worried that Rena would start calling Kaitlin Tink.

"Would these creatures be angry about Kaitlin's change?" Michael asked, not really expecting an answer.

"They rarely mess with humans, though there are a few tales about wayward Fey mating with people. Those human-Fey hybrids are supposedly outcasts shunned by the rest."

"Meaning that they might not be too happy about Kaitlin being part wolf," Rena suggested.

Michael needed time to think on his own, without the others being part of the process. He hadn't been alone since first meeting Kaitlin near this very place a few days ago. His thoughts had been filled with nothing but her since then. His body missed hers. He could hardly keep focused on other things. But both Kaitlin and his pack were quite possibly in jeopardy from a nebulous new direction that no one could actually pinpoint.

Was there another world behind that ebony spot?

The thought that came to him now was that if these Fey creatures shunned hybrids, maybe Kaitlin would be all right. Wolf aside, maybe the reason she had been a college student was due to the fact that Kaitlin had been another kind of hybrid to begin with. Possibly she had been one of those human-Fey beings Dev said the Fey didn't accept.

It could be that these Fey creatures had merely come here to see what was going on, and would eventually leave everyone alone. If Kaitlin wasn't like them, they might leave her to him.

He was all for that.

His attitude had gone way beyond possessive. Plus, he wasn't sure what happened to imprinted pairs if one was taken away, or even if one could leave such a pairing. Under dire circumstances, did imprinting reverse? After his mother had been killed by hunters, his father had never chosen another mate.

Cade nodded to Michael and turned away, heading toward the street and Michael's house. The big Were paused near the far grove of trees to wait for Dylan, giving the two Lycans some private space.

"He's a good Were," Dylan said, looking after Cade.

Michael nodded. "The world would probably be astounded to learn that young Viking banker Cade Willis has a very private life after hours."

"And that Dylan Landau, a Miami attorney by day, hails from one of the largest packs in the East," Dylan said.

"Yes," Michael agreed, thinking that both Weres managed their secrets well.

Rena reluctantly followed Cade, glancing at Michael over her shoulder every few steps to make sure he wasn't going to call them back. He had no intention of doing so.

"Would you like me to wait with you?" Dylan asked, eyeing the sparkling anomaly beside them.

"No. Thanks. If anything comes out of there, I'll let you know."

When Dylan didn't move, Michael sensed that the Lycan had more to say.

"Speak," Michael said.

"I have a feeling that something already has come out of there."

Michael said in agreement, "I think so, too."

"So, you're hoping to catch this visitor?"

"I'm hoping that whoever or whatever that visitor is doesn't try to take Kaitlin back with them when they go home."

"You have imprinted with Kaitlin," Dylan noted.

"It seems that I have."

After letting that comment settle, Dylan spoke again. "I'll watch over her until you return."

"You have my gratitude for that, Dylan. I owe you one."

Dylan said, "Maybe I'll call in that chip someday," as he headed toward Cade.

Alone at last, Michael turned his attention back to the possibility of the female he had bonded with being taken away to a place he could not access…and to Kaitlin's having a bloodline that possibly either predated or ran parallel to his own.

No longer a full-blooded Fey—if Fey was what Kaitlin turned out to be—would Kaitlin's species shun her?

The growl that bubbled up from his chest was a menacing warning for all intruders to keep off his turf. To his complete dismay, that growl was answered by a sound that was twice as deadly.

Sensing movement, smelling trouble, Michael whipped around to fix his attention on the area where the sound had come from. His wolf vision picked up two Weres coming his way, some distance from where he stood.

They were moving fast. One of them came in from his right side. The other unwelcome newcomer circled to his left as if the two were part of a hunting pack that had found viable prey. Their scent was feral and more animal than human, though they appeared to be human now. The area picked up the stink of raw, misplaced animosity directed at him.

"You're trespassing," Michael called out, readying for what might happen next and guessing these were two more of the rogues the creep named Chavez had created with a savage bite or two.

"Obviously no one has taught you the fine art of manners," he added.

As they approached, the beast on his right spoke in a harsh, gravelly voice that indicated a recent injury by way of a blow to the throat. "We don't need manners or ruffled shirts to be able to hunt wherever we like."

This guy wasn't crazed like the Were in the library, Michael noted. That didn't help matters. Intelligence was hard to work around in criminals bent on utter destruction of the things others held sacred.

"Why is that?" Michael asked, feeling his claws press against the inside of his fingertips, just seconds from his own big reveal. "You have no respect for the rights of others?"

"We're passing through," the Were announced. "Here and gone." He blew out a breath to mimic a fast-moving rush of air and added, "Plenty of harm, and no foul."

"What do you want?"

"Fun."

"You can have fun elsewhere."

"Are you kicking us out, Alpha Dog?" the Were taunted.

"As a matter of fact, if you come any closer, I'd love to give you the boot."

"That would be hard when it's two against one."

"Piece of cake," Michael said as his claws slid through the skin that had hidden them, causing no more discomfort than a light, familiar sting.

"How did he do that?" the other Were asked his partner with a ring of surprise in his tone.

"Fancy trick," the Were on Michael's right concluded. "Special effects."

Michael smiled. He couldn't help it. Shit was raining down on Clement, and here two of those jokers stood.

"Okay," he said, fed up with everything that embodied the word *nasty.* "Let's do this."

The Were on his right took a moment to process what

Michael meant. Then he came at Michael with the force of a battering ram, snarling like a rabid dog, head down, fists raised. Inspired by that, the other Were joined in.

Michael swung his arms, wielding his claws like blades, getting in a few good strikes that sliced Were hides and made rivers of blood. Fatigued beyond belief from the night's events, he wanted to hold off a shape-shift for as long as possible, fearing that shift would take longer than usual and leave him momentarily vulnerable to these two greedy trespassers.

The fact that neither of these guys had weapons made things easier in an uneven playing field. Brawn was the universal calling card of Chavez's creatures, Dylan had told him. Though one of these Weres had shown a glimmer of intelligence, they were basically nothing more than fighting machines.

He took three hits to the chest that sent him spiraling backward, and rebounded. He had sent the pack home a few minutes too early, and could have used some backup of his own. These Weres had been trained by a master. The stronger they were, the longer they would last in Chavez's world.

However, Michael was no newbie to the fighting scene. His father's pack had taught him well. Working wood all day honed his muscle and kept him in tip-top shape. Being physical was what he liked. *The more opponents, the better.*

"Beasts like you threaten Were anonymity and place innocent people in danger," he said, rallying for another strike. "You have gone after a friend of mine, and I cannot allow that kind of behavior to continue."

He fought with all his strength and the fluid grace built into Lycan bloodlines—dodging blows, ducking flailing arms and returning to deliver his own brand of trouble. In this Lycan dance, he avoided real harm as the fight went on, with no one giving up or giving in.

Suddenly, there was another presence added to this skirmish, coming in from street side at high speed. For a moment, Michael was worried about those changed odds. But when a familiar voice said, "Need some help, Michael?" he could have kissed the Miami cop, Dylan's pack-mate Adam Scott, square on the mouth.

The intruders didn't seem to appreciate losing their advantage. Howling through human throats, they fought with all their might, no match for two of Clement's defenders. In the end, both rogues turned their battered bodies around and sprinted in the opposite direction, with Michael and Adam close on their heels.

The idiots ran straight toward the shimmering veil stretched between the trees, seeming not to notice the density of that particular spot. They hit that black curtain at full speed, one after the other…and disappeared. Poof. Gone.

Michael grabbed Adam's shirt and hauled the cop to a standstill. Adam hadn't seen this anomaly. He had not heard the suggestions about its origins, and therefore could not possibly have understood what happened to the rogues.

There was no sign of them at all.

"What the hell?" Confused, Adam scanned the dark spot in front of him.

Before Michael could explain, a rolling ground tremor staggered them both. The black curtain wavered. A flash of light brightened the area, nearly turning night to day ahead of schedule.

Through that curtain came a projectile of bones, tossed by invisible hands back into the world Michael lived and breathed in. Those bones, Michael knew by scent, were the remains of the two rogues who had dared to trespass where they were unwanted.

Michael met Adam Scott's eyes with a startled look that said *You might have missed something important.*

"You think?" Adam returned.

Chapter 20

"Kaitlin? You all right?"

She recognized Dylan's civilized scent of aftershave and laundered shirts without having to see that Michael had sent reinforcements to watch over her. She had been going after the curious visitor, and had made it only as far as Michael's small front room.

The strange visitor in her doorway had left her feeling out of place and hollow inside, when tucked inside her was a wolf, all curled up and readying for its next appearance. She had no idea how to set that wolf free. Possibly some things happened according to a preordained plan, like Michael's wolf calling to hers. Becoming a wolf had been like a sexual response to Michael's nearness.

"He will be back soon," Dylan said, appearing from around a corner.

For a minute, she wondered if the visitor had been Dylan, realizing that Dylan would have spoken back to her.

"Michael is in trouble," she said. "And I'm grounded by a promise to behave."

"You would go to help him if you could?" Dylan asked.

"Why haven't you?" Kaitlin countered.

"Michael wanted to be alone. This is his area, and I am his guest. I'm obligated to follow his wishes."

"Yes. He said Weres have rules."

"Rules keep us civilized, at least on the surface."

"And below that surface?"

"We're not always quite so obliging."

Kaitlin studied the handsome Miami Were, whose features were as chiseled as Michael's, but whose scent wasn't the one she craved. "Michael can handle himself," she said.

Dylan agreed. "I'm sure he is capable of handling most of the things that come his way."

Did that reply contain an underlying message about Michael being unable to handle his affection for her? Should she feel guilty about that?

"And," Dylan said, "Adam is out there tonight."

Adam would help Michael. That news brought relief.

"Michael asked you to watch over me?"

"He is concerned."

"Are you older than Michael? I get that impression, no matter how much courtesy about adhering to a neighbor's wishes passes between you."

"Older by a few years. Nevertheless, age has nothing to do with how we treat an Alpha in a different territory."

"I see." She was beginning to view the shape of more of the rules these Weres lived by. "And the bad ones? The bad Weres? Like the old clichés, they are evil and ignorant?"

Dylan said, "Some of them merely choose to ignore the things the rest of us believe are good for Weres as a whole."

"Does that apply to the guy you chased here?"

"Unfortunately, Chavez is the worst of the lot. He kills Weres and humans alike, going out of his way to do so."

"Weres never kill other Weres?"

"Not if they want to live for very long among us."

Kaitlin leaned against the wall. "You police your own kind?"

"Seems like every damn day."

She saw that Dylan was tired, and changed the subject. "On your way in, did you pass the guy who left here?"

Dylan's eyes met hers with a strong, intense gaze. "Someone was here?"

"Yes. Minutes ago."

"Who?"

"I don't know. Whoever it was didn't speak to me, but left when I asked him to, so I figured he had to be all right. One of the good guys."

"Scent?"

"I couldn't tell. Maybe I'm not ready to detect some of the nuances."

She witnessed a flash of apprehension in Dylan's eyes. "Well," he said. "Can't be too bad, then, if whoever it was behaved."

She might not have been one hundred percent up on scent, and yet Kaitlin sensed Dylan was lying about his thoughts on that. Like Michael, Dylan didn't want to frighten or upset her further. He tried not to overtly sniff the air in order to get a whiff of her visitor, but the action was uniquely Were and hard to camouflage.

Dylan's long fair hair swept across his shoulder, almost platinum in color. His eyes were light. His skin was a mild golden tan. All the Weres she had met were beautiful. She wondered if all the bad guys would look like the fiend in the library, and also wondered how much these friendly Weres knew about the depth of her feelings for Michael, her growing ability to read other Weres and what had gone on tonight when she and Michael were alone.

"I'm aware of most of what goes on around me, as most Lycans are," Dylan said. "I'm not here to point a finger at anyone, for any reason, since my mate was human not all that long ago."

Dylan offered her a brilliant smile and a further explanation. "Reading other Weres is a degree of telepathy that saves us a lot of time and repeated conversations. That ability is stronger when we're in wolf shape, though it never disappears completely."

He smiled again—a nice, earnest smile. Charming.

"Your mate," Kaitlin said. "If she was human, doesn't that mean you broke the rules?"

"It means exactly that," Dylan replied. "Some of us have found that love usually wins in the end, and over everything else."

He waved a hand at the room. "Now, would you like to share something to eat, or do I really have to earn my keep by avoiding the kitchen?"

"Earn your keep by keeping me in your sight?"

"That was the task assigned to me. However, if I don't get something to eat soon, we'll have to worry about my partner, Dana, coming here to see that I do."

"She keeps tabs on you?"

Dylan grinned. "I wouldn't have it any other way."

Kaitlin looked to the door. "Capable or not, Michael might get hurt out there."

"I doubt a Were or two can get the better of a Michael and Adam team. Michael seems to have a good handle on what goes on around here."

"Does that include the mysterious black curtain in the park?"

"Do you know something pertinent about that?"

"It doesn't scare me the way the vampires do."

"That's curious, since it rubs everyone else the wrong way." Dylan glanced over his shoulder. "Can you tell me anything else about your visitor here tonight?"

"Afraid not, other than that the room seemed cooler when he was in the doorway, as though he'd left the front door open."

"You said *he*. The visitor was male?"

"That's just the impression I was left with." She pointed to Dylan's nose. "What do you perceive?"

He didn't have to reply, Kaitlin supposed, but he did. "There's a lingering scent of nature. Trees. Flowers. And straw. No species I know of smells like that."

Another chill wafted over Kaitlin. Those were the same things she had smelled. Trees. Grass. Open spaces. She had dreamed of those things, and had placed Michael in the dreams. The fact that Dylan had sniffed them out and, as experienced as he was, didn't have a conclusion to the question of who those scents belonged to, was disconcerting.

Expecting more of an inquisition from this tall blond Were, Kaitlin was surprised when she didn't get one.

"Do you think you might find the kitchen while I have one more look around?" Dylan asked.

"Then we can have a nice chat at the table while bad guys and vampires threaten the town?" she volleyed.

"The first thing to learn about vampires," Dylan explained calmly, "is that daylight isn't their friend. That much, Hollywood got right. As for the other bad guys, we have that covered for now, and will remain vigilant."

Kaitlin glanced to a shuttered window. Dawn had a distinct taste that coated the back of her tongue. Daybreak wasn't too far away, and she couldn't wait to see the sun.

"Hell of a day," Dylan agreed. "Michael will be back

shortly. For now, we do the best we can to ensure that we'll be ready if a call to action comes. That readiness includes fuel. So, how about it? Kitchen?"

Kaitlin closed her eyes. "I can't."

"You'd be surprised by what the smell of a good sandwich can do. If that won't entice you, it would be nice if you'd keep me company until my friends arrive."

"All right," she conceded. "I can rustle something up for you. I need to keep busy. I hope you're not disappointed though."

"In the company?"

"In my lack of kitchen skills."

"It's not so easy to hide a pile of bones," Adam Scott said, staring at the heap of them on the grass. "I guess we could always throw these back."

"They did this in seconds," Michael mused. "Unless they have a different sense of time than we have, and the two time frames don't align. That's about as possible as anything else that's gone on here tonight."

Adam kicked at a femur bone with the toe of his boot. "Dylan mentally included me in your earlier conversation, Michael. I just wasn't sure where this thing was. Another layer of the world was how one of your friends described this place, right? I have to admit that it's been a long time since I personally have encountered something completely new."

"As a cop, I thought you'd have seen it all."

"More than I would have cared to see, believe me. But the real world has nothing on the supernatural one. That's where the truly interesting stuff is."

Adam absently touched his scar before continuing. "I thank whoever counts as being thankable that most of the people in this world don't yet know what goes on beneath their focus."

Michael pointed to Adam's scar. "Chavez did that?"

"Not himself personally. The wily bastard put me in the ring with a bunch of hyped-up, drugged-up, drooling monsters. That was my first sight of werewolves, my first inkling that they existed. It was also my crude initiation into the moon's cult."

Michael shuddered to think of how that had gone down. "You survived."

"Tory, whom I had met prior to that incident, raced to the rescue and called in the good guys. That's how I lived to see another day."

"And your life changed," Michael said.

"Yes." Adam's hand dropped from the scar on his face. "While a maniac named Chavez got away."

Adam moved another bone with his foot. "Got a big bag handy? There are a lot of bones, and I'm guessing we can't just leave them here."

"We can wrap some of the bones in my shirt." Michael began to unbutton as he studied the black curtain. "I don't suppose we can thank whoever is back there for taking care of these two idiots, or that they'd want to hear anything from a couple of werewolves."

"I don't suppose they would," Adam agreed. "This might have another meaning altogether, you know."

"A warning? Our visitors showing us an example of what they can do?"

"We can't rule it out."

"Then why don't they come here and finish us?" Michael asked.

"Who's to say they won't if we stand here long enough?"

When nothing jumped out at them to make that suggestion a reality, Michael spoke again. "You can take the bones back and dispose of them. I'm not leaving this spot, in case some unsuspecting human stumbles in."

"What if it stays here permanently?"

"We'd have to post a red flag. Seriously, I don't think it will remain."

"You think this, why?"

"Sooner, rather than later, we're going to have to find out exactly what it is, and what they want. We're going to have to deal."

"By bringing Kaitlin here?"

Michael opened his shirt. "If I have to."

"Okay." Adam looked down. "I'll cart some of these things away. You can bring the rest with you."

They kept their eyes on the black curtain as they scooped up the bones that made the bad-guy tally two less than before, hoping this would cramp Chavez's style. When they were done Michael sensed yet another Were's approach. Adam didn't have to intervene. This scent was now familiar to Michael.

"Go," Tory said to Michael with her eyes on Adam, the mate she had played a big part in rescuing, much in the same way Michael had rescued Kaitlin.

Tory understood longings and needs. She also had seen what Kaitlin could do to a glow factor. No doubt she had been listening in on the Were hotline and heard about what they were facing here, as well.

"Go to Kaitlin. I'll stay here," she said, waving a hand to ward off any protest. "Perhaps, if hybrids aren't their cup of tea, they'll like me. If not, I hope whatever comes out of that black hole tastes good."

There was something to be said about a tough Lycan female with a sense of humor, Michael decided as he helped Adam hoist the detritus of a branch of their bloodline that had gone bad.

He would have liked to spend downtime with all of these Miami Weres, and vowed to do that one day if things in Clement got settled. He would take Kaitlin, as Tory suggested. Having already met three members of that pack, Kaitlin might be at ease among them. Since Tory and Adam were accepted by the others in the Landau compound, he and Kaitlin also stood a chance. It seemed that the Miami pack didn't mind too much about breaking old Lycan rules.

He'd also take Rena, Cade and Devlin. He would see his father after two long years spent in Clement, which he told his father were designed to form a small pack of his own.

He had chosen misfits for his pack-mates—humans who had been bitten and turned and now were in need of a family. He had helped to ground Rena, Dev and Cade, explaining about the species they were now part of. That had turned out well. He had found a home among them.

"Is Tory this fearless and formidable all the time?" he asked Adam as the street came into view.

When Adam smiled, Michael took that for a yes.

"I have questions," Kaitlin said to Dylan. "Before Michael gets here."

Her bones still ached. Being in Michael's house gave her feelings of comfort that she feared might not last long if there was going to be a war between species in Clement. Daylight, arriving soon and welcomed, would eventually turn into night, with more action for the pack and more surprises for her.

She was sorry she used to think that school was boring.

"Wouldn't it be better for Michael to hear what you want to ask?" Dylan said.

He laced his fingers together, which seemed to her such a normal thing for a werewolf as powerful as Dylan was to do. He had polished off the sandwich they had made in record time. Weres had fast metabolisms, Michael had told her not long ago. She had made Dylan another sandwich, and toyed with her own.

"No. He'll be…" she started to say.

"Preoccupied? Tired?"

Kaitlin nodded. "And you're…"

"Not involved, other than in my hunt for Chavez," Dylan said before grinning sheepishly. "Sorry. I'm used to thinking ahead of people. It's part of my job as a DA. When we're around other Weres the telepathy process speeds up. Please excuse me for finishing your remarks, and go on."

Kaitlin drew in a breath, failing in her attempts to make sense out of all of this. "The visitor who came here tonight might have been looking for Michael."

"Possibly," Dylan said tentatively.

"You believe this person came to see me?"

"I think that's more likely."

"I don't suppose you'd have any idea why."

"I do. And so do you, Kaitlin, if you think about it. You're not what you might have seemed to be all this time, and others are taking notice of the changes."

"This visitor wasn't Were, and if it had been a vampire, I wouldn't be sitting here. Plus, Michael mentioned that vamp and Were blood don't mix, in terms of wanting to suck some of mine, so I don't get what the appeal might be for the vampires."

She eyed Dylan soberly. "Do you believe that visitor came from behind that curtain in the park?"

"I'm almost certain of it," Dylan replied.

She had to take a few seconds to ponder the meaning of that, shook up by the adamancy of Dylan's reply.

"Michael thinks so, too?"

"That makes the most sense," Dylan explained, "given

that the curtain appeared very near to the place where you were originally attacked."

Kaitlin glanced at him. "You know about that, too?"

"Michael hardly thinks about anything else, and beams his fear that you might be harmed again."

Michael was taking on the world for her.

"Given that vampires don't like wolf blood, why would they be after me now?" she asked. "Do you have a theory?"

"That's a big question mark, isn't it, and why we're leaning toward believing you must also be something of a delicacy to them."

Kaitlin shuddered. "Delicacy? Why? What are the beings that live beyond that curtain?"

"As frightening as it might sound, there has been a suggestion that the Fey species lie beyond that black veil, and that you could be one of them."

Yes. She had heard this and had to at least consider it.

"I don't know anything about that," she said. "I'm lucky to be here at all, and am breathing only thanks to Michael. I've been over this and can't come up with any explanation to suggest that the hypothesis about being connected to that thing in the park is true."

Dylan moved his plate to the side. "Maybe these others sense that you were hurt and have come to see for themselves. Wolves can perceive when a pack-mate is in trouble from quite a distance away. This could be true of your…"

She didn't let Dylan finish that statement, and turned the tables on mind reading. "My species? That's what you were going to say, isn't it?"

"I wonder why you don't know about that, and about what else you might be, other than like the people you've been living among. It's fairly clear that you are connected to that dark spot somehow."

Her protest was vehement. "I was beside that curtain tonight, and no one came from behind it to confront me."

"I believe you might have been a wolf at the time," Dylan reminded her. "That shift might have been enough to confuse the issue and postpone a meeting."

Damn it. Did everyone know about her transition tonight? Weren't werewolves able to hold any secrets sacred, and keep things to themselves?

On the other hand, Dylan wasn't treating her any differently than he treated the others in Michael's pack. He showed no sign of prejudice against another species that didn't have fangs…as far as they knew. Dylan was calm and rational when she wanted to scream.

"I don't understand how I shifted," she said, modifying her voice so she wouldn't come off as hysterical. "I think Michael drew that part of me to him."

She didn't add that she also believed her transformation might have been sexually sparked, and that her emotional reaction to Michael at the time had been overtly passionate and possessive.

"That thought was personal. Sorry." Kaitlin avoided Dylan's watchful scrutiny.

"It's all personal. You can learn to block certain thoughts with practice."

She glanced at Dylan again through half-lowered lashes.

"That's often how this wolf mojo works," Dylan explained. "Wolf calling to wolf is a powerful lure that rivals the call of the moon in many of us. Lycans are particularly susceptible to emotions trapped in the body. In this case, however, becoming a wolf might have saved you from becoming something else."

A cold feeling came over Kaitlin, because Dylan could be right in believing that whoever had brought that dark spot here had come to see her. They might have been surprised, confused and angry with her shape-shift. Maybe they hadn't recognized her. If they had truly come for her, that is. And if she was half something else, and that half was like them.

"Just who the hell are they, anyway?" she asked.

Kaitlin felt the twitch of her own anger rising over her ongoing ignorance. The heat caused by her tremors began to chase the chills away.

"All I have to do to prove any of this is to go out there and knock," she said. "Questions would be answered pretty quickly."

"Sure," Dylan agreed. "Yet I wouldn't rush out there right now. The sun's almost up and the others are on their way here. Together, we can decide what the next move will be."

Dylan was right again. She perceived Michael's nearness as strongly as if he had been sitting beside her. She wanted him here, and also viewed this meeting with trepidation. They had made love and would have to deal with that face-to-face, along with everything else, when she would have liked nothing better than to have stepped off the emotional roller coaster for a while.

Eyes shut, Kaitlin voiced the last question she'd have time to ask before Michael arrived. "What kind of creature do you suppose a wolf-Fey hybrid might turn out to be?"

She didn't like anything about the look in Dylan's eyes when she risked a glance at him, and the chills made a comeback.

Chapter 21

Michael allowed Adam to precede him into the kitchen. He was just about to move toward the bedroom when he realized Kaitlin was sitting at the small kitchen table with Dylan.

He felt silly, and slightly out of his element observing the warm scene. It all looked so normal on the surface. Michael wished it truly was normal, but he wasn't one to have his wishes come true.

Kaitlin was dressed in his oversize T-shirt, with a sheet wrapped around her waist. He waited for her gaze to connect with his. When it did, he heard the rumble of a rising protest inside her. Her eyes were gray again.

"Cozy place," Adam said, helping himself to water from the tap.

"I like to keep my walls close and the front door handy," Michael returned without taking his eyes off Kaitlin. Her heart beat in sync with his—a further sign of their bond.

"Smart building philosophy," Adam said. "Tory and I have a similar one. We have a bungalow beside a park that we keep a tight watch on."

A hush fell over the room after Adam stopped speaking. Everyone here waited for pleasantries to be out of the way so that the real discussions could begin. Where to start was the temporary stalling point.

Kaitlin spoke first. "Fey. That's what you believe this is? I'd go home to confront my parents and demand some information if I was sure my wolf wouldn't make an appearance and ruin a perfectly good argument."

Michael turned his attention to Dylan, who sat at the table with Adam standing at his back. "This isn't your problem, Dylan. Whatever the Fey are or aren't, Chavez can't be allowed to get away again. We need to be discussing a plan of action for that, with you taking the lead. I said I'd help, and my word is good."

"I think a good plan," Adam said, "would be to chase everyone in Chavez's gang toward that damn dark curtain if it remains here for another day or two." He recounted what had become of the creatures that had gone through. "Whoever is on the other side likes outlaws about as much as we do. They did us a service tonight, though I suppose they might not see it that way."

When Kaitlin spoke again, her voice was steady and pitched low. "That anomaly is seemingly here because of me, so I'll deal with it. You catch the bad guys, and I'll find out what that curtain hides."

"How do you propose to do that?" Michael asked.

"She wants to go out there and knock on the door," Dylan answered in Kaitlin's place. "And she could be right about that being the only way to get the answers she needs."

"She can't do that when we don't understand what that thing is," Michael protested.

"So some of us can go with her," Adam said. "We go tomorrow, when the sun is up and before monsters wake and get hungry."

Michael said, "And Chavez?"

Dylan took that one. "Chavez is another kind of bloodsucker and only comes out to party after the sun goes down. We have that possible place in mind for where he has been hiding, but to go there at night without an army would be suicidal if he has brought more of his old pack with him. That's when they're at their most lethal. Who says we can't face that strange Fey portal first, in the morning, and then go after the prey Adam, Tory and I are hunting here?"

"No." Kaitlin pressed against the table to get to her feet. She addressed Dylan. "You go after Chavez as planned. I don't think anyone here can afford to let anything get in the way of that agenda. I'll go to the park and take one of Michael's pack-mates with me to see if that thing is still there."

"I'll go with you," Michael said.

Kaitlin shook her head, which made her tousled auburn hair tumble over her shoulders. "Only Rena," she said. "Rena can go with me."

Michael's argument was interrupted before he could make it.

"I'm volatile when you're around," Kaitlin said to him. "Your wolf calling to my wolf is how you once explained that to me. It's better if Rena accompanies me, assuming she agrees to do so, because I won't have to worry about retaining the ability to keep my shape or speak in a human voice."

"I'll worry," Michael said softly.

Dylan stood. Like a gentleman, he took his plate to the sink and spoke over his shoulder. "Tory, Adam and whoever you have available, Michael, will head out after the sun comes up. Adam and I will leave you two now to hash out the details of how you'll handle things on your end. Michael, that closet with the blankets you mentioned is where?"

Defusing the standoff easily and quickly, Dylan drew Michael's focus. Expecting to see something other than the sympathetic expression Dylan wore, Michael backed to the kitchen doorway. "I'll show you."

He tossed Kaitlin a purposeful glance that asked her to wait for his return. Her ethereal thinness made him actually believe for a few seconds that he could almost picture, rising from her shoulders, the nearly invisible outline of the small, iridescent fairy wings that Devlin had nixed.

Of all the pairings, wolf and Fey had to be the most inconceivable.

And there was no way in hell he was going to let Kaitlin go anywhere near that damn portal without him.

She was determined to go out on her own. Kaitlin had already made up her mind to be braver than she had ever been and to stop involving everyone else in the next few steps on her life's path.

Since the Weres supposed that black hole in the park had appeared because she was somehow tethered to it, chances were decent that she could find out what it, they, them, the so-called Fey, wanted. Otherwise, the pack's attention would be riveted to it, splitting their attention from the gravest threat, which was the wolf named Chavez.

"I'm no damsel," she repeated for the twentieth time in forty-eight hours.

Having told Michael she'd take Rena, and with no idea

where Rena lived, she supposed that information was now at her fingertips, and that all she had to do was open up her mind and put out a call to the pack's only female. Rena, like everyone else around here, would hear that call and either ignore it, or respond. Kaitlin didn't really care what the outcome was. This next bit was up to her, and her alone.

She returned to the bedroom to find her clothes hanging in the closet, which was the last place she looked because neatness had never been her own strong suit. Michael had racks of clothes, mostly jeans and shirts, all necessary since he ruined or ditched so many of those items every time he decided to change shape.

She had one leg in her jeans when she looked up, feeling the heat of the sexy, sometimes volatile, Alpha's stare.

Michael was lodged in the doorway, his expression grim.

She sat down on the edge of the bed without bothering to finish dressing. Stripping in front of him in the park was only a dim memory. Dressing beneath that green-eyed gaze of his was out of the question.

"You might turn around and let me get my pants on," she said.

"I'm afraid to take my eyes off you," Michael returned. "One blink and you might disappear."

Kaitlin put a hand to her temple. Like the rest of her body, her head hurt, and the intensity of Michael's observation doubled the erotic feeling of being in his bedroom, partially undressed.

Her pounding heart didn't help the ache behind her eyes. Michael was only six steps away and could have covered that in seconds. Breathing was always difficult when he was around.

"It isn't safe for you out there," he continued. "Please don't get any ideas about slipping out while I rest. What am I supposed to do? Sleep in the doorway, in case escaping is what you have in mind?"

"Am I a prisoner?"

"Certainly not. Well, maybe."

"I'm not brave enough to run," she said. "I would like to be clothed, however, in case any other visitors come calling."

Michael focused on that. "Dylan told me about the one who showed up. It's odd there was no scent left behind."

"Dylan thinks he came for me."

Michael took one step into the room. Kaitlin's heart beat faster.

"I won't let them near you, Kaitlin. I won't come near you, either, if that's what you're afraid of."

Damn that mind reading trick. Could he hear how rapidly her heart was racing?

"I'm not afraid of you," she said. "I'm wary of what you can do."

"I'm fairly sure it's the other way around, and it's me who is wary about you."

"That's supposed to make me feel better?"

"No. I do want to get close, you know," Michael confessed. "You've become like an addiction, and are drawing me to you when…"

"When you don't want to act on that?" she finished for him.

Michael stared openly, blinking his brilliant green eyes as if trying to come up with a line that might appease her fear of falling prey to so many more things than merely being a new species. He had blocked his thoughts from her, a trick she needed to perfect if she was to retain her dignity in his presence.

She wanted to jump him again. Have him fill her again. Beneath the aches and discomfort she was experiencing, and between her legs, a bigger, deeper ache was demanding satisfaction that only Michael could supply. She hoped that craving was more than just a wishful distraction.

"Are you in pain?" he asked.

"No. And you need some sleep."

He glanced to the shuttered window. "Can you feel them out there? Anything?"

"No. Not now."

"You felt them before?"

"I can't separate all the new feelings at the moment. I can't trim them down to who makes me feel this, and who makes me feel that."

She was glad she couldn't see past the shutters. Night would never be the same for her after this.

"I won't get far if I tremble every time I see a shadow, or if I'm accompanied by a bodyguard each time I move. Is that what's in store for me, Michael?"

"I wouldn't wish that on anyone," he replied.

Kaitlin sighed wearily.

Michael took another step. "How did you react to the visitor earlier? Were you afraid?"

She didn't have to think hard about the question. "I thought it might be a wolf or a vampire at first."

"And then?"

"Then I knew it wasn't either of those things."

"Could it have been a person? A human?"

Kaitlin briefly closed her eyes, letting the words *person* and *human* take on shapes that no longer described her. Strangely enough, she didn't miss them.

"It won't go away." She glanced at him. "That thing out there won't disappear until it gets what it came for. Isn't that what you've decided?"

"It's only a guess."

"Why else would that visitor appear, unless he wanted something?"

Michael was almost close enough to reach out to. With fatigue etched on his face and his hair curtaining his cheeks, he still gave the impression of being an angel. It was, she thought, a wonder that people didn't see that on a daily basis.

Her inner wolf dared Michael to take those last few steps, but reaching her wouldn't accomplish anything in terms of solving the puzzles confronting them. Still, he was so very tempting. So masculine, alluring and safe.

"Do you believe it's here for you?" he asked.

"What I don't know is giving me a headache. I do know you've spent most of the night seeing to my safety, with little regard for yourself."

All one hundred and ninety pounds of Alpha behavior had been extended to her. With benefits. Kaitlin gritted her teeth to stop from remembering how warm his hand had felt between her thighs, and the way she had anxiously anticipated what would happen after that. Every damn second she had known Michael seemed like a dream—unreal, made up, the concoction of an overactive imagination—when the time was past for getting that straight.

His sad smile went a long way toward doing her in.

"Dawn," he added. "We'll go out there at dawn and finish this."

He had something else to finish, as well. Two giant steps later he was beside her, pressing her onto the bed, his musky scent filling her lungs.

There was no place for *nice*.

Michael didn't even try.

Stretched out on top of Kaitlin, leaning on his elbows

and meeting her eyes, he felt their connection ricochet through him, uncontainable and potent in scope.

Kaitlin's legs, sliding open, making room for him, were an exhilarating invitation. Her eyes—warm, wide, unblinking—dared him to delve deeper into their mysteries.

He desired it all…all of Kaitlin, as if there had been no previous liaison in the park, and these were the first moments of discovery.

Her skin, warm beneath the sweater she now wore, shivered as his right hand skimmed over each curve, each angle that formed the enigmatic whole of Kaitlin Davies.

Kaitlin's hands weren't idle, either. She retraced the remnants of the grooves she'd made in his bare back with her fingers and nails, reopening the scratches that had already mostly healed. Hurting him gave her pleasure, though not in the way others might have imagined. Hers was an intrinsic need to hang on to him by digging in, as if she feared these magical moments would stop and he'd go away. As if he could.

He really would have to tell her more about imprinting. She'd need to know what these ongoing cravings meant. Werewolves were the hungriest beasts on the earth in terms of seeking sexual gratification with their mates. It was a primal instinct that never faded or went away.

Kaitlin moaned.

He had shut his eyes, and now, again, met her frank, greedy gray stare.

"I'll never get enough," she whispered breathlessly, gripping his shoulders and lifting her hips. "And I have no right to this, at this time."

Michael growled as he angled his head. The meeting of their lips created a new storm system. The air grew heavy with silence. Michael's body felt suddenly weighty as he pressed Kaitlin deeper into the mattress.

His mouth was demanding, brutal, unyielding. He took in her breath and gave his breath back to her, completely possessive in directing the necessity for air. Kaitlin's tongue met his, licking, enticing, tempting, luring. His tongue darted in and out of her mouth as if it were a surrogate for the body part stiffening between her slender pelvic bones. And still, with great effort, Michael waited for a sign that she wanted this as much as he did.

Already, he was burning up. Their mouths, sealed together, were on fire.

Kaitlin tore at his waistband, sliding her fingers through the gap at his lower back. His next thought was that he had been caught, if not tamed completely.

When the sudden burst of cool air ruffled over him, Michael's skin rippled. His muscles bunched.

Kaitlin made a disturbing sound that sent chills up his spine. The chills were a warning.

He backed up in a fluid motion, and was on his feet seconds later. But he could not move toward the open doorway in front of him. He could not call out, growl or complain about the untimely interruption.

Something stood in that doorway, camouflaged by shadows that were as unique as Michael's inability to sense the approaching danger. His eyes were useless in clarifying what this visitor was.

In a wave of disturbed air, the visitor entered the room, bringing the shadows along. The entity moved to the bed, to Kaitlin, and Michael could only watch, horrified, frozen in place, as that entity extended a semi-visible hand to Michael's little panting wolf.

Was Kaitlin as helpless as he felt? As immobile as he was? His legs wouldn't work. He could not turn his head.

As if mesmerized, Kaitlin's gray eyes closed. Slowly, and as Michael fought against the invisible bonds holding him hostage, Kaitlin sat up and placed her fingers in the offered hand.

Michael's mind fuzzed over. He had to work to breathe. Helplessly, he watched Kaitlin stand. Half-naked, and with her oversize sweater reaching nearly to her knees, she walked past Michael, now a captive of someone or something else.

Howls of distress bubbled up in Michael's chest. His skin, so icy that it was beginning to burn, quaked as he fought, strained, groped for a way to move…a way to keep Kaitlin from harm.

But it was too late.

Before the howls reached his throat, she was gone.

Chapter 22

It was the longest five minutes of Michael's life. Robbed of the ability to move or speak, all he could do was to continue fighting the spell rendering him useless to protect his mate.

He heard footsteps as the chills finally subsided. The doorway became occupied by another interloper, this time an ally.

"Michael?" Dylan met his eyes. His familiar Lycan heat broke the icy, invisible bonds chaining Michael to the floor. Michael rolled his shoulders and punched the air. He let loose another howl.

"I felt a disturbance," Dylan said with concern.

"They took her." Michael rushed past the Lycan who obviously had sensed the very thing Michael hadn't seen coming. That discrepancy in his awareness was unforgivable. Worse, he couldn't even describe what had happened, since he hadn't seen much of the bastard that had taken Kaitlin away.

"Right behind you," Dylan called out as Michael made for the front door.

"My problem," Michael shouted over his shoulder.

He heard Dylan yell Adam's name, though Michael's senses were firing enough to know that Adam Scott wasn't in the house and had likely gone out to join his mate... and that Dylan was concerned enough to issue a warning.

Michael was outside, running as fast as his legs would take him as the sky adopted the pink hue of a new dawn.

This time, he knew exactly where to go.

In a daze, Kaitlin allowed the stranger to lead her from Michael's house.

The being next to her was luminous in dawn's early light, shining with a rainbow-hued glow that was difficult to see past. As they entered the park, the entity began to take on a more familiar form. More of its arms appeared, and also legs and a torso. Slender, slight of bone, white-skinned, with hair as fair as Dylan's, this new being was a fragile fantasy figure come to life. Beautiful beyond belief. And female.

Another layer of the world was what she had heard Michael thinking as she'd left him behind out of necessity, fearing to involve the Weres in her problems when they faced so many more of their own. The incredible being beside her proved that this was a case of genetics and secrets that were a big surprise to the person in most need of clarity.

She wasn't afraid, even when this unnamed being turned pale eyes her way. Gray eyes, like her own. She had the feeling this entity was trying to see through the half-wolf part of her, and that made Kaitlin want to laugh.

They walked in silence. The shimmering curtain wasn't

far. Her fate would be dealt with in minutes. This march had the quality of sleepwalking.

Her feet didn't really touch the ground in any natural way. Like her strange companion, she seemed to glide over the earth. Each patch of grass they passed created a single note that attached to the next one, and so on, until the looming dawn was filled with music. The music seemed familiar.

"Kaitlin!"

The shout from behind made the music stop.

"Kaitlin!"

Michael...

In thinking his name, Kaitlin felt again the moistness of the grass between her bare toes. Her body seemed to access its former weight. But the spot that waited for them in this green landscape lay just ahead, and was shimmering between the trees. *Wolf* was a concept behind her now. The glow of completing this puzzle was on the horizon, twenty steps away.

Fifteen steps away.

Michael, I'm going to do this.

Ten steps.

Five.

Kaitlin turned her head when the pressure of leaving the world squeezed the air from her lungs one last time... and saw her lover running toward her.

Michael desperately tried to reach her. Dylan was on his heels. There was no sign of Adam, or Tory, who was supposed to be monitoring this anomaly.

Now, he had lost Kaitlin.

Michael sprinted toward the black curtain, cursing out loud and feeling as though someone had cut out his heart.

He knew heartache. The real reason he had left home

was to avoid the pain of remembering what a pair of nasty humans had done to his mother, and learn to adapt to living among them.

Devastated by the loss of his wife, Michael's father had never fully recovered. As the male losing a mate tonight, even if his bond with Kaitlin had been recent, Michael understood what his father had felt. As was the case with his father, he had not been able to protect his mate, and that lapse in attention went against every principle he had held to a high standard.

Michael stopped in front of that abysmal curtain of unknown origin and fisted his hands.

"Do you think Dev was right?" he asked Dylan.

"How can anyone know for certain?" Dylan replied, sending out a second silent call for the missing Miami pair.

Michael could see the concern blossom on Dylan's face when no answering reply came. Chills were taking over. Tory, Adam and Kaitlin had disappeared.

His nod to Dylan said everything he couldn't utter. *Find your friends. Take care of my pack. Get help with Chavez and kick that sucker to kingdom come. If I don't come back.*

Sucking in a deep breath that he figured might very well be his last, Michael dropped his jeans. If humans couldn't trespass in Fey territory, maybe a wolf could.

Holding a breath, and with an image of Kaitlin stretched out on his bed, Michael lunged toward the wavering curtain and whatever a bunch of fucking fairies might have in store.

Chapter 23

Kaitlin opened her eyes to a brilliance that hinted at potential retinal damage. She tried to shield her eyes and couldn't, because her hand was not a hand. It was an auburn-colored paw.

Somehow she had shape-shifted again.

She looked past her muzzle at a landscape populated with trees and grass in colors she'd never imagined existed. There were actually too many shades of green. The sky was a cloudless amethyst blue.

The portal that had transported her here fluttered against her backside, which meant that she had just stepped through. She had no idea how she had shifted, but all she had to do was turn and jump, and she'd be back where she belonged, in a world with fewer shades of green and with the wolf she loved.

Did this place hold any answers for her?

Where was the welcome committee?

She saw them then. Two beings like the one that had brought her here stood a slight distance away, staring at a wolf instead of the female who might at one time have been coded to be like them. Without speaking, their thoughts were as clear to her as Were thoughts had started to be.

What's done is done, said one of these beautiful beings in a voice that was softly feminine.

Shame, really, the other agreed.

What do you want with me? Kaitlin studied them with her enhanced wolf vision. It didn't take her long to see that their beauty was managed by a cloaking device meant to protect a truer image. That device, aura or glamour, wavered around them like the curtain one of them had brought her through. Though she focused hard, Kaitlin couldn't see all the way through the spell they had cast for themselves.

"We wanted to welcome you." The taller being spoke aloud and waved a thin hand. "But look what we found."

Wolf is a new part of me, Kaitlin sent back to them.

When the tall being cocked her head, some of the glamour sifted off. Kaitlin saw a dark expression cross the pale, otherworldly features.

Dread began to set in. These beings didn't seem light, upon closer scrutiny. Her senses told her there wasn't anything light about them at all. They weren't happy to see her like this.

The dark curtain moved again. A heavy moving mass came leaping through the portal, knocking Kaitlin over. Sharp teeth caught her by the back of her neck. She yelped as she was dragged backward. Her overwrought senses reeled as her exhaled breath exploded into a thousand tiny fragments of color, each tinted shard as sharp as broken glass. Then she was robbed of breath until the familiar world again opened its arms to welcome her back.

More green confronted her, this time a pair of eyes

in a face that was as darkly wolf as the faces across that veil had been darkly ethereal. She knew these eyes. She loved these eyes and had run from them to find out more about the secrets tucked inside her. At the moment, she was sorry she had tried.

Change back, Michael silently directed.

They weren't alone. Dylan was there, waiting for what would happen next, and she and Michael were still wolves.

Change back, Kaitlin, Michael repeated.

Can't, she panted, mustering her courage to face this latest challenge.

See yourself in the other form. Believe it. Be it.

I can't be like them. They didn't appreciate the new me. She sounded winded.

If you are like whoever they are, it's only in part. The other part is like me, and I am going to change back.

"Someone is coming," Dylan announced, spinning to sniff at the early morning breeze.

Michael growled menacingly. *We can't be seen like this, Kate. This is Clement, not Colorado. There are no wild wolves here.*

With a body-jarring snap of ligament and bone that made Kaitlin want to howl, Michael's wolf form began to disappear as if he merely tucked his fur back inside. Naked and always gorgeous, he crouched beside her and placed a hand on her head.

He said, "You'd think others might be wary of this, too. So unless you want me arrested for strutting naked near a college campus, I suggest you hurry."

Michael then spoke to Dylan. "Not Tory's or Adam's scent in that wind?"

Dylan shook his head. "It's not a good omen when monsters dare to show up in daylight."

Kaitlin willed herself to shift, to no avail. Her first

shape-shift had been automatic in both directions. This one had come on just as suddenly, and now she seemed to be stuck.

"Damn it." Michael took hold of her fur, tucked his arms beneath her and lifted her up. "What did those Fey bastards do to you?"

Oddly enough, Kaitlin wanted to tell Michael that they hadn't done anything to her except stare at what had crossed over in that portal. She had a feeling she'd failed their test, and had been rejected.

"We need reinforcements," Dylan said. "Chavez might have my friends, as impossible as that seems."

Kaitlin knew Dylan was thinking that Tory and Adam had been taken by that evil trespassing gang, and she couldn't see that happening. Tory was Lycan. On her own, Tory was terribly strong, with Adam a close second. Together, the pair should have been unstoppable. She couldn't begin to imagine a force comprised of Michael, Dylan and the others being unable to secure any outcome they chose.

What mattered at that moment was shifting back to her usual body and watching her Alpha in action. Michael was already sending out a call to rally his Weres.

She sent her mind inward to locate the key for turning off a shape-shift. She was tired of being at the top of everyone's prey list, and through with being the underdog.

Michael held her tightly. She felt the beat of his heart against her shoulder. His wolf's pulse was slowing, unable to maintain its feverish pitch in a man's body. Kaitlin concentrated on those beats, breathing through her open mouth, demanding that her body obey the command to change.

Michael's extensive tattoos kept her mesmerized. The inky scrolls became fluid as he moved. Each flexion of his chest muscles set the intricate scrolls rolling and produced a reaction in her that was very close to being hypnotized.

With a long pink tongue, she gave one scroll a lick. Michael was salty from the effort of changing. He tasted like sex.

Her transition began as a distant pulse, like the first hint of an impending orgasm. That pulse didn't roll or rise. Instead, it spread sideways like a plague that would take over her organs, one by one. In this case, it was a wolfish sort of glamour that was calling to her. Those Fey beings behind their curtain would have appreciated it, surely.

Kaitlin's heartbeat matched Michael's as her lungs filled with air. When her body began to convulse, she doubled over in Michael's arms, folding up like an accordion.

They had been heading toward Michael's home when her physical gyrations prevented him from taking another step. He swore out loud and loosened his grip enough for her to drop from the safety net of his strong arms.

She landed on her feet, both of them, as her body swelled from an auburn-furred wolf to the likeness of a young human female before she hit the ground. This older, familiar shape was a lie, of course. A sinking feeling came to Kaitlin of not knowing where she truly belonged, though this shape would have to do for now.

Michael used a tight grip on her wrist to turn her abruptly around. He leaned down to peer into her eyes. "It doesn't matter," he said, his voice reflecting his impulse to get her out of sight. "Use everything available to you and consider yourself lucky to have made it this far when the odds were stacked against you. Your specialness makes you who you are. Own it."

He was right. She knew what half of her was, and that half was something she could use to help this pack. Michael's pep talk had helped.

On tiptoe, Kaitlin rose to look at him. With her face close to his, she said, "I'll race you home," daring herself to test the parameters of a current status she wasn't quite sure she could completely master in so short a time.

The comment took Michael back until she swayed on her bare feet, spasmed as her spine crackled and realigned, and her body began to turn itself inside out. Words became impossible to transmit. Thoughts became longings. She was once again a wolf.

Rendered immobile by the surprise of this victory, Kaitlin swiftly regrouped. After the first wobbly few steps, she took off at a lope, glancing over her shoulder only once to see the few seconds of stunned surprise on Michael's face before he ran after the wolf he had created, flinging four-letter curses to the wind.

Kaitlin didn't change back when they reached his house. She kept her wolf shape, Michael supposed, because she wanted to, since she had successfully reverse shifted in his arms.

He wasn't sure what the others would say. It was a sure bet they'd be as stunned as he had been when first encountering Kaitlin's handy little trick. He still wasn't used to it.

As he dressed, she circled his room, watching with her wolfish gray eyes made greener by her infusion of Lycan blood. She brushed against his legs once, careful afterward not to remain within touching distance. Being close to him had to be the key to her transition reversal. He sensed her anxiousness about what might happen next.

Rena, Dev and Cade burst through the front door at the same time, equally as anxious, all of them paler than usual from lack of sleep. They slid to a stop when Kaitlin appeared, and exchanged puzzled glances.

"Long story," Michael said.

"Is that Kaitlin?" Rena asked.

"Yep." Michael moved quickly past the myriad of questions he perceived in their minds. "Tory and Adam are missing, and Chavez's minions are loose in the light."

"Shit," Rena muttered. "Does that freak have a damn army?"

Kaitlin growled, and all eyes turned to her.

"That," Rena said, pointing to the auburn wolf, "isn't normal. Tell us how you did it."

"Bigger fish to fry," Michael said. "We join Dylan to hunt for his friends in the daylight and in public. I hope to God Dylan is wrong about Tory and Adam being caught, and they're out there somewhere, not daring to call in."

Devlin inched closer to Kaitlin, looked down at her and whispered, "You have the smell of that mysterious place on you. Is this a spell?"

For Devlin, at least, a spell might have explained Kaitlin's current shape, Michael thought with relief as he strode to the door. "Dylan is searching. You know what to do. At the first whiff of trouble, call. Those are the rules."

"Aye aye, Captain," Dev said. "Over and out."

Rena blocked Kaitlin's departure by straddling the threshold. From the porch outside, Michael let Rena say whatever she had to say.

"There was something strange about you from the start, Kaitlin. Still, if you're willing to help, you can cover way more ground than we can in that shape. Be careful. Keep out of sight. You probably already know that you don't blend real well with Clement's people world. If they find you, they're likely to call in the posse, the pound or the closest zoo."

Rena cleared the doorway to allow Kaitlin to exit. Proud of Rena, Michael waved for them both to follow.

"Rena means well," he said to Kaitlin, marveling how quickly she had adapted to a shape she wasn't used to.

"The hell I do," Rena remarked. With a wave of her hand, Rena took off after Cade in the opposite direction and called back, "Just making conversation."

"Dev, can you monitor the area near that wavering thing in the trees that, with any luck at all, will be gone by now?" Michael asked.

"Shouldn't she do that?" Devlin replied, alluding to Kaitlin. "Maybe she can get the fairies to help."

"I don't think she'd like that, Dev."

Devlin shrugged shoulders that were covered this morning in a tight black T-shirt. After a lingering glance at Kaitlin, he saluted and took off to man his post.

"You dodged a silver bullet," Michael said to Kaitlin, who shadowed him like a heeling hound. But he immediately wished he hadn't used that phrase. An image of his mother's dead, skinless body returned to haunt him. Because that's what wolf hunters did. They scalped and skinned their prey in order to make money on the black market, or hell, just for bragging rights.

Worry began to consume him as he glanced to the wolf beside him. There weren't any wolf hunters in Clement that he knew of, but a sleepy college town would be a short enough distance from Miami and possibly, to a wolf hunter's crazed mind, live with potential new pickings.

"What if they followed Chavez here?" he said.

An answering reply came from the wolf frequency.

To hell with Chavez and the pelt he loped in with, Dylan said. *If there weren't so many nice wolves here, I'd call those wolf hunters myself and leave them a direct map to their worst wolf nightmare.*

Kaitlin was growling. Michael glanced down, deciding to tell her more of the things he had never spoken of to anyone.

"Wolf hunters left my mother's bloody carcass for us to find. Not much of her was left to identify, other than a locket my father had given her. I moved to Clement in part to try to lose that memory, and made myself believe I came because of wanting my own pack."

He drew a deep breath. "You don't have to stay here. You can go home, or someplace else, and start over. Chances are good that you wouldn't shift without me beside you. Maybe your family can help."

What was he saying? They had imprinted, and those chains, once forged, could not be broken. If Kaitlin left him, odds were good that he'd never find another mate. He'd never want another mate. It would be the same for Kaitlin, unless her other nebulous half could overrule that bond and set her free.

Sharp teeth dug into his leg. Kaitlin might have heard some of that last bit.

"I didn't do this on purpose," he said, studying the trickle of blood she had drawn. "I didn't think that in rescuing you I'd want you so very badly."

Kaitlin's growl got him moving again, though not very far. She circled around and planted herself in front of him on the pathway. Her eyes, like the rest of her, were undecided about what color to be, and which species should rule such a small detail. Gray, green, gold...the colors flashed in a revolving, never-ending cycle that Michael found as fascinating as everything else about Kaitlin Davies.

Rena would have said he was smitten, when in fact imprinting changed a wolf's cell structure. He felt that connection deep in his bones, as if it had always been there and had merely grown up with him. His need for Kaitlin was strong enough, and perhaps senseless enough to make him want to leave everything and take her home, where the world and its problems could pass them by.

Alpha.

Her voice in his mind caused a misstep. He had blocked those last thoughts from her, and she might have read him anyway.

"Yes," he said to Kaitlin. "I know my where my duties and allegiance lie."

Scenting Dylan cut that conversation short. The Were was walking fast in their direction and had agitation written all over him.

"Chavez doesn't have them," Dylan said with a hint of relief as he announced Tory and Adam's fate. "I think that whoever lives behind that damn portal does."

Chapter 24

Dylan knelt down to speak directly to her. "Can you go in there again, Kaitlin? Behind that portal?"

Kaitlin twitched her muzzle, forgetting about being a wolf at the moment before sending a message the wolf way. *Not welcome.*

"Then Tory and Adam wouldn't be welcome, either. So how far could they get, if in fact they did get through that portal?"

I believe the gate might be guarded.

"By whom? What are they, and what are they like?"

Fey is the name Devlin used to describe them.

"You've seen them. Tell me what we're dealing with."

They're beings who aren't to be reckoned with. Their appearance was deceiving. For me, they were more like a feeling rather than beings with substance.

Dylan looked around. "Would they lure a wolf in there for bad reasons, if my friends didn't go by their own accord?"

Kaitlin shook her head. *Don't know.*

Dylan sighed. "I'm not sure Tory and Adam would try anything so risky when we have a serious agenda here, and yet I've traced their scent back to that damn place."

"Maybe they didn't go past the curtain," Michael suggested. "Both of them were there earlier. Their scent might have lingered."

"True," Dylan admitted. "Yet the scent was strong, so I'm thinking that might be a reason for the loss of communication. If they aren't with Chavez, I should be able to sense them elsewhere."

Kaitlin growled again to regain their attention. They both had to realize that Chavez, seeing that everything Dylan had told them was true, might be playing tricks and using some kind of sleight-of-hand to disguise his own agenda. Surely Dylan already knew that.

She let both Lycans in on that thought, while her gut told her that wasn't the case with Tory and Adam. The beings that had met her beyond that portal would not have allowed more werewolves to cross their borders. They hadn't been happy with her. Who knew what they thought after Michael's wolfish rescue?

Dylan and Michael stared at her for several seconds before swearing in unison. For a brief moment, Kaitlin saw the similarities of their Lycan heritage. Both of these Weres vibrated with a metabolism that virtually hummed. Both of them were gorgeous examples of physical perfection, and incredibly smart.

They moved with a special degree of muscle awareness. Their eyes were deep-set and bright. Both of them seemed to prefer long hair, and were unfazed by naked bodies. They would have turned the heads of any and all females of multiple species, and the females they chose as mates would be extremely lucky to have them.

But there was no mistake about how dangerous each of these two Lycans were, despite the fact that her insides rumbled with the thought of being one of those chosen females.

"Show me where Chavez is hiding," Michael said as they formulated a plan to start toward the college. "Maybe they've chased Chavez's creatures there and are blocking communication for defensive reasons."

To Kaitlin he added, "I don't suppose you'll go to my place and wait for me there."

Because it wasn't really a question, Kaitlin didn't bother to answer. She was this Alpha's mate, and had to prove herself worthy. Nevertheless, she had to be wary. The new day had dawned and people were starting to show up in the distance. She would have to slink through the trees on a parallel path to the route Michael was taking.

Their current direction was the result of Dylan's insight into the last communication he'd had with his pack-mates, and he transmitted that information silently to Michael.

She heard every word.

Chavez, they believed, had claimed a basement for himself in one of the older buildings at the edge of the campus—an old warehouse that had fallen into disrepair. Students sometimes went there to fool around, believing the place to be haunted. All in all, it was a perfect place for monsters to choose. And if they had chosen it and brought their victims there, *haunted* would take on a much deeper meaning.

Clement truly was in trouble, and the images that trouble kicked up in Kaitlin's mind were sickening.

"Kate," Michael said, turning. "You can't come along. You know that. You're like catnip for some of these guys, and who knows if that lure extends to daylight. Let me do what has to be done without worrying about you. Please."

Michael's apprehension was contagious. The fur lifted on the back of Kaitlin's neck. This was her Alpha. Her mate. He had said *please*, and she didn't like that he had to resort to that word.

Go, she sent back to him.

Still, he waited.

Erase me from the picture, she said. *I will take care, I swear.*

Michael dropped to his haunches in front of her, put his hands on the sides of her head and looked into her eyes. Wolf to wolf was how she wanted him now, her hunger for Michael tripling in intensity. Was more hunger in her future, too, if this fight with Chavez and Clement's vampires turned out well?

She bared her lupine teeth in honor of that idea, and was rewarded with Michael's brief, dazzling smile. He understood this desire perfectly, because he shared it.

"You will undo me, Kate," he whispered.

As Michael joined Dylan, Kaitlin experienced an emotion that was like being torn apart. He had said *please*. She had to respect his wishes. Didn't she? One good turn did deserve another.

She watched the Lycans move off, her wolf motor revving. When they had disappeared past the closest stand of trees, she lifted her head, sniffed the air and backtracked to find the place where she was going to press the advantage of being somewhat like those strange, sparkly, colorful entities that had offered her a hand in this world and made her unwelcome in another.

Fey. That's what Devlin had called them. And if Fey DNA ran in her blood, at least one half of her had a right to use that portal whenever she wanted to.

Fearful that Michael might be aware of her plan, and that she hadn't fully mastered the fine art of the mental

mate block…worried that he might turn around, angry with
her propensity for ignoring his requests… Kaitlin utilized
all the speed built into her wolf limbs as she raced for the
site of what everyone called *that damn portal*.

The building was vacant, and spooky in its sad state
of disrepair. Michael was aware of the college's plans for
an entirely new campus rising from the ashes of the older
version. Building had already started. While the unused
brick structure in front of him still had good bones, time
and increased university budgets had rendered it useless.

He and Dylan paused to look the place over. The foul
odor of werewolves in residence was easy for another wolf
to pick up. Anyone human who ignored the posted warnings and trespassed here would have chalked the smells
up to the odors of age and decrepitude.

It was likely that vampires had been here until the monsters had moved in. Although the place carried the stink of
bloodsuckers, rogue Weres were the bigger threat. Rogue
Weres could move around in the daylight hours and crip-
ple a nest while the vamps enjoyed the breathless naps of
the undead.

Perceiving nothing to stop them, and with no Weres
to bar their way, Michael led Dylan into the dark, aban-
doned hallway. Stairs leading up to a second story were
cordoned off. That left the stairway down, and another
moment of déjà vu.

Unlike the other building where they had gone after
Cade, this one had only one lower floor. Michael and
Dylan crept quietly downward, sure they were alone for
the time being, but on guard.

The stairs emptied into a one-room basement that was
also dark and eerie.

Several rectangular windows, high up in the walls, that

should have shown the feet of whoever passed by, had been boarded up. What light there was came from three plastic-covered fluorescent lights that buzzed overhead.

The room itself was large and square, with a gray concrete floor and no real insulation to protect it from the elements. Urine, feces and blood had been used to scratch graffiti onto the walls. Two words were repeated over and over in a fiendish mantra. *Wolf.* And *kill*.

Some poor sucker's claws had done that. The blood was Were blood. There was no evidence of humans here. Chavez was indeed setting up a fight club. The bastard had wasted no time at all.

"Does Chavez allow some of his victims to live, adding to his private army after they've been brutalized by virus-dipped teeth and claws?" Michael asked.

"Survival of the fittest, maybe, in terms of Chavez requiring a stronger race of beast," Dylan replied. "As long as that victim isn't a cop. He shows no mercy for law enforcement, or the people his victims leave behind."

"Women, too?"

"As far as I know, the fight rings are for males."

Michael mulled that over. Tomorrow a full moon would rise and this bite-and-claw club would see action, unless it was stopped. Tonight, Chavez's beasts wouldn't look and act like the monsters they were: part man, part wolf; both of those parts lethal.

"There's no time to lose," Michael said. "The only way to close this place down and sanctify the ground would be to light a match and watch it burn."

"That's what we will have to do," Dylan agreed. "But not with his crew loose in your town. If we wait until the beasts return, we can turn the tables and trap them here."

"Along with a few innocent people."

"No. We see to it that doesn't happen. We stand guard."

"And Chavez?"

"He will be here. This is what he does. What he likes. He gets off on the show."

Michael again scanned of the room. "There's no sign of Tory and Adam. If we burn this now, Chavez might migrate to someplace else."

"Possibly," Dylan said. "Can we take that chance?"

Michael gave Dylan a sideways glance.

"I doubt if Chavez can be included in whatever the reason those vamps had for showing up," Dylan said. "Chavez was in need of an escape from Miami, and ended up here."

Michael shook his head. "The Were in the library was focused on Kaitlin. He said things to assure me she was his target."

"Then something happened to put them on her trail. Maybe they followed the vampires on this one and discovered an unusual treasure."

"Fey," Michael said.

Michael felt his jaw begin to tighten. *Yes*, he thought. *That's what this is. That's what some of this is about.* But were Chavez and the vampires aware of the appearance of the Fey on Clement's doorstep? Were the Fey what made his town the apex for the hell that was breaking loose, or was it a coincidence?

"In a fight between us, we'd be sadly lacking without Tory and Adam. We have to trap the beasts here."

Dylan's light eyes flashed angrily in the fluorescent lights. "I'm ready to do whatever it takes to get Chavez, even if it means that I die in the process. And I swear to you, Michael, that if I were to go down, I'd take that nasty sucker with me and leave the world a better place."

Michael said. "Tory and Adam showing up would be a bonus."

Insight suggested to Michael that he, too, had fallen

victim to the Fey's intrinsic charms buried inside a female who didn't realize what she was. So, who stood a chance against the Fey if they were undetectable? Without smelling or sensing their presence, if those creatures beyond the portal wanted to, they could wreak havoc on anyone.

The Fey were the problem, and also the answer.

In the pit of Michael's stomach, an excitement began to grow that had tentacles in both dread and the higher aspects of hope.

"Hell, Dylan," he said. "We have to find them."

Dylan glanced over. "Tory and Adam?"

"Those Fey creatures."

Dylan waited for him to explain.

"They are the key, and possibly the path to ending this future small-town Armageddon. Kaitlin has to use that portal again and find out what's going on."

Michael had already reached the stairs.

They exited the basement quickly, inhaling the fresh air outside. Rena and Dev came sprinting in from their search of the park to meet them, wearing grim expressions.

"Oh, hell," Michael snapped, predicting what they were going to say. "You didn't find Tory and Adam."

Chapter 25

In the early hours of daylight, the Fey's curtain had taken on a pink glimmer that reflected the color of the rising sun. Anyone else, Kaitlin thought, would have missed it. The thing was very nearly imperceptible to the naked eye. She, however, didn't have to see it. She felt the portal's presence.

She was connected to this gateway the way she was connected to her wolf, and stood before the wavering curtain in human form, naked and curious.

She needed answers, and this was the only way to get them. With her head held high and her quakes in check, she said softly, yet adamantly, "I'm back."

Nothing happened. No glittering hand appeared to invite her inside.

"Really?" she said. "You can withdraw your offer after having extending it?"

The curtain undulated as if it were alive and wanted to address her remark.

"With your blood in my veins, shouldn't I be able to claim kinship? Isn't that kinship why you've come? Everyone here believes that's the reason, and their opinions have convinced me. Come out, or let me in. Those are the only choices if I was ever one of you completely, before fate changed that."

The curtain rustled in a cool breeze that Kaitlin now guessed was of her making, since it had appeared each time she was about to face the unknown. As incredible as that was, the thought occurred to her that if she could do that, maybe her Fey side had other surprises in store.

"I won't leave," she added in a steely tone. "Since my family didn't prepare me, I'm not to blame for having no information about you. I'm here because I need your help. My friends also are in need of your help. Possibly I have a right to ask that of you."

The curtain waved, then began to dissolve. Kaitlin saw nothing where it had been hanging except for one blinding flash of light that she figured had to contain the power, spell or magic to allow her passage.

Without understanding what awaited her and where this portal might lead, or if it actually was still a gateway to another place or realm, Kaitlin took a giant step forward.

Two strong hands pulled her the rest of the way inside.

Michael, Dylan, Rena and Dev moved away from the building together, but stopped when they reached the trees. Someone was coming toward them, and it wasn't just anybody. It was Adam. And though Tory wasn't anywhere in sight, three Weres Michael didn't know accompanied Adam.

"Brought reinforcements," Adam said as he approached.

Dylan rushed forward to greet the newcomers, one of which was a she-wolf with dark hair that Dylan appeared to know particularly well. The other two had the same look of clear-eyed experience those in Dylan's pack had.

From behind Michael, Rena muttered, "More visitors."

Michael exhaled with relief.

Adam had gone for help. There hadn't been time for a six-hour round trip to Miami so he wasn't sure how Adam had gotten these Weres here so quickly.

Any way Michael viewed it, however, these additional Weres were a godsend.

Dylan made hasty introductions. "Matt Wilson, Cameron Mitchell and…" Dylan grinned when his eyes met the dark-haired she-wolf's eyes. "Dana Delmonico. Miami, meet Michael, Rena, Devlin."

Adam moved to the front of the group. "Where's Tory?"

Dylan stiffened. "She wasn't with you?"

Adam's thick neck muscled twitched. "She was watching that portal. I left her there."

Exchanging another look with Dylan left a bad taste in Michael's mouth.

"Tory figured that Kaitlin would return to the portal," Adam explained, "and wanted to be there when she did."

"Damn it," Dylan whispered, turning. "She wasn't there a while ago."

"You haven't heard the rest of it," Cade said, striding forward from wherever he had been lately. "Kaitlin went to the portal a few minutes ago. I saw her moving across the park and followed. By the time I reached the portal, she was gone."

Michael whirled. "What do you mean by gone?"

"I couldn't reach her in time," Cade said. "She went through."

The sun was rising higher over their heads. Michael's energy was waning when it was needed in full form. They had monsters to chase down and people to protect. They had plans to make and a mad, brutal beast to thwart. In spite of all that, he had to find Kaitlin.

He searched the new faces and found them set. The new Weres gave off no vibes of being frightened over what was going on. Michael got the impression that all of these wolves were in law enforcement, and were therefore used to dangerous situations. He identified the smell of metal, which told him that all three of these Weres carried concealed weapons.

There was no time for further explanations. All he had said before he took off at a run was, "Have to get there. To her."

He heard Adam utter a curse, but barely heard the sounds of his pack running behind.

Kaitlin stumbled to a halt once she got on the other side of the portal and took in a big breath of air. She scanned her new surroundings.

The colorful landscape she had seen during the last visit beyond the curtain appeared, this time darkened by an overlay of midnight-hued clouds. She glanced up to see a twinkle of stars.

She guessed that this realm had an opposite time schedule to the one she was used to. Sunrise in the world she had left was counterbalanced by nightfall here. The difference was disorienting, as was the implication of actually having been transported to another time and place.

When she looked again, she saw that she wasn't alone. Two beings, perhaps the same ones she had encountered on her last brief visit, faced her. They must have ushered her through the portal.

"Thank you." Kaitlin said this sincerely once she got her breath back. Going through the curtain had stolen her air.

The tall being across from her inclined her head.

"You know me?" Kaitlin asked, garnering another nod. "I was one of you until…" She couldn't finish that remark since nothing made sense.

"Am I welcome here, in spite of what has happened?" she managed to ask, her voice deep, tremulous, hoarse.

No nod came from these Fey creatures, and yet both of them remained.

"I would have died," Kaitlin explained. "I almost did. Michael saved me and I owe him for that and so much more."

A reply came at last in a voice as deep as Kaitlin's. "You carry his smell, even while walking on two legs."

Kaitlin shook off her discomfort and rallied. "His actions have bonded us together. That's the way he explained this to me. I am at the mercy of the wolf's ways, and yet I seek your help in saving one of those wolves and his friends from an evil creature far worse than any you might imagine. That creature is a monster maker, like the vampires that came after me."

"We sense their presence," the tall being said, still cloaked in the sparkling glamour that hid the rest of her features.

"You don't care?" Kaitlin asked.

"It does not concern us."

"Then why have you come?"

"To help one of our own."

"Do you mean me, or is there someone else?" Kaitlin pressed.

"We came for you," the tall Fey replied.

The wind ruffled Kaitlin's hair, providing welcome relief from the heat of her recent transition. She didn't dare close her eyes for fear that all this would disappear.

"We came too late," the tall Fey admitted. "The wolf had already cursed you."

"I'm alive, and grateful for that."

"You're no longer one of us."

"Enough like you to come here and speak with you. Enough like you to be able to call the wind and see visions of what this place is like when it's hidden from me."

These remarks were met with more silence. While waiting that silence out, Kaitlin's eyes began to clear, as if the wind she had somehow called up was whisking away the spell cloaking this foreign landscape from her.

There were mountain peaks in the distance, and trees of all kinds. She knew the names of each of those trees, and what their shadows hid. In the back of her mind, Kaitlin remembered believing she had known these things once before, and wondered how she had forgotten that.

"Yes," the Fey spokeswoman said, perhaps reading the wonder on her face. Possibly reading her mind. "You begin to understand what would have awaited you here."

"If you had gotten to me first," Kaitlin challenged boldly. "Before someone else rescued me."

Another moment of silence ensued before the Fey spoke again.

"He comes," the tall female said.

Kaitlin glanced over her shoulder. "The monster?"

"Your wolf."

She nodded. "Michael would rescue me again. He would risk a lot to do so. You must see that these Weres are deserving of help from wherever they can get it. They watch over the people in this town and in others. They live in secret, having to hide in plain sight for fear of being persecuted by prejudices such as the ones you hold, and without the magical ability to disappear through portals to a safer location."

"You do not understand about your lineage, Kaitlin Davies."

"You are right about that."

The other Fey spoke. "We are not uncaring. We do not travel easily, or to wherever we choose. You brought us here. Your call created this bridge to the mortal world."

They had come to her rescue, perhaps hearing her calls and prayers the night she almost lost her life. But they hadn't arrived in time to claim her as one of their own. Instead of becoming wolf that fateful night, she might have been like these two, Fey and shimmery and magically inclined. She had some kind of connection to them still.

She was also a wolf. And Michael was here, at the curtain, searching for her, waiting for her. She felt his distress and his need for her in a time of danger and strife.

Her body responded to him with a throb of desire strong enough to make her sway on her feet.

"I might have been Fey once, but that part of me has been trumped by Lycan blood," she explained. "In order to be with Michael and be his mate, I need to be a wolf. I choose to be wolf."

Suddenly, Kaitlin found she wanted that more than anything. More than the powers these Fey beings wielded. More than anything that anyone could have offered her to change her mind.

"I'm asking for your help, just this once. I'm pleading for you to help save those who saved me," she said. "Please."

The stars glittered overhead. Branches in the colorful Fey trees waved and creaked in the wind that surrounded her. Finally, before she could say anything further, the tall Fey female glided forward.

Kaitlin made herself stand her ground.

"Granted," that beautiful Fey creature whispered, resting a pale hand on Kaitlin's shoulder. "When the time is right, you have but to call on us."

Then the atmosphere changed. Colors swirled around Kaitlin until she believed she had been swallowed by a rainbow. She felt as if she were tumbling end over end. Her breath whooshed out. When she opened her eyes she was standing in front of Michael, who without hesitation reached for her.

She was back in the arms of the wolf, where she belonged, having been dismissed by her what? Blood kin? Distant relatives? No matter the title, they had agreed to help if she asked. And that, Kaitlin figured as Michael's arms tightened around her, had to be a step in the right direction.

"Well, I'll be damned," Rena said, her words echoing thunderously inside Kaitlin's unsettled mind. "Dev was right."

Chapter 26

Kaitlin was naked, gleaming with moisture, alive and in his arms. Because she was quiet, Michael feared she might be in shock.

She didn't tremble, didn't quake. Her body molded to his the way it had when he had stretched out over her on the bed. His hands remained motionless when the desire to run them over her lush bareness was all he could think about. Hunger for the secrets her body held returned with fervor.

Her hold on him was equally as tight.

"I thought I had lost you," he whispered to her. "Hell, Kaitlin."

Her voice was smooth, calm. "They will help us."

Michael loosened his grip. Holding her at arm's length, he searched Kaitlin's white face. Sweat dampened her hair at her temples. Several auburn strands clung to her neck, hiding the remnants of the wound that had sent her into his arms in the first place.

Gray eyes showed no glint of the wildness he was feeling. Something had happened behind that curtain that had changed Kaitlin again. He saw determination in her expression, and an angularity to her cheeks that he hadn't noticed before.

"What did you say?" he asked her.

"They will help us. They have agreed."

"Great," Devlin said from behind them. "And what will that cost?"

Kaitlin turned her head.

"There is always a cost for soliciting help from the Fey," Devlin explained.

Michael said, "Such as?"

"The first-born son. A pretty daughter. The soul of your grandmother. Who the hell knows for sure? As I mentioned before, the Fey aren't charming little beings prone to dishing out good deeds to anyone who asks."

"Maybe not to humans," Kaitlin said.

"Or half-breeds," Devlin remarked. "So the stories go. In the Old World countries, the Fey were, and probably still are, feared."

"Could be that they took her clothes as payment," Rena suggested wryly when the silence grew too thick to cut through any other way.

As if to punctuate that statement, Rena unbuttoned her shirt, exposing her sports bra, and handed the shirt to Kaitlin. "I'd appreciate getting this back sometime. I don't have time or the cash to hunt for a new wardrobe."

Michael saw that Rena's wryness and her heart didn't go hand in hand. She'd been quick to offer what help she could to Kaitlin. In this case, Rena's sarcasm disguised real concern for Kaitlin and what Kaitlin might have been through on the other side of that curtain. Devlin hadn't painted a pretty picture of the Fey.

Devlin then handed Rena his shirt to cover herself with. When Devlin looked to Cade, Cade said, "Not going to happen. I gave Michael my best blue shirt earlier."

The moment of awkwardness had passed. As Michael glanced to the portal one more time, his wits made a comeback. His hunger backed off. With Kaitlin safely on this side of the portal, it was time to go after Chavez.

It had been suggested, perhaps in a moment of anger, that all they had to do was chase Chavez's beasts here, to this spot. He had already seen what damage the Fey could inflict, so if they were willing to help, burning down the building housing the fight club didn't have to be the only option for getting at the werewolf monster maker.

"Time to move." He barked the order as his mind whirled with ideas on how to accomplish the plan. "We have to find the beasts and keep them away from the school. We need to bring them here, one by one if need be..."

"And shove them in," Rena said, finishing his thought.

He directed his next words to Kaitlin. "As a wolf, you were noticeable. Like this..." He smiled in spite of the dire situation they were in as she put on Rena's shirt. "Like this, you're equally as noticeable."

Rena moved up. "Home first for more clothes, and then sprinting toward your relatives comes after. Deal, Kate?"

Kaitlin looked at him with eyes that were no longer so innocent. With his heart beating hard and fast in his chest over the need to let Kaitlin out of his sight again, Michael pressed his lips to her forehead. His mouth slipped to her ear.

"If this works," he whispered to her, "I'll be damned before letting them take you or any of the others as payment."

Kaitlin severed the connection that always left them both breathless. Michael watched her go with Rena, stifling the shout that would draw her back. Kaitlin was loath to leave him. Her body language telegraphed her fear of what the future might bring.

But his help was needed elsewhere. Now that they had a plan that Kaitlin had placed herself in danger to secure, that plan demanded his full attention. He couldn't afford to soften or appear to be torn. This was serious stuff, and dangerous. Chavez was a monster, and they had to keep innocent people away from him.

Could the Fey be trusted to honor a deal? He sure hoped so.

If they managed to get Chavez here and those portal gatekeepers didn't like the taste of a real beast, Adam and Tory surely would.

And, Michael added in afterthought as he, Dev and Cade eyed the visiting pack...if the newest arrivals from Miami had silver bullets in those guns they carried, one good shot from the hand of an expert would end Chavez's antics forever.

After that happened, he'd consider everyone in Miami his new best friends.

Rena laid a hand on Kaitlin's shoulder, bringing her to a stop. "They're here," Rena said in a steady voice. "Werewolves," she added, as if werewolves and Weres were two entirely different species. "Change of plans, Kate."

Kaitlin followed Rena's gaze to the front of her apartment building. Copying the she-wolf, she sniffed at the sultry breeze and immediately picked up the scent.

"It's not like your scent," she noted.

"Thank you for the compliment. If I smelled like that, I'd off myself and save everybody the trouble of doing it for me." Rena pointed. "There are two of them. I guess monsters prefer to travel in pairs."

"How did they find my apartment?"

"Wolf recognizes wolf. Things are easier that way."

Kaitlin heard Rena's silent message to the others in the pack as if the she-wolf had shouted it out loud. She also heard the wolfish yip of a reply.

"Those two can't hear your message?"

"We have a closed frequency. All packs do," Rena explained. "Those two idiots will detect us in a minute, so detouring to my place will have to do. We can't take on these guys by ourselves no matter how much I'd like to."

"I'm still the weakest link," Kaitlin confessed.

"You have other talents."

Kaitlin glanced sideways. "Were you human, Rena? Before—"

"Yep. Although I like to think of my former status as *rebel*."

As they walked swiftly toward what she assumed would be Rena's abode, Kaitlin couldn't help being curious about the female beside her.

But trouble was in the air she breathed, and had been since she opened her eyes Friday night. While in human form, the two werewolves by her apartment building had the look of bikers and smelled like rotten fruit. Rena didn't appear to be put off by that. Was confidence a trait that could be learned as a person adapted to the particular strengths of being Were?

As a baby wolf, was she actually stronger than she felt at the moment? Was the ability to shape-shift without a full moon, like Michael did, one of those talents Rena was referring to?

She'd told the Fey that she had accepted being a wolf but wondered if they had gleaned that she hadn't been telling the whole truth.

She didn't feel like a wolf, even when she shape-shifted.

The feeling inside her was more like *theirs*. Devlin's notorious Fey.

Right then, her wolf filled that hollow space, and yet the wind sang to her. Trees whispered their names to her as she passed. She silently recited those names.

"What if I'm not wolf enough?" she asked aloud without meaning to.

Rena slid her a glance. "Then you're torturing Michael for nothing, and I won't stand for that."

"You love him."

"Always have. Always will," Rena admitted. "Then you came along."

Kaitlin laid a hand on Rena's arm to slow her. "I'm sorry."

Rena stopped walking and faced Kaitlin. "For what? No one seems to be able to look past that pretty exterior of yours. Except maybe Dev, who despite his well-honed muscle, remembers his childhood stories too well. These guys can't help themselves. I'm the only one immune to your charms."

Kaitlin turned. Rena pulled her back. "Let me finish, Fey girl. I was about to add that even I have been swayed by your courage and your loyalty to a species you've only just met the hard way. I wasn't nearly so ready to accept the fantastical implications of being a werewolf as you are. You have questions. I get that. You have doubts, like we all did. Still, I find your kindness inspiring. Shit, Kaitlin. Maybe I should be in love with you."

Rena's conspiratorial grin didn't quite reach her eyes.

They moved off again. Kaitlin said, "Did Michael rescue you?"

"Is this the Inquisition? If so, the timing is really bad."

Kaitlin winced.

"Cade did," Rena said, picking up the pace. "It was Cade who first found me."

The big blond Were who always had Michael's back would have made a great mate for Rena, Kaitlin thought.

"You aren't bonded to Cade?"

"I already had wolf blood in my system by the time Cade came into my life. Some guy at a party took a swipe at my throat when no one was looking, and the next full moon I got a big surprise."

Kaitlin stared at Rena, but kept up with the she-wolf's strides.

"Imprinting is different," Rena continued. "It's a look in the eyes that snaps a permanent connection in place. A desire to have another person, body and soul, that never eases and can't be forgotten. We don't have that. Cade brought me to Michael, and here I stayed. End of story."

Rena had more to say. "You've hooked up with Michael and I envy you that. Who wouldn't? But I've noticed that you don't seem to be very happy about it."

"I'm in love," Kaitlin said, confessing her innermost thoughts.

"And?"

"I'm not like any of you."

"Old story," Rena said. "Heard it before."

"I feel as though the term *wolf* can't contain what I'll turn out to be."

Now Rena looked at her soberly, and the time for sharing confidences was over. Kaitlin was beginning to notice another kind of pull on her system that made her stomach tighten and her throat close up.

"Yeah," Rena said, glancing up at the sky. "That's what she does. That's what you feel, whether or not you see her."

"She?" Kaitlin choked out the word.

"Madam Moon. She waits in all her silver glory to direct the antics of all her children."

Kaitlin closed her eyes briefly.

"You might be special, Kaitlin, but you're not exempt. Tonight the moon will start to change Michael and change you, even if tomorrow is the full. What's worse is that it will also affect the freaks that are hunting here, putting all of Clement at risk."

"Then," Kaitlin said, stiffening her spine and glancing over her shoulder, "we need to get rid of those two beasts behind us, and narrow the field."

Rena shook her head. "Do you have any weapons on you? Of course you don't. Have you been up against pure evil and lived to tell about it? Of—"

"Yes," Kaitlin said, cutting Rena off. "Looking into the soul of pure evil is the reason I'm here."

Rena went quiet for several seconds. Then she grabbed Kaitlin's wrist and said, "Okay, Fey girl, I believe you. So, how fast can you run?"

As they circled back toward the street, Kaitlin heard Michael shouting on that special wolf frequency. *No!* he exclaimed, cursing under his breath like an angry sailor. *Damn it, Rena. Don't chance it.*

But it felt good to have an objective, a focus, and Kaitlin followed Rena, hoping she had this, and that they weren't going to end up like lambs at the slaughter.

Chapter 27

Waiting was tough. Waiting was hell. In Michael's mind, he heard Kaitlin ask, *Are you looking for me, werewolf?* She wasn't speaking to him. He knew who and what she had found.

It took all of his willpower to stay where he was in front of the portal. He couldn't blow this operation, not now that a group of wolves had been sensed nearby. Both Kaitlin and Rena knew their plan. Both females were fast on their feet. Kaitlin could shift at will if needed and Rena was incredibly bold and strong.

Working against them was the raw power and brainwashing of the hyped-up rogue Weres. They'd be itching for a fight. With the full moon so close, the beasts' blood would be boiling. The two Weres that were nearing him and the others now had that look—hungry, solicitous, itchy.

"We're almost there," Dylan said to him. "Whatever happens after this will flush Chavez out of hiding. He will have scented us in his den. We will have tainted it for him. He can't afford to start over, with the moon showing up tomorrow. Out of necessity, he will come out of hiding."

Dylan was right. All Weres had to either accept the moon when it was very near to full, or full, or go mad, even when madness didn't sound like such a stretch for a character like Chavez. This need for the moon was also true for Lycans carrying the special gift of being able to shape-shift at will. When the moon showed up in all her silver glory, ultimately that moon was the master.

Michael's head ached. His body ached, not in any way that could be helped without reaching out to Kaitlin.

Run, my lover, he sent to her. *Run like the wind and pray that a Fey deal is a real one.*

Dylan stepped out from under tree cover to confront the two battle-scarred henchmen. They stopped. Forgetting they were in human form, their lips drew back to show blemished human teeth.

Full of themselves, partially moon-whipped from the night that was still hours away, the two undercover beasts came after Dylan. Sensing Michael as well, they fixed their attention on both without realizing that two crazy fledgling werewolves against two pure-blooded Lycans was a no-win situation. Chavez had not taught these poor bastards a thing.

As the angry Weres drew closer, some of Dylan's group closed in from the sidelines. Matt Wilson, Cameron Mitchell, Dana Delmonico. Perfect tributes to the best of their species. Proof that good guys could remain good guys after being on the wrong side of a raw deal.

Sensing this welcoming party and dissecting their rapidly fragmenting odds, the beasts veered left, catching sight of Tory in the distance. Michael didn't have any idea where she'd been, but was relieved to see her now, and that she was all right.

In daylight the beautiful flame-haired Lycan she-wolf was a delicacy these bastards could not resist. Coveting that beauty and hungry, they ran toward her. Addled by finding a type of Were they were unfamiliar with, they followed when Tory led them away with a lure they obviously were stupid enough to fall for.

Everybody followed. Only Adam was missing in this parade, and Michael had a bad feeling about that. It seemed that members of Dylan's pack often went off in their own direction without checking in, turning off their lines of communication. Did he blame Adam for wanting Chavez to himself, hoping to dish out some long-overdue retribution for throwing Adam in a fight ring?

He wanted to have Kaitlin beside him. When Weres loved, they loved with their heart and soul. Bonding was immediate. Love was furious. No dating, sharing chitchat and getting-to-know-you stuff was necessary. Humans had nothing like this. Hell, meeting his mate was like being hit over the head with a rock. His entire way of thinking had been rearranged.

And if Kaitlin was harmed in any way…any way at all… Michael hoped that Adam would step aside and allow Michael Hunter the opportunity to throttle Chavez with his bare hands.

Kaitlin easily kept pace with Rena as they raced through the park. Students scattered out of their way, unconcerned about a couple of runners out for some exercise. No one paid much attention to the runner who was only half-dressed. None of the few students in the distance gave a second look to the beasts giving chase, because those beasts were in man shape.

The portal wasn't far from where they had started. Kaitlin could have found it with her eyes closed. The closer she got, the stronger it tugged on her mind. The thing was like a vacuum, sucking her closer, and from afar, it glittered in the sunlight like one of the stars it hid.

What do we do when we get there? Rena messaged to her, Rena's legs moving effortlessly as they covered ground.

Not sure.

They ran as though their lives depended on speed… which was true. She could probably go through that doorway, Kaitlin reasoned, and let the beasts follow her. Rena likely wouldn't be welcome in any circumstance. They'd have to separate at the last minute and hope both of Chavez's Weres would follow her through the portal.

She perceived sounds on the periphery. Rena heard them, too, and tossed her a glance. More than sounds. She felt Michael getting closer. Michael had others with him.

She ran the last bit of distance with her heart bursting in her chest. This portal was the answer to their prayers, in part, if the Fey honored their word. What the fate would be for Chavez's beasts wasn't in the realm of her imagination. Had she made a deal with the devil in order to save this pack from harm?

The portal wavered, then cleared in her vision. Behind her, the two beasts growled with human throats. They were heading into the unknown. If this worked, it would be a miracle.

"Now!" she shouted to Rena. "Turn now!"

Rena obeyed, throwing herself to the right three steps from the curtain. Kaitlin bounded through the opening with her eyes wide-open, hearing Michael's voice echo inside her head.

Come back to me, Kate.

* * *

Michael ran as fast as his legs would allow, and still couldn't reach Tory. Dylan and his mate ran beside him, sober-faced and determined to get the job done.

He began to sense the portal because Kaitlin had reached it. There wasn't far for him to go. He knew this area of the park like he knew the back of his hand. He knew Kaitlin enough to realize she would forfeit her life if helping him demanded it.

Michael's message to her was heartfelt. *Once you're through that portal, circle back. Do not hesitate.*

He didn't realize he hadn't blocked that message until Dylan's mate, Dana, glanced his way. Of all the Weres here, he figured that Dana would understand. She had mated with a Lycan and had the bonding drill down.

The portal was just ahead. Michael saw Kaitlin go through. He saw Rena duck aside. As soon as they disappeared from sight, Tory reached the curtain. But at the last second, merely a breath away from possible death, Tory was yanked back from the wavering Fey doorway by a strong female hand. Rena's.

Tory stumbled to the side as the rogue Weres tried to slow. They weren't as agile as they should have been, and weren't able to stop in time. Both of the rogues skidded into the veil and disappeared.

Michael and the rest of the wolves pulled up, staring at the curtain. He saw nothing beyond the almost invisible glimmer between the trees. There was no sign of Chavez's beasts.

And there was no sign of Kaitlin.

The curtain's motion stilled. No one on this side of it moved. Michael couldn't draw in a decent breath. His heart was pounding hard.

He waited for what seemed like a century. The others

waited with him, without speaking. But Kaitlin didn't return.

"I'm going in there," he announced.

"That's not wise," Dylan said. "They might mistake you for one of those rogues. You're needed here."

Tory, staring at the onyx curtain, spoke softly to him. "She will return, Michael. Let her do so in her own time. Allow her access to what she is."

"We have to go now," Dylan said. "We have to find Adam. We have to find Chavez and could use your help, Michael. I know you'll want to stay here, and I can't ask you to accompany us, but this is your area. Knowledge of it could mean the difference between life and death for more innocent people."

"Kaitlin will return," Rena seconded, adamant about that statement.

He had to go, had to leave the last place he'd seen his lover, his soul mate, his very special little wolf. He had to help save more innocent people from the clutches of a madman whose gang had taken a hit. There was a possibility that Chavez had no henchmen left...until tonight, when foaming at the mouth for revenge, Chavez might start all over again in claiming his next victims.

Michael actually felt his heart break. His soul was being torn from him piece by piece and there wasn't a damn thing he could do about it.

I owe them this, Kate. I'm obligated to help. Don't you see how much I hate having to leave you here? Find me. I will leave a trail of messages until you do. Find me, Kaitlin, as soon as you can. Don't prove that I'm as weak as I feel.

Turning from the portal that might have become as treacherous a threat to his future, Michael resigned himself to fulfilling his part of the deal he'd made with Dylan.

Find me, he repeated, sending that message to Kaitlin over and over as he hustled back toward the college with the rest of the Weres, who also had a quest to fulfill.

Find me.

Chapter 28

The wolf packs backtracked to the basement where Chavez had created his new domain. As before, the place was empty. The hope Michael and the other Weres held was that they had taken care of the small gang, and Chavez was on his own.

Adam was waiting on the steps when they came up for air. He got to his feet. "No use waiting this out until dark. No other Weres have returned here, so you must have done a good job in putting a kink in this party."

Adam knew what had taken place in the park. He looked past them for Tory. Muttering "Damn it," he kicked at a concrete step with his boot. "Lycans," he added as if he'd uttered a curse, but he kept the reason for that to himself, and Michael understood why. Tory again wasn't with them. The red-haired wolf was a wild card in the Were cop's love life.

"We'll scour the campus and set watch until dark," Michael said, glad for the chance to get back to the portal, and relieved to hear about the current lack of beasts.

"There are nine of us," he added. "Pretty good odds for hooking up with one monster and a few more rogues, don't you think?"

"With luck on our side," Adam said seriously. "Other rogues might have scattered for the time being."

"I'll take the area on the west side." Michael's comment garnered empathetic looks from more than one of the Weres in attendance. They all knew what he was waiting for, and what Kaitlin had done to help the cause.

"We'll remain here," Cade said, gesturing toward the building as he breezed in with Devlin in tow. "No sign of more monsters anywhere we checked. I'm positive they can't be experts in camouflage."

Michael nodded. "Cade, go with Dylan and whoever he wants with him. Rena, go with the rest. Dev, I'm taking you with me."

"I figured as much," Dev said affably. "I can feel the heat of that hot seat from here."

They split up. After one more sweep of the campus and grounds, they'd have a few hours to wait out until darkness fell and the moon Michael already sensed hovering behind early-afternoon sunlight would render camouflage useless. Chavez would have to come out to play, and his foes would be waiting with new strengths of their own.

This sounded to him like a decent type of showdown. Wolf to wolves. Although a clawed hand wouldn't be able to pull a trigger, and a spray of silver bullets had darkened every nightmare he'd had since he was a kid, silver in the hands of the good guys, used to take down a criminal like Chavez, would seem appropriate, and not quite so bad anymore.

He wasn't certain Adam would feel the same way about

a quick disposal, after what Chavez had put Adam through in the past.

In the meantime…

I'll be waiting for you, Kate. Right on your blasted doorstep.

He was, in fact, already on his way.

Kaitlin opened her eyes without remembering why she had shut them. All was quiet. The bad wolves had not caught her, and she saw no hint of them in the circle of beings that were looking at her.

She was surrounded by Fey, and they weren't speaking. The voice in her head that repeated a message on continual loop wasn't theirs. That voice said, *Find me.*

She would have given anything to have complied with that request.

"Thank you for your help," she said to the gathering crowd. Without changing her mind about finding the Fey beautiful, a darker undertow passed through her that brought her to her feet.

"I'll be going back now," she said.

Her declaration was received in silence.

"I belong with my kind." Hearing that always surprised her. She added a statement similar to what she had told them before. "I don't know about you, or what I would have been if this was my world. I was never offered that choice."

More silence. They seemed to be waiting.

"I would have liked to be like you." She glanced down at a body that was very different from theirs. "Who could have predicted what this body hid?"

One of the circle of Fey finally spoke. Kaitlin recognized the voice.

"Payment is due, Kaitlin Davies, for services rendered to you this day."

Chills shimmied up Kaitlin's spine. "Was that in the fine print?"

"Because you're of our line, our demands are simple."

"And those demands are?"

"You stay."

Kaitlin's chills intensified. Michael's voice resonated in every cell in her body. *Come back to me, Kate. Don't hesitate.*

"Out of the question," she said, facing them all and refusing to back down.

"Payment is due," the tall Fey repeated.

"Then choose another one. You get that I'm no longer like you. You can see that. One of the Weres said that you shun halflings, and that mating with another species is not allowed. My body has merged with a Lycan's. Do you sense the blood in my veins?"

"Your family is powerful," was the response. "And of our own kind. Kaitlin Davies began as Fey, not human. One of us did not mate with an outsider to produce you. We can overrule the wolf blood coursing through you. Your future can be altered."

"What?" This news enhanced the chills, and sent them in all directions. "Are you saying that I don't have to be a wolf, and that you can change that?"

The Fey all nodded in agreement. The tall spokeswoman said, "We can, and will."

This was her choice. She was being given the opportunity to reverse the actions that had changed the direction of her life. But how was that payment for helping the Weres?

She asked that question.

"We take from those who ask for our help the thing they want most," the tall Fey said.

"In Michael's world, that's me?"

Michael's voice was more insistent. *Do not hesitate, my lover, my little wolf. My love.*

She was what Michael wanted most. He had rescued her. He loved her. The Fey had come to help, and had arrived too late. Without Michael's timely interference in a vampire attack on a person who looked human, but wasn't, she wouldn't have been standing here now, faced with such a choice.

Over her head, the stars twinkled, beaming another kind of message to whatever was embedded inside the part of her DNA that Michael's nearness did not affect. However, that part had grown noticeably weaker. Whereas she might have, in the past, wanted to stay here and learn about her family's heritage, she couldn't recall a time when her family didn't stress about being normal and never standing out from the crowd.

Were her body, her face and its features, controlled by a glamour such as the kind these Fey used to cloak themselves? Had her family purposefully chosen to live among humans, instead of with the rest of the Fey in a wonderland-like alternate realm? They had to have made that choice for a reason.

Maybe they assumed she'd never find out about the tweak in her genetics and live out her life among humans, ignorant and happy with the simplicity of human life. What about when she married, though? What would her children be like with diluted Fey blood that would no longer gain them access to what she was seeing right that minute?

Come back to me, Kate. Choose me, my love. Choose this world over any other.

Kaitlin's spine snapped straight. There had to be reasons for all of this.

"I'm going back," she said clearly, backing up as she

spoke. "You'll have to take a rain check on that payment, because I refuse to give it to you now."

All they had to do was stop her. Surely if they could redirect her fate and remove the wolf from the veins, they could simply block her from using the door.

They didn't try to do so.

"I will offer you a gift," she said thoughtfully. "A werewolf so vicious that stopping him will halt the flow of wolf blood to many people, and possibly keep you from facing these same problems again."

A murmur went through the Fey gathered there. Kaitlin felt the wave of their interest go through her, as well, as if she truly were one of them.

The tall Fey moved forward. Kaitlin had to look up to find the pale gray eyes looking back at her. "Deal," that Fey declared. "For now."

When Kaitlin smiled, she was again in the park, on the opposite side of that glimmering portal, surprised to see that stars shone here also, in a sky gleaming with the silver light of a huge round moon.

A werewolf moon.

She'd been gone a full day at least in the Fey time warp. Michael wasn't there, waiting, as she had hoped. As the wolfishness coursing through her veins began to twist her into her alternate shape, Kaitlin howled.

Chapter 29

The entire pack had no further reason for guarding the building where Chavez had been. Without his full horde of beasts, this master had to search for replacements. He'd be flushed out of hiding tonight by the pull of the moon.

Michael acknowledged the others waiting with him with an inclination of his head. Beneath tree cover that was lacy and insufficient for stalling transformations, some of the pack had already shifted into the man-wolf hybrid combination of Were that walked on two feet and still wore their clothes.

He wasn't like them. Neither was Tory, who stood a little apart from the others, still in human form, a feat that told Michael that like him, the red-haired wolf might also have a special ability that separated her from the rest.

He hadn't been ready to leave his post at the portal, and had sent messages to Kaitlin until his mind was weary, hoping she'd hear him, receiving no replies. He had felt her nearness to that damn Fey doorway, and had held himself back from leaping through it to find out if he was right.

And still, she had not appeared.

And the damn portal had vanished, as if it had never been there in the first place, rendering his search for Kaitlin useless. Leaving him heartbroken.

It's time, Dylan said, looking as fair and formidable furred up as he had been in human form.

"Yes," Michael agreed.

A rustle of accord went through the group. Above the din, he swore he heard Kaitlin speak a few words in the unfathomable language he'd heard her use once before.

Was she calling to him? In need of help? He couldn't find out without the damn portal.

Had the entire world gone mad, or just him? Because he sensed her. Felt her, as if she was nearby and might appear at any moment.

And then he heard her howl. He hadn't made that up. The others had also turned toward the sound in the distance.

Michael shouted, "Follow me. This way." Excited, and with his heart in his throat, he followed the echo of that howl.

He ran like the wind, feet churning up the ground, senses flooding with hopeful thoughts. It didn't take long to find her. God yes, Kaitlin was there, in the center of the old part of the college's overgrown, grassy field, standing on all fours and as motionless as a statue. She was in a state of full transition, all wolfed up, her glossy fur shining in the moonlight. Her eyes tracked his approach, but she didn't call out.

He wanted to reach her, hold her, thank his lucky stars for her return. Something in her stance stopped him from doing any of those things. She was waiting for something, and focused on whatever that was.

Several students passed her by, perhaps thinking her a dog waiting for its master. In truth, she had another agenda altogether. Kaitlin wasn't waiting for him to find her. She had not planned on him coming in time. Kaitlin had someone else in mind to lure, and every Were with Michael knew who that was.

Suddenly he appeared. Chavez. The devil himself. Had to be. Tall, his body partially covered in dark hair, waking upright on two legs…and Lycan.

Holy hell… The gaps in Michael's mind filled in. All the dots lined up. Chavez wasn't any old werewolf. He was a pure-blooded atrocity. A Lycan gone bad. That was where the monster's power, strength and insight came from.

Michael saw no mask of madness on Chavez's face. The beast had to realize that Michael and the others were there. Lycan senses were nothing short of miraculous. Yet Chavez didn't appear to care about having an audience. His eyes were on Kaitlin, the Fey wolf with a power to lure most species, as she waited for him to make a move.

Her welcoming growl rolled to meet this monster maker. Her fur ruffled in the wind that was her particular calling card and proclaimed her secret of being something other than entirely wolf.

Mesmerized, Chavez moved toward her.

Michael inched forward. The pack at his back did the same.

Two more feet, and Chavez put out a hand, the way a person might do to allow a dog to determine if that person was friend or foe.

"Kate," Michael whispered. "What game is this?"

She growled again, and backed up. Chavez followed with two more steps toward her. For Michael, that was two steps too many. He moved, breaking into a sprint. Kaitlin, in wolf form, and after who knew what else had happened to her behind the portal, had the faster reflexes.

She ran, virtually flying over the ground. Chavez, in full hunting mode that made chasing down prey a foregone conclusion, followed her. He might even have believed he was invincible. But there were far too many of his enemies here.

Kaitlin slid to a stop beside the building that housed Chavez's ill-fated fight club.

"No!" Michael shouted to her. *"Stop!"*

Two more beasts ruled by Chavez appeared on the roof and began to climb down. Michael heard Cade growl. Rena seconded the sound, already heading for the wall to greet those monsters. Two Weres from Dylan's pack followed.

A figure stepped into Michael's sightline. In the shadows, and while under the cover of the roof's overhang and out of the moon's reach, Adam Scott was suddenly at Kaitlin's side. There was a flash from the weapon Adam carried. *Silver bullets*, Michael chanted to himself. *Use them, Adam. Put an end to this.*

Of course, that was too easy, was the unanimous thought that came from the group beside Michael. After successfully avoiding capture for so long, the mad beast could be bested by a bullet?

Kaitlin's next howl split the silence. Loud, harrowing, her call seemed to herald the arrival of a much worse outcome than Adam's bullet had promised.

Though Adam had a finger on the trigger, and Michael and the pack barreled forward, Kaitlin's call was answered in a faster manner.

Clouds covered the moon, throwing the scene into darkness. A fierce wind whipped at them all, holding Michael and the others back with the force of a hurricane.

Adam's back hit the brick wall behind him with a smack that had to have rattled his bones, but his gun was still aimed at Chavez. Michael could feel Adam's finger begin to squeeze, as if his own finger was moving.

In the time it took for the gun to fire, a hole in the atmosphere opened up and a second blinding flash of light lit the area. The bullet sailed toward Chavez. He flailed, howled menacingly, and thrashed the air with his claws as hands nearly the same color and consistency of the light winking around them pulled him backward through a brand-new portal.

The two remaining beasts fought to go after their leader, and the good guys helped them along. The last thing Michael heard before the portal disappeared was the sound of Adam's silver bullet striking its intended, if invisible mark. And then his eyes moved to Kaitlin, and found her looking back.

He could have sworn that she smiled.

Michael had said his goodbyes to some of Dylan's friends. Tory and Adam, Dylan and Dana were camping out in his living room and making the best of it. He heard laughter and the recap of events, as well as the clink of glasses toasting Chavez's defeat.

Kaitlin was nestled in his arms on his bed, and Michael didn't wish himself anywhere else. He didn't want for anything else, either, and imagined he never would.

His she-wolf was breathing softly against his neck. Despite what she had been through, she was still smiling. That smile alone could have done him in.

"You'll tell me about it someday?" he asked her, rolling over to stretch out on top of her feverish body for the third time in less than an hour. "All of what you went through in that other place?"

"Is nothing scared?" she replied, lifting her arms over her head to take hold of the bedposts, bracing herself for what was coming next.

She had assimilated her Lycan blood and was game to indulge in the physicality of a passion that was likely to last all night, every night, if he had his way. Michael refused to think about the price the Fey had exacted from Kaitlin for letting her return to him. Someday, she would be able to talk about it.

"You are my drug," he whispered to her, placing a trail of kisses on her forehead, her cheek, her nose, before landing on her lush, waiting mouth. "I can't get enough."

"It's a Fey thing." She accepted the pressure of his lips and moved her hips seductively against his hips.

"Maybe I'll learn to like the Fey," Michael teased, feeling every inch of her gleaming nakedness beneath him, from the raised pink buds of her breasts to her long, lean thighs. He'd had his mouth on all of those places tonight, and promised himself he would soon start all over again.

Right then, his patience had taken a hike.

In all honesty, though, patience had never been one of his best virtues.

He inched Kaitlin's thighs apart with his own and settled his hard length between them, affirming again that he was not wolf-whipped, and that an Alpha had to maintain some dignity with which to command the respect of his pack. He'd use Kaitlin's Fey lineage as an excuse for being unable to keep his hands off her. Hell, he wasn't entirely sure that wasn't part of the real reason he loved her so much, anyway. She certainly was like no other.

Kaitlin's gray eyes bored into his. Her breath was warm and sweet, when she had proved herself to be anything but passive and sweet in the past few days, and in the hours since their return to his bedroom from the battlefield.

"I am the Alpha," he reminded her as she nipped at his tattoos with her human teeth.

"Yes," she said, grinning. "And I am no mere wolf."

"Hell. You have that right."

Michael matched her grin and eased himself inside her moist inferno. Her head hit the pillows. Her eyes closed. Maybe, he thought, he could take advantage of her weakened state.

"How did you do it? Get them to take Chavez off our hands?" he asked.

Kaitlin, withholding a groan of delight, said, "Payback." As she wiggled her hips, she added, "It's not over."

"No. This is just the start," he taunted, sliding further inside her and observing how tight her hold was on the bedposts.

"Vampires," she whispered, gasping as he stroked her insides the way she liked it best, and as he returned to her mouth, determined to capture her next breath.

"I think our pal Chavez will have taken care of a fair share of the bloodsuckers, maybe even giving us a break for a while. He cleaned out two nests in those basements," Michael said, pausing, drawing his hips back.

Kaitlin's hands left the posts. She snaked her arms around him, letting her hands slide sensuously to his lower back, and then to his buttocks. With the force of her passion alone, she pulled him back, raised her hips, urged him on.

There was so much he needed to find out about Kaitlin, and about her family's secrets. He had to know what had gone on behind that portal, and how she had solicited the help of a species that loathed mankind and included werewolves in that despicable roundup.

Because of her, Clement, and possibly other cities, had been saved from bite clubs. But Devlin had stressed that the Fey always demanded payback for a favor. An eye for an eye. So, what had Kaitlin promised them in return for their help with Chavez?

Would he ever realize the extent of things left unanswered? He wanted to ask her about it now. His form of payback would be one kiss in return for one answer. Or maybe something better than a kiss. After all, a long lifetime together lay ahead.

"I can hear you, you know," Kaitlin said, blinking up at him.

And then…

Then…

The consummation of their love, their desire, their bonding, became all. As Michael pressed the evidence of his love deeper into Kaitlin, she muttered another stream of unintelligible Fey words that ended in a deep, rumbling growl.

And hell, he knew what to do with that.

* * * * *

MILLS & BOON®

nocturne™

AN EXHILARATING UNDERWORLD OF DARK DESIRES

A sneak peek at next month's titles...

In stores from 14th July 2016:

- **Enchanted Guardian** – Sharon Ashwood
- **Lycan Unleashed** – Shannon Curtis

Available at WHSmith, Tesco, Asda, Eason, Amazon and Apple

MILLS & BOON®

Mills & Boon have been at the heart of romance since 1908... and while the fashions may have changed, one thing remains the same: from pulse-pounding passion to the gentlest caress, we're always known how to bring romance alive.

Now, we're delighted to present you with these irresistible illustrations, inspired by the vintage glamour of our covers. So indulge your wildest dreams and unleash your imagination as we present the most iconic Mills & Boon moments of the last century.

Visit **www.millsandboon.co.uk/ArtofRomance** to order yours!